ABERRATION
OF
STARLIGHT

RANDOM HOUSE
NEW YORK

GILBERT
SORRENTINO

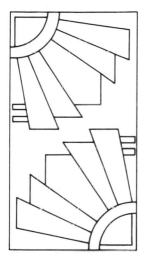

ABERRATION
OF
STARLIGHT

Library of Congress Cataloging in Publication Data

Sorrentino, Gilbert.
Aberration of starlight.

I. Title
PZ4.S717Ab   [PS3569.O7]   813'.54   80–5280
ISBN 0–394–51189–1

Grateful acknowledgment is made to the following for permission to reprint previously published material:

Chappell Music Company: Lyrics reprinted from "On Miami Shore" by William Le Baron and Victor Jacobi. Copyright © 1919 by Chappell & Co., Ltd. Copyright renewed. Published in the U.S.A. by Chappell & Co., Inc. International Copyright Secured. All rights reserved. Used by permission.

Columbia University Press: Excerpt reprinted from *The New Columbia Encyclopedia* by permission of the publisher, Columbia University Press, New York.

Dodd, Mead & Company, Inc. and William Heinemann Ltd: Excerpt reprinted from *Kashmiri Song* by Laurence Hope from the book *Indian Love.* By permission of Dodd, Mead & Company, Inc. and William Heinemann Ltd, London.

Edwin H. Morris & Company: Lyrics reprinted from "Prisoner of Love" by Leo Robin, Clarence Gaskill and Russ Columbo. Copyright © 1931 Edwin H. Morris & Company, A Division of MPL Communications, Inc. International Copyright Secured. All rights reserved. Used by permission.

Charles Scribner's Sons: Excerpts from "Invictus" by William Ernest Henley and "Envoy to the Toiling of Felix" by Henry Van Dyke are reprinted courtesy of Charles Scribner's Sons.

To Jack O'Brien

aberration of starlight . . . The true path of light from a star to an observer is along the straight line from the star to the observer; but, because of the component of the observer's velocity in a direction perpendicular to the direction to the star, the light appears to be traveling along a path at an angle to the true direction to the star.

—*The New Columbia Encyclopedia*

¿Quién no escribe una carta?
¿Quién no habla de un asunto muy importante,
muriendo de costumbre y llorando de oído?

—César Vallejo

Ils n'égalent pas leurs destins
Indécis commes feuilles mortes

—Guillaume Apollinaire

Although our information is incorrect, we do not vouch for it.

—Erik Satie

ABERRATION
OF
STARLIGHT

There is a photograph of the boy that shows him at age ten. He is looking directly into the camera, holding up a kitten as if for our inspection, his right hand at her neck, his left underneath her body, supporting the animal's weight. The sun is intensely bright, and he squints at us, smiling, his white even teeth too large for his small face. Because of this squint we cannot see that his left eye is crossed. Behind him are the edges and planes of farm buildings faded watery red, and the deep shadows that they cast on the ground. In the shade of a haymow a half-grown Holstein calf lies, also looking directly at us: although we cannot see them, because of her distance from the anonymous photographer, flies swarm and settle, rise, swarm and settle around her pacific eyes. The kitten is striped, her eyes slits in the sunlight.

The boy's hair is black and freshly combed, glistening with a brilliantine known as rose oil, given to him by Tom Thebus and bought at the five-and-ten in Hackettstown. To the boy, this dark-pink, almost cerise liquid, its odor unlike any rose ever grown on this earth, is a palpable manifestation of a world of beauty and delight. In this world his mother will be happy. In this world the memory of his dead grandmother will fade subtly into lies about her goodness. In this world his grandfather will be, always, the confident and arrogantly serene gentleman that he is when he plays croquet.

The thick, smooth croquet lawn that borders the white farmhouse a hundred yards away is not visible in the photograph, but the boy may be able to see one corner of it, and on wooden lawn chairs in that corner, in the thick shade of umbrella trees, his mother and Tom Thebus, the latter's hair gleaming with the same rose oil that the boy wears. White smoke from his pipe hangs in the calm late-morning air.

One might say that the boy is arrested at a moment of happiness, although photographs, because they exclude everything except the split second in which they are snapped, always lie. Still, one stares at them, urging them to give up their truths: here one wishes to see trapped forever in the boy's eyes the image of the photographer, to know whether that irregular shadow that blots the gravel next to the cooling shed is cast by Louis Stellkamp, the owner of this farm, to see, not merely what is behind the boy, but what is in front of him. Perhaps the lawn chairs are unoccupied.

Perhaps the boy's smile is caused by the fact that the photographer is Tom Thebus, and that next to him stands, in a pale-green slack suit that sets off her blond hair, his mother. If this is so, it may be that a moment after the picture is snapped, the boy's smile disappears, for he sees in that corner of the croquet lawn visible only to him, the figure of his grandfather, in white shirt and flannels, a croquet mallet over his right shoulder, standing and looking at them, stiff with resentment. White smoke from his cigarette hangs in the calm late-morning air until a brief cat's-paw tears apart and disperses it.

Dear Danny,

How are you? Is the City hot? I'm fine. I was going to write
this letter before but I had to wait until I could get some stamps
in Hakketstown when we go there Friday nights. Thats fun
because we go to the five and 10 and, then walk around and then
go to the Warren house, that a guy called Dave Warren owns a
guy going to marry Eleanor Stellkamp whose mother and father
own this place. Eleanor is pretty ugly but she's nice. They have
clams and I get orange drink and they have pokas there. And they
have potatoe chips. I bet the City is hot. It gets hot up here too.
We go to a lake, Bud Lake or, a little river they call the locks
every day. There is a man up here this summer called Tom and
he is neat. He drives us mostly and yesterday I sit in the rumble
seat with a girl who is up here this summer too. I never sat in a
rumble seat before. A funny thing is that they have milk here at
supper that is still warm. From the cows. Well I have to wash up,
for supper. This guy Tom made me a sling shot and I'm going to
try after supper in the field. I hope that your feeling fine and say
Hello to your perents.

Your old pal and see you soon, Billy

Your gramps can really play croquet! A champ! He just beat me without half-trying.

I think *you're* pretty good, Mr. Thebus. You give Gramp a good game.

Ha! *And* I keep asking you to call me Tom. What's the matter? You don't like me? *Mister* Thebus! I'm not a schoolteacher. Do I look like a schoolteacher?

Mom told me I should call you Mr. Thebus.

What about your gramps?

What?

What did he say you should—? Nothing. But your mommy doesn't call me Mr. Thebus . . . she calls me Tom just like you should too.

Mom's different. I mean that's different. I'm a kid and I'm supposed to show grown-ups respect. Mom says.

Billy, if you call me Tom you'll show me all the respect I want. I'll have a talk with your mother about it so you won't get in dutch. How's that? O.K.?

O.K. That's swell.

How's that slingshot coming along?

Neat! I can almost always hit a bottle and cans from about, oh, a pretty long way, twenty feet. Mom says I can't take it back to the city.

And she is absolutely right. That's a dangerous thing.

I wouldn't shoot it at anybody.

But supposed you missed and hit somebody anyway? Or a window? It wouldn't matter if you didn't *want* to hit anybody. Your mommy's got the right idea . . . do you realize how lucky you are to have a mommy like her?

I always just call her Mom. Just Mom. *You* know.

Well. You're a very fortunate and lucky young fella. Believe me. I hardly knew my mother, she died when I was younger than you. How old are you?

Ten and a half, about. But I could maybe shoot it in the backyard in Warren's house who's a friend of mine in the city around the corner.

Yes. I was about nine I think . . . there's an old saying that you never realize what a mother is until she's gone. That is very true. Believe *me.* God couldn't be everywhere, that's why He made mothers.

Or down at the pier where the kids go crabbing maybe? You can't hit people there. Mom don't allow me to go there because she says the crabs have disease and you can fall in. A kid got killed there last year when he fell in down between the pier and a barge. He got squashed.

As usual, I have to agree with your mother. We see eye to eye on a lot of things.

Is she a good dancer? Mom?

Dancer? Your mommy? Mom?

She said you might go dancing with her. At the WigWam? They have a real band there, you know that?

Oh. Oh, we just talked about it—maybe, maybe. Almost like a joke. I haven't danced in years and *years.*

I hate it.

Well, when you get older you'll see it's a good thing. A young man . . . it's a thing you ought to know. You escort a young lady out . . . it's a gentleman thing. My Tommy always said he hated it too. Another wise guy—like you! Put 'em up! Come on! I'll knock you for a loop! Think you're tough!

Hey! You're too big!

Aha! That's what they all say! All the tough guys! All the wisen-heimers! Hey! Ouch! Not so hard, Dempsey.

I don't *really* not like dancing. I mean if you go with Mom dancing at the WigWam it's O.K. I mean if you like to. Do you? Are you a good dancer?

Well. I don't know, really. My Tommy's mother thinks so—she used to think so once upon a time. God knows what . . .

What?

I said at least I don't have what you call two left feet.

What's that? What's two left feet?

It means that you just can't—Well, suppose *you* had two left feet. How do you think, with these two left feet, you'd walk around?

Oh, yeah.

Pretty dopey, right? Well then, imagine two left feet, dancing.

Oh, yeah, sure. Sure. Oh you couldn't dance at all good.

That's the idea right on the noggin. That's where they get the expression.

Is your boy as old as me?

Just about your age. You'd like him a lot, I bet. He's a lot like you are too.

He looks like me?

No, I mean he's *like* you in a lot of ways, he's just sort of . . . like you.

Has he got to wear eyeglasses like me?

No. But so what? What's so important about eyeglasses?

I hate them. Kids call me four-eyes. And cockeyes.

What? You don't have any cockeyes! Those kids must be nuts. What you have will most likely just go away by itself when you grow up. I knew a couple kids with that when I was a kid. They call it a lazy muscle. It just went away, like that!

Just went away?

Just like that. I swear it.

I wish that—I wish—But *how* is he like me?

Oh, a lot of ways. You feel like sitting down in this shade? It's pretty hot for an old man.

What old man? Oh! *You're* not an old man. Gramp is old.

He's a wonderful gent, your grandfather. I wish I knew why he didn't like me too well.

I didn't know Gramp didn't like you. I thought Gramp sort of liked you.

Well. I don't mean that your gramps doesn't *like* me, I mean you know, that he *hates* me. I just get the funny idea that he doesn't actually, you know, like me.

Well I like you. And Mom likes you too.

Thank you, Billy. That's very nice. And nice of your mom. How do you know that?

What? Know what?

That your mother likes me. Too.

Well she sort of told me. I don't really remember.

She told you what? How did she tell you?

Well she didn't really I guess tell me really. Things. Stuff she says about you and all. About what a swell guy you are and a gentleman. And you make her laugh and things like that. And you're spic and span. Just stuff like that.

Well I like her a lot too. I think that maybe she's one of the nicest ladies I ever met. Your mother is a real lady.

I sometimes make believe that, you know, that you are sort of my father. I kind of sometimes wish that you are my father. Sort of my father.

Well . . .

I mean that I hardly even know my real father. The last time I ever really saw him for about an hour was when I was really little. I was about maybe seven. He took me to Coney Island and the penny arcade. I love to go there.

Me too.

With about a thousand pennies, I had about that many. I played one of those steamshovel games where you pick up the prizes from all these little candy beans or some stuff. It's hard. You know that one?

Oh yes. Tommy loved that one too. See? You and him are just alike. I told you, Jack.

Jack?

Dempsey. Jack Dempsey.

Oh. I got a big round lighter for the house, for the table. I started to give it to him but he said to take it home and give it to Gramp.

Ah. That was nice.

Yeah. Gramp don't even fill it. He never filled it once. He never even once used the rotten piece of junk shit!

Hey, hey, kid . . . take it easy . . . you don't want to cry. Hm? Come on. O.K.?

I wish I had a real father I could see . . . like you. If you could be like my father.

Well. Well, I don't know about that but I'll see if maybe we can't fix it up so that we get to see each other in the city?

Really? You mean it, Mr. Thebus?

I mean it. *Tom* means it. Right?

Right. Tom.

You like football?

I don't know. I don't know how to play it.

No. I mean to watch it, you know, real football with men.

Oh. I don't know much about it. I used to listen to it on Saturday sort of on the radio with Janet at my Cousin Katie's house in Jersey City when Mom and me lived there. But I was really a baby then.

Well, maybe we can go to some games this fall. How does that sound to you? You think your mom would let me take you?

Sure! Sure she would. She really likes you a lot. That would be really swell.

Now if I can manage to only get your gramps to like me a little— just a little bit—everything would be just hunky-dory.

He'll like you. I don't really think he don't like you. Sometimes he just makes you feel like he hates you. Me too I mean. Even my mother. When he talks about my granma who died from a sickness last winter in her blood. When he does he makes you really feel like that. It's really stinky. And other times too.

Well, it's his privilege, Billy. It was very very sad for all of you, I'm sure. Come on, let's start back, O.K.? That old dinner bell will be ringing soon and we should wash up.

I think that's Mom over there coming over to us. Yeah, she's waving.

Yes, that's your mom. Let's go and meet her, O.K.?

Can I tell her about the football games?

Why don't we sort of—? Why not? Sure.

What did Billy remember of the abrupt termination of his parents' marriage?

The sudden turmoil of their one-family house in Flatbush the day that he and his mother left it for good and moved to his Cousin Katie's house in Jersey City. The empty rooms seemed strange and frightening to him, the moving men huge and loud, and his mother wept when he asked her where Daddy was and was he going to Jersey too. That night he was put to bed on a couch in Katie's living room and fell asleep listening to his mother and Katie talking in the kitchen, its light falling in the hallway eerie and unfamiliar. He woke up in the middle of the night and wondered where his metal zeppelin was.

Note some specific if disjointed recollections he had of the nights his father came home late for supper.

A bowl of salad made from lettuce, tomatoes, and green pepper rings. His father with tie loosened, sleeves rolled up, and vest unbuttoned, eating angrily and silently. A bottle of Worcestershire sauce. The cold coming in from the back porch as his father stood there, the door half-open, pulling his rubbers off. "Margie." His mother sullenly washing dishes, her back to the table. A Big Little Book of *Terry and the Pirates.* "Your home is on Wolcott Street!" *The Sun.* His father carrying him up to bed. Darkness. Loud voices. Long periods of silence. His mother crying.

What were some things that Billy most liked?

Playing at being driver in his father's parked car; stirring ice cream into a soup; tying his shoelaces very tight; walking in falling snow; smelling the gum packed with baseball cards; watching badly drawn slides about personal hygiene and/or nutrition in the school auditorium; playing running games like Caught Caught Blackwell and Ring-aleevio; listening to his grandfather tell stories about Irish wakes, especially the one about the drunken men who pulled the dead man out of his coffin, sat him up in a chair, and tried to give him some whiskey; going to the penny arcades at Coney Island; the howling wolves on *Renfrew of the Mounted;* hearing his mother sing "Poor Butterfly."

What was the single most awesome and terrible thing about his grandmother?

Her corset. The first time he saw it on a chair in his grandparents' bedroom, he did not know that it was a garment. It seemed, rather, a mysterious object that his grandmother used for some malicious purpose secret to herself. Seeing it for the third or fourth time, he realized that it was something that his grandmother wore, hidden, for some strange reason, beneath her clothes. The vast expanse of white cloth, tinged yellow with age, the enormous elastic straps with their cruel-looking metal clips, the bony stiffness that permitted it to lie so rigidly on the chair—all these things together frightened him. That she should place this horrible thing on her body: perhaps it was the magic that made her so mean.

What further thoughts did these reflections give rise to?

He thought of his grandmother removing the corset, standing naked. He felt slightly sick and light-headed when this idea came to him. He wondered if she made his grandfather watch. He then wondered if his mother wore such a thing, and at this felt absolutely dizzy and sat down. Each time this latter thought subsequently came to him he exorcised it thus: He bit the flesh inside his mouth on the left side and said, silently, "one, two, three." Then he bit the flesh inside his mouth on the right side and said, silently, "four, five, six." Then he pressed his lips tightly together and said, still silently, "seven." He then concluded by whispering, "that's all, no more."

Note a few curious things that happened after the move to Cousin Katie's.

A ragged boy in the adjacent backyard asked him if he wanted some soup. When Billy said that he did, the boy handed him a rusted Campbell's Soup can filled with worms and earth. Katie's mashed potatoes had hard lumps in them, and he was expected to eat them all if he wanted dessert. Dessert was almost always lemon Jell-O, which latter possessed a tough and rubbery film on its surface. Katie's younger son, Buddy, fell in the school gym one day and hurt his back and a few weeks later he died. Janet, Katie's only daughter, taught him how to listen to college football games on the radio and smoked cigarettes in the bathroom. He was sent to various stores in the neighborhood to ask for wooden crates that Katie used for kindling in the big black kitchen coal stove. A month after the incident with the can of worms, the same boy threw some dead flies in his face, after asking him if he'd like some of the candy he had in his hand; Billy then hit him across the shoulder with a dead branch and was awed at seeing him scream, cry, and run away. Katie's husband, Leonard, sat in a rocking chair all day, looking out the window and listening to the radio; he was something called "retired" and had a disease called "disability."

How did he feel when his grandmother got sick?

He was glad that she now stayed in her bedroom all day.

How did he feel when his grandmother died?

He was frightened that she was not really dead because of how she looked in the funeral parlor.

The occasion for his mother's first slapping him across the face?

His grandmother's funeral. Walking toward the limousines from the gravesite, he asked if they buried Granma with her corset on and if they did, who put it on her.

What disturbing adventure did Billy have just about the time his parents began to have their quarrels?

Cookie and Honey Neumann, a brother and sister aged seven and five years, respectively, called him into their next-door garage one day. While Cookie giggled hysterically and pointed to a neat pile of fresh human feces, Honey lifted up her coat and dress and pulled her underpants down and he saw that someone had cut her birdie off. Although he later could not decide just *why* he ran home, he felt sick and knew that there was something wrong about what had happened.

What was his grandmother's method of persuading him to do what she told him to do?

She hit him across the legs with a thin leather belt that came with one of her crepe de Chine dresses.

Did she thus discipline Billy only when alone with him?

No. She often did it when Marie was present, and when Marie protected her son from her mother's anger, there was invariably talk about "roof over your heads" and "three meals a day" and "being eaten out of house and home" and "your poor father working like a nigger." For some years after, Billy thought that all "niggers" worked in "credit," whatever that was.

When it became clear to Billy that Margie was somehow the reason that his parents argued, and then left each other, and that he and his mother had to go to Jersey City, what did he feel?

He was chagrined because he liked Margie. She had shown him how to play jacks, she had taught him to put sugar on rice when he went to the Chinese restaurant, she smelled kind of nice—even his mother said she smelled like a five-and-ten counter—she called his father "Tone," which sounded fancy to Billy, and she had bright-red hair.

As he grew older, what did his mother tell him apropos Margie?

That she was a snake in the grass. That she was cheap. That she had used him. That she had blinded his father. That she had broken her heart. That she was shanty Irish. That she lived in a cellar with rats as long as your arm. That her brother was a Judas. That she was older than *she* was. That she had even fooled his grandmother. That she was strictly dese dose and dems. That her mother kept coal in the bathtub. That she walked like a tramp. That his father would live to rue the day. That she liked her liquor. That she wasn't even pretty. That she was shameless to call herself Mrs. Recco. That her brother's gimp served him right and was the judgment of God. That she was a bad woman and he'd understand someday what she meant. That she hadn't but one dress to her name when she met his father and that one from Namm's. That her idea of a good time was a plate of boiled potatoes and a growler of beer. That she was Red Hook through and through. That she was the scum of the earth. That she needed rowboats to fit her feet. That she had wormed her way into her friendship. That she took and was glad to get one of her old winter coats, old, yes, but better than anything she had on her skinny back. That she had the nerve to come to Billy's fourth birthday party, and all the time she, well, she wouldn't go into it. That she'd go to fat like all the

shanty donkey women in ten years. That that slob of a Jimmy Kenny
liked her and *that* should have warned her. That she never even got
out of grammar school. That her teeth were as green as grass, disgusting to look at. That you give a man a clean, fresh girl and he has to
go and find one like Margie in the sewer. That God sees everything
and that He is good. That time wounds all heels.

Apropos his father?

That she didn't know what had happened to him. That they'd cast
a spell on him. That they'd put the evil eye on him, it's been known
to happen. That he needed someone dirty and low. That some old
witch had told Margie to dip one of her dirty stockings in his coffee.
That he'd turned his back on all his brothers. That he was ashamed
to look his father in the face. That *she'd* given him everything he ever
wanted but it wasn't enough for him. That she'd been a good wife, an
angel to him. That she couldn't see how a man could just abandon
his own flesh and blood that way. That he'd been a prince when she
first met him. That he'd never liked redheads, not that that was her
real hair. That men are no good. That if *he* ever fell for anyone like
Margie, she'd cut the legs out from under him. That he'd had the
nerve to take her into her own house. That she'd be damned if he was
going to get away with his phony Florida divorce. That *she* was Mrs.
Recco and that she'd *always* be Mrs. Recco. That if he showed his face
in New York before her final decree she had a good mind to have him
arrested for bigamy. That she knew he'd have that shyster kike lawyer
give her the runaround. That he didn't care if they starved. That he
very conveniently forgot when he was a greenhorn off the boat without a pot to piss in, excuse her French. That now he was the big shot
high mucky-muck to people who didn't know him when. That she'd
heard how embarrassed he'd been when some man, some lovely man,
told him that he'd met his *real* wife and *lovely* boy. That he bought
a toupee and walked around like an accident looking for a place to
happen until everybody was laughing fit to be tied at him. That he was
no better than Jimmy Kenny with *his* cow of a floozy. That he'd
treated her father like dirt when he went to try and talk some sense
into him. That he didn't know what to do with a clean, decent girl
from a decent family. That he'd spent whole afternoons away from
the office in the Wolcott Street cellar, someday he'd know what she

meant. That he'd been married in the church just like she was and would have to meet his Maker some day. That he would get his because God is good. That time wounds all heels.

How did Billy's left eye become crossed?

He tripped on the stairway carpeting, fell, and struck his forehead, just above his left eye, on a small knickknack table on the landing. Two days later, while he ate breakfast, his mother looked in his face, made him stare at her, had him move his eyes to follow the movements of her index finger, after which he became frightened enough to cry when his mother gave a short shriek and clasped her hands at her bosom.

To what did Billy assign the cause of his eye becoming crossed?

His mother and father's separation.

What did his mother persist in calling his crossed eye?

A "tired" eye.

What did he most hate about his crossed eye?

The fact that certain boys and girls his age called him, on occasion, "cockeyes." The glasses that he began wearing at age six, when he entered the first grade; there, certain boys and girls called him, on occasion, "four-eyes." The black celluloid patch that his mother made him wear over the lens covering his "good" eye upon returning each afternoon from school. The monthly visits to the clinic at Brooklyn Eye and Ear. The eye drops administered by the doctor, which drops half-blinded him for the remainder of the day.

What was most puzzling to Billy in terms of his grandmother's attitude toward his mother after he and she had moved from Flatbush to Jersey City?

She seemed angry with his mother, not his father.

How did Billy think of Tom Thebus?

As a hero; as a movie star; as a possible new father; as someone who would maybe go and beat his father up; as a man his mother liked a lot; as someone who made him laugh without even trying to.

Recount Billy's sweetest and most mysterious memory.

One morning he awoke and realized from the way the sun looked on his window shade that it was Sunday. He heard his mother and father laughing quietly and got out of bed, walked down the hall to their bedroom, and opened the door. His mother was sitting up in bed, propped against two pillows. His father was sitting on the edge of the bed in his undershirt and shorts, his face turned toward his mother. He was bouncing up and down on the bed and Billy noticed that the bed seemed lopsided and close to the floor at its foot. His mother and father turned toward him as he entered and his mother said, "Your father broke the bed." At this she began to laugh, putting her hand over her mouth. His father, wagging his finger at her, got up, grabbed Billy in his arms and sat down again with him on his lap. "Don't believe Mama," he said. "*She's* the one who broke the bed!" Then *he* began to laugh. Then he shouted, in mock anger that made Billy giggle, "Pancakes! Bacon! Gallons of coffee! Eggs! Rolls!" His mother reached over and put her hand on his father's shoulder with a tenderness that gave Billy a chill of intense delight. There was, he considered, nothing more wonderful and funny than breaking a bed if you were a mother and father.

Dear Daddy,

How are you? We are having a nice time. I feel fine. There is a
man here called Tom Theboss that made me a sling shot and
takes us swimming also, he is a lot of fun and tells a lot of jokes.
And he acts more like my father than you ever do. Well how are
you? I don't know why, I ask, because I don't really care because
I hate you. Mom told me how you walked out on us and didn't
give us any mony. She says I am old enough to know the truth,
now we live with Gramp who is old and mean sometimes, well
you know him. Granma died last winter and I was sad for about a
minute and then I was happy about it. She used to hit me on the
legs and back with a belt and yell at Mom all the time about
mony and things like food. Also she used to give me three rotten
Woolworth cookies for desert every night. All this crapp because,
you left us. It is your fault. I hope Tom Theboss will marry Mom,
and I Really hope so. Because I am sick of thinking about you
and wishing that you would come and say Hello. You came and
see me about twice in many years and I allways hoped that you
would say Hello on my Birthday or Christmas but, you never did.
What a pain you are, what a Louse. Tom can do anything. And
reads books all the time, I even think Gramp likes him, anyway,
they play crokay together allthough Gramp allways beats him like
he can beat anybody. But, Tom plays crokay pretty good, Mom
said you use to play crokay but you stunk. I hope that it is real
hot in the City and you are really sweating a lot and can't sleep.
By the way it is Nice and Cool up here. It would serve you right

anyway. Mom allways says that every dog will have his day. I
guess that means we are the dog that will have their day but, as
far as I am concerned you, are the Real Dog. And guess what
kind of a Dog I mean. Mom told me the story that you and
Margie got married in some phoney way and I just wanted to ask
you if Margie still had green teeth, Mom said, it was the only real
Irish thing about her and, she said that she was a snake in the
grass and she really is a snake. She even looks like a snake. Mom
also said that you and her deserve each other. When Tom is my
real Father soon I will ask him to go and punch you and Margie
in your face.

Yours very truly, your Son,
Billy

How great everything is panning out! Mom really admires Tom and loves him a lot too and Tom thinks Mom is as swell as they come and a great sport and he loves her too!

Even better than this is that Gramp likes Tom a lot and thinks it is a capital idea that Tom wants to marry Mom and she wants to marry him. He thinks that Tom is a real gentleman and a go-getter and says he is the only man who can give him a decent game of croquet.

Tom in fact loves Mom so much that he asked her to marry him so that he can be her husband just like Daddy was and also be Billy's father.

Gramp thinks it is about time that he popped the question and that it is jake with him and thinks that they should not even wait to get back to the city but they should tie the knot right here this summer and get married in the Warren House in Hackettstown!

Suddenly one fine morning Daddy comes up to the Stellkamps' farm and says that a little bird told him that Mom was getting married to Tom and that he has looked into Tom and found out that he is a prince of a man and that as far as he is concerned he thinks it is one of the best ideas he has heard in a long time. He wonders if he would be a fifth wheel if he came to the wedding at the Warren House because he certainly doesn't want to butt in where he isn't wanted.

Of course you can come to the wedding Mom says and so does Gramp and Tom too says sure it is fine with me, hunky-dory, and that Mom has told him an awful lot of good things about Daddy and Gramp says that he shouldn't make himself a stranger and what in hell has been the matter with him that nobody sees hide nor hair of

him anymore? Is he getting too good for everybody now that he is a
big mucky-muck?

Daddy says that there is no substitute for old friends and that blood
is thicker than water and that he will be glad to come to the wedding
and he will stand in the back so that he won't be in anybody's way.
And Gramp and Tom say what do you think you're doing? Stand in
the back my foot! You will be the guest of honor and Mom says oh
yes Tony and that she bears no grudge or hard feelings, it is all water
under the bridge.

Daddy is so happy that he starts to laugh and says well this is more
than I bargained for because I did not know exactly what kind of a
reception to expect but this is really tops in my book, it is aces. What
Daddy really came up to the country for he says is to ask Mom's
permission to take Billy on a little trip to the Pyramids of the Nile
and Borneo. That is such a cunning idea Mom says and gives her
permission in a sec. There is nothing like foreign lands for an educa-
tion she says, as long as you come back finally to the good old U S A.

Of course Gramp says this will be after the wedding in the Warren
House because not only is Daddy going to be the special guest of
honor because he used to be Mom's husband and he is Billy's dad and
I think the world of you and if I can add two and two you and Tom
here are also going to hit it off but also Billy is going to be the ring
bearer. Which reminds Gramp to tell Tom that he better skedaddle
into Hackettstown or Netcong and select a ring from one of the
diamond jewelry stores there. Tom slaps his forehead with his hand
and laughs and says wow! I am so excited and happy that I almost
forgot about the most important thing of all! What a dumbbell jerk
I am! You certainly are Gramp laughs and slaps him on the back and
says it's lucky his head is attached to his shoulders or he'd forget that
too!

Suddenly that afternoon Father Donovan from Our Lady of Angels
comes up and says that he is carrying a message from Monsignor
O'Hara and he stands on the porch and opens an envelope while Tom
and Mom and Daddy and Gramp all sit in rocking chairs and there
are some other busybodies there too with their ears cocked like the
Sapurtys and Mom is pulling at her hankie and Tom is patting her
shoulder. Billy doesn't know exactly what the heck is going on but he

remembers Mom saying that Father Donovan is a very strict priest because he is a Back Bay North of Ireland convert and they are the worst kind and Billy figures that Mom is nervous because the Catholic priests do not like people to get divorced or to get married twice or something like that, it's like eating meat on Friday. Daddy is looking at him with a little kind of wisenheimer smile because as far as he is concerned priests all eat roast beef on Friday and live like kings except for Father Bucafusco at St. Rocco's who was a saint on earth.

Father Donovan looks at the message and says that as far as Monsignor O'Hara is concerned and all the other priests and the good Sisters of Charity at Our Lady of Angels it is fine by them that Mom and Tom should get married because they are both good Catholics and Catholics should be happy. Besides Monsignor O'Hara adds a P.S. to say that just that morning before Father Donovan got on the Erie to Netcong, which is why he is all covered with grime and soot, a special-delivery telegram came to Monsignor O'Hara from the Pope Pius and he has thought the case over and decided that he wants Mom and Tom to get married right away because he knows from special reports what a wonderful lady Mom is and what a good Catholic she has been all these years and also what a fine man Tom is. As for Gramp although he is not a real Catholic as far as the Pope Pius is concerned he might as well be because High Episcopalians are just about Catholics.

What a relief for everybody! They all pile into a big black Packard limousine that Our Lady of Angels has sent up special with a chauffeur and rush into Hackettstown and stop off for a minute to buy a stunning wedding ring. Then they go to the Warren House so that Mom and Tom can get married right away and they do. Father Donovan stands on the little platform that the dutchie polka band plays on on Saturday nights and they are married in a jiffy and everybody says that Mom is a beautiful bride in her white summer dress and that Tom is a handsome groom in his white polo shirt and white knickers that he sometimes wears to play croquet and his white stockings and shoes.

Then Father Donovan buys the house a round of beer except for Billy and the Copan girls and he buys them orange drink and a whole bunch of potato chips. And when they start dancing to some records on the jukebox like "Beer Barrel Polka" and "Careless" and "Darn That Dream" and "Deep Purple" and "Hold Tight, Hold Tight" and "If I Didn't Care" and "I'll Never Smile Again" and "My Prayer" and "South of the Border" and "Three Little Fishies" and some other hit tunes Daddy comes up to Billy and says well Billy are you ready to leave tomorrow with me to go to Egypt and the Mysterious Nile and then to Borneo to see where they get pure rubber? And Billy says wow! *Am* I!

Daddy comes home late, he can tell because it's been dark for a long time and he ate while Jack Armstrong was on and that was also a long time ago.

"I am really sorry, honey, but I was working so hard and working my fingers to the bone to make plenty of money to buy us all some nice things and also maybe put a down payment down on a new Packard."

"Oh, my darling husband Tony, that is perfectly all right! I have kept this nice Swiss steak nice and warm and juicy and I will make you some mash potatoes and a nice crispy green salad!"

"You are just a peach, Marie, dear wife."

"I am so sorry and I apologize for being so late that it is dark already, my darling wife."

"Oh, that is O.K., adorable Tony, my husband. I do not mind one iota you coming home late. I know how hard you work down by the dockyards."

"Well, I have to be square with you, sweetie, I was not really working late, I had to meet an important mucky-muck and sign a contract with him for a big job that will be about a million dollars or maybe even more."

"You are the smartest and most wonderful hubby who ever lived! Here, sit down and I will give you your favorite supper of spaghetti and chocolate pudding!"

"It is certainly getting mighty cold and it feels just like snow. Well, it serves me right for getting home in the dark and cold windy night.

Will you accept my apologies, beautiful bride of mine?"

"My dearest Tony! Will I accept your apologies? Ha ha ha! Just go and sit in the living room and put your feet up and shake up a cocktail. I will fix you a nice hot dinner of caviar and pheasants that were on sale today at Bohack's."

"Dear! Soon, and you can mark my words, you will not have to be worrying about buying things at sales. Our ship is going to come in soon."

"Of course, sugar pie. You know how I have such full trust in you and how smart you are. Now, just go in and sit down and have a highball cocktail or two."

"It is sure enough cold out there, Marie honeybunch. There is enough snow to make it like the North Pole! I hope that you have not waited for me for supper."

"I will whip up some roasted chicken in a minute, don't you worry about a thing, and also some salad with French dressing just the way a hard-working man likes hearty foodstuffs."

"How swell you are, my cuddles! I was late because I had to help that poor kid Margie in the office with her cheapskate Jew landlord because she don't have heat in this subfrozen weather. Can you beat that? I told him where he could get off and that I would call up the police chief if he did not act square. That is why I am so darn late."

"Tony, you darling! You have a heart of gold to help that poor nice girl out like that. And good for you that you talked turkeys to that Jew skinflint. Now, sit down and let me toss up some roasted chicken for you!"

"Hiya, dear. Gosh almighty, I tried and tried like heck to get off work early tonight but you know how things go for a young boss."

"Don't aggravate yourself, hon, I will just fling out this Swiss steak stew dish and snap beans and mash potatoes and gravy in the garbage since it is all dried out. And I will run to the butcher in a jiffy and get you a couple of nice tender lamb chops for supper and stop off for a banana split too because I know how you love it."

"Gosh almighty, Marie sweetness, don't you bother your pretty swell little head about it. Go out in this weather? It is blowing up a blizzard tonight! Are you nutty? Just serve me whatever odds and ends you have left over and I will fill up on Bond bread too. Gosh, you know how I love your Swiss steak better than anything except that great stuffed roasted turkey you cook on special occasion holidays. Your dried-out and ice-cold Swiss steak is better than a meal fit for a king!"

"You are such a thoughtful man, and meanwhile darling, while I heat up these few things, just sit down and read your paper and listen to the radio in your socks. Supper will be ready before you can say Jack Robinson."

"Jack Robinson!"

"Oh, Tony! You're always such a kidder!"

"Boy, the traffic was really heavy tonight and on top of working late at the old grind mill no wonder I am so tardy for supper. Heck, I am sorry, sugar cake."

"You do not have to worry, dearest, I have a special emergency supper all ready to cook for you here, see? Fruit salad and alphabet soup and roasted steak sandwiches on toast. How does that sound?"

"Wow! That is what I call a hearty meal! But if you would not mind saving it, I thought that we could all go out for supper if you do not mind eating another supper or just watching me eat while you and Billy have a hunk of bread and butter or something."

"Go out, my lamb?"

"Yes, my dreamboat. Because today I signed the papers to become partners with a millionaire and soon we will also be millionaires! So let's put on our duds and go out, maybe we will drive out to Nathan's?"

"Oh Tony! It is so hard to believe! You have worked and prayed so hard for this chance to show them!"

"Yes, sugar, it has been a long haul but we are on our way to the moon!"

"Oh gosh, gosh! Let's go! Let's go to Nathan's! It will be a swell treat!"

"Hi, honey! Excuse me for being so late for supper but I have been up to my ears in important meetings with a bunch of millionaires like the Rockefellers and the Vanderbilts. Business, you know."

"Darling! Maybe this is the chance you have been praying to God for."

"I certainly hope so, angel. But I am afraid that I have to disappoint you about after supper again. Instead of staying here in our cozy living room with my slippers on and listening to some good shows, I must eat and run because I have to get back to the meetings. Those rich bozos do not watch the clock, as they say. So if you can just make me a ham or baloney and American sandwich on Bond bread with a dill pickle I will be in seventh heaven."

"Dearest Tony! Of course! Gosh, you don't have to explain why you have to go out after a bite of supper. I pride myself on understanding your work. I will whip up a big club sandwich for you in a jiffy! There is a mouth-watering recipe for one with crispy bacon and tasty cheese in the new *Liberty.*"

"Swell, sugar. And meanwhile, I will change my clothes and shave because I probably will not be home until tomorrow night late. Time waits for no man."

"O.K., my beloved, just hurry now and I will have this scrumptious sandwich that they often serve at the White House ready for you in two shakes of a lamb's tail!"

"You are a real princess, my darling wife."

His mother was going to go out on a date, a real date, just like Helen Copan did with the lifeguard, but she wasn't going out with any *lifeguard,* but with Tom Thebus. And they *were* going to go to the WigWam, just like she had said they might and like he had talked about a few days ago with Tom. His grandfather didn't seem to like the idea, so maybe Tom was right when he said that he didn't really like him. That was something that Billy couldn't figure out at all. But he knew that his grandfather and mother had been arguing, his grandfather's face got long and sour and he spent a lot of time sitting on the church steps and taking walks all by himself, sometimes as far as the Bluebird, and that was really far away. For some reason, Mrs. Schmidt talked to his grandfather a lot. She smiled like you would at a baby. Today his grandfather *really* had a sour puss.

His mother had gone into Hackettstown that afternoon with Dave Warren, who had come up to the farm to get some eggs for the Warren House just like he did every Saturday, and he was going to come back for supper like every Saturday too. When she came back she had a bag with her from the five-and-ten and two other bags. The five-and-ten bag had presents for him, a big white metal China Clipper, white as snow, really swell. And also his own bottle of rose oil just like Tom's. She was smiling and happier than he ever remembered seeing her, except when he got that Certificate for Clear Speech from P.S. 170 in June. And maybe a few other times, but anyway, she was happy, that was for sure. In one of the other bags she had a pair of white summer shoes, all open on the top and with high heels and the other bag she didn't open. She pulled off her canvas shoes and put the white shoes on and pulled her skirt around her legs so she could look down

and see how the shoes looked. She almost did a kind of dance right
there in her room, turning her feet different ways so she could see how
the shoes looked when she moved. When she asked him how the shoes
looked on her he told her that they were beautiful. They *were* beautiful. His mother had really small feet and these shoes made them look
even smaller, maybe because they were all open on the top with only
little strips of leather crisscrossed and a strap around the ankle and
the heels were thin and high. It was a cinch that she would be able
to dance better in them than in any of the other dress-up shoes she
brought from the city, they were O.K., but they didn't look like these
and most of them, maybe all of them, were black anyway.

The idea of his mother and Tom going dancing at the WigWam
fascinated him. He had imagined the WigWam a hundred times, but
he only knew what it was like from the outside and he had only seen
it at night once. But he remembered it perfectly. There was a sign in
neon lights in the shape of a wigwam and written over it in script it
said, also in neon lights, THE WIGWAM. Under the wigwam sign and
a little to the right of it, and also in neon lights, a smaller sign said,
DANCE DINE COCKTAILS. The night he passed by, one time that they'd
gone last summer with Eleanor and Dave to the amusement park at
Lake Hopatcong, there were cars outside, a lot of cars, and the signs
were really bright in the dark, and he could see men and women going
in and coming out, laughing, and he saw one man kiss a woman he
was walking with. From inside came music and you could tell it was
a real band from the way it sounded. He'd heard a band at the Warren
House but this was a different kind of band, you could hear that they
really could play real songs, like "Maria Elena." With trumpets. It
wasn't a dutchie polka band. He didn't know what it was like inside
but he thought that it was probably really big with tables behind a
little low wall and a big shiny dance floor and the band had fancy suits
on, the kind with the black bow ties. If people weren't on the dance
floor dancing they would be sitting at the tables, laughing and chatting
and smoking cigarettes and drinking terrific cocktails. Really fancy
drinks in all kinds of colors in those glasses with stems on them. The
bartender was wearing a short white coat and shook these drinks up
in a solid silver shaker while the band played. Once in a while when
two people could really dance great, everybody else stopped and got

off the dance floor and watched them. The bandleader probably had
a moustache and a skinny stick that he waved to tell the band how
to play all the songs. And also he knew that the place was all white,
floor, walls, and tables. The works. He would go there every night in
the summer when he got to be a man.

As soon as his mother got back from Hackettstown, his grandfather
seemed to get more and more mad. Really sore. He came right into
his mother's room without even knocking when she was showing Billy
the new shoes and told him to go out and play but he went into the
bathroom just down the hall and tried to hear what they were saying.
But his grandfather closed the door and the bathroom door was also
closed, so he couldn't hear much, just once he heard his grandfather
say "a patch on a man's ass," and he also heard his mother say *some
life*," and something like "cook and bottle washer," and he knew that
had something to do with his grandmother being sick in bed so long.
He left the bathroom and ran down the stairs and out, then crossed
the road and went into the churchyard where it was shady and cool
under the big elm trees. He figured that his grandfather must be mad
because he thought that maybe Tom Thebus and his mother were
doing something bad like his father and Margie did. The bad had
something to do, he was sure, with what was fucking. But his mother
would never do that. He felt funny and sad even thinking about that
word when he thought of his mother. And he didn't think that Tom
would ever do that either. It was different with his father and Margie,
if that was the bad that they did, because his father was married to
his mother when he was going out to see Margie and dancing with
her or going out on dates or visiting, and Margie was a tramp which
was the same as a hooer and Kickie told him a year ago that all hooers
did was fucking. If you were married to a person, whether you were
a man or a woman, and you danced and visited and went on dates with
another person who was not married or who was married to some
other person themselves then that was doing something bad, that was
probably about fucking. But if you weren't married, like his mother
and Tom, what was bad? They were going on a date, like Helen
Copan. Nobody thought that she was being bad when she went out
with the lifeguard. Everybody thought it was cute. Mrs. Saputry even
said, "Aren't they darling?" on the porch one night when they were

going to the movies. So what was his grandfather so mad about? Tom was a great guy. It was easy to see why his mother wanted to go dancing with him. Billy *wanted* her to go and he'd tell his grandfather that if he asked him. His mother was pretty and should go dancing with a guy like Tom Thebus, who liked everybody and was always making everybody laugh. And maybe Tom would come and see them in the city and take him to a football game. And maybe sometime he would really be his father. Maybe his mother would get married to him. Once you were married you couldn't do anything bad with the person you were married to, *priests* married you, you wouldn't have to worry about fucking. If his mother and Tom got married his grandfather would have to stop.

He moped around the rest of the afternoon, only it wasn't really moping, even though he wished that he'd gone to Budd Lake with Mr. Copan and the girls. He was just waiting for the time to pass because he wanted to see his mother and Tom get all ready and leave in Tom's car. He fooled around on the lawn with a croquet mallet and Mr. Sapurty came out and asked him if he'd like to have a game and he said sure. It was always embarrassing to play with Mr. Sapurty because he could usually beat him and Mr. Sapurty would get annoyed and chew away at his cigar and say something about the wrong glasses he had and how he meant to get them changed. But he was just a lousy player. It was really funny to see him play his grandfather or Tom, they could beat him without paying attention to the game at all.

As usual, he beat Mr. Sapurty and he was going to play him another game when Tom came out on the lawn and sat down under the umbrella trees near the vegetable garden. Mr. Sapurty said that he had to clean out the inside of his car, but Billy knew that he didn't want to play him and get beat with Tom watching. Billy went over to Tom and they sat together and Billy played with his China Clipper for a while but Tom didn't say a word about the WigWam and he thought maybe that his grandfather had told his mother that he wouldn't allow her to go. But just as he was thinking that maybe that was exactly what had happened, Tom said that he hoped it would be a cool night because he had to wear a tie. He said "a goldurned dadblasted tee-eye," to make Billy laugh. Well, that was that. Tom would never wear a tie unless he was going somewhere special.

At suppertime everything went along as usual. Tom sat at their table and talked about Germany and how things looked bad and the Depression, and his grandfather looked at him with a kind of disgusted look. Billy knew that Mrs. Schmidt was a German and so were the Stellkamps and he figured that when Tom talked about Germany and that things were bad there he was probably doing what his grandfather called mortifying everybody. His mother smiled at Tom when his grandfather wasn't looking and Mrs. Schmidt at the table with the Copans and Dave Warren was smiling every once in a while at his grandfather like she was sorry for him. Once she said something to Mrs. Copan, who was the skinniest woman Billy had ever seen, his mother said she was a bag of rags tied in the middle, and after she said it Mrs. Schmidt shook her head like she was very sad and smiled over at his grandfather again.

Then Billy just sat on the porch with the Copan girls and Dave Warren. His mother and Tom were getting ready and just about the time it was getting shadowy over in the churchyard where it always got dark first, Tom came out on the porch smoking his pipe and dressed in his blue coat, white pants, a white shirt and blue tie, and his white shoes. He sat on the porch railing and talked to Billy about the Dodgers and Giants and looked at his wrist watch once. The Copan girls were giggling and whispering together and Dave Warren sat smoking a cigarette and said just one thing, that it looked like it was going to be a nice evening. Then his mother came out. She had on a white dress with a white belt and a string of white beads that matched her earrings and her new white shoes. She was wearing silk stockings. She was carrying a white crocheted shawl and she looked really swell with rouge and lipstick on, really pretty and young, better than Helen Copan. She and Tom smiled at each other and he looked at his watch again and said that it was time they got going because it was kind of a drive. Dave Warren got up from the steps to let them pass and the Copan girls told his mother that she looked just beautiful. His grandfather came out on the porch and stood there with his hands in his back pockets and Billy kissed his mother and then looked over at his grandfather but his face was stiff and angry, even though Billy thought he said to his mother to have a nice time. He didn't say anything to Tom. Tom and his mother walked down the path to the gate that opened on the road and everybody on the porch stood at the railing and watched them and Billy wished and wished that his mother would take Tom's arm like Helen Copan but he knew that she wouldn't in front of everybody, she looked, even, like she was blushing. When they got in Tom's car and started off, everybody waved except his grandfather, who just stood at the railing with his arms folded the way he did when he made a good shot in croquet and he was waiting to see what the other player would do. Tom backed the car out of the spot he always parked it in next to the church and they started down the road the way you went to the Hi-Top and the Copan girls and Billy waved and his mother put her hand out the window and waved back and Tom blew the horn twice, just two short little beeps.

Billy went inside for a while and looked at the Stellkamps' Sears, Roebuck catalogue, skipping all the pages with ladies in their underwear because Eleanor was still there pulling off the tablecloths and polishing. The pictures made him feel very strange and sometimes a little dizzy and hot. He couldn't figure out why a lady would let somebody take a picture of her in her underwear. Maybe they were hooers. The pictures fascinated him because he learned the names of all those things that ladies wear under their dresses. There were a lot of pretty ladies wearing corsets but they didn't look like his grandmother's. He put the Sears catalogue back and went out on the porch again. His grandfather was sitting next to Mrs. Schmidt, both of them rocking back and forth. He was smoking. He told Billy that he had been looking for him to tell him that he was going to take a walk and that he expected Billy to take a bath and get to bed at the usual time. "Nothing special about tonight, young man." Then he went in and came out a few minutes later with a sweater, a flashlight, and a bottle of citronella, and he and Mrs. Schmidt left together. It was funny that while his grandfather was gone, Mrs. Schmidt told him what a wonderful man his grandfather was, that he was a lucky boy to have such a man to take care of him and his mother, and that they should always be grateful to such a prince. Billy said he was glad she liked his grandfather and she got red and said that that was not exactly what she meant.

He didn't take a bath but just ran water in the tub to get it wet. He washed his hands and arms and face and skipped brushing his teeth. It was a strange but very good feeling that his mother wasn't there to make sure he took a bath and everything else. Maybe if she got married to Tom she wouldn't pay so much attention to him. When he turned the light out in the bathroom he looked out the window that faced the farm buildings and the fields beyond and saw that it was a clear night but that there was no moon that he could see. The dark was full of fireflies. He went into the room he shared with his grandfather, said his "Now I lay me," and got into bed. Right now, he guessed, his mother and Tom were at the WigWam, probably having a fancy drink in one of those glasses with the long stems, a Horse's Neck or a Manhattan. He knew a Manhattan was a *really* fancy kind of drink because when they first came up this summer they had to wait for Louis to pick them up at Netcong and they went into a little café to get out of the sun and cool off and his mother said she felt like a Manhattan. He remembered his grandfather said, "These hicks will give you a *Brooklyn,* damn all they know about it," and his mother laughed and had a Tom Collins instead and gave him the cherry.

The WigWam *must* have white everything. He figured that's probably why his mother wore white and Tom had on white pants and stuff. Sure. He was absolutely delighted thinking of them dancing and talking and Tom smiling as he lit his pipe. Maybe they'd do this again. Maybe Tom would come to see his mother in the city all the time and take her out to the movies and to night clubs over in New York, maybe even to Coney Island and they could go to Feltman's. That would be great, the waiters sang songs and everything. He fell asleep thinking of his mother and Tom chatting over a little bite of something, little sandwiches cut like diamonds. They had that liquor you put in a pail.

His grandfather was shouting at him from the roof to come up! come up! and he woke up and saw his grandfather in the dark, leaning out the window, shining a flashlight down and across the road. He was yelling and really mad, and he kept yelling about the time! the time! and what did he think his daughter was, and telling somebody to come up, goddammit to *hell!* Billy suddenly felt sick when he understood that he was yelling at his *mother.* And at Tom, too. But really mostly his mother. He said "Gramp" and his grandfather turned his head and told him to go back to sleep. Then he just stood at the window without shouting anymore but he kept standing there, shining the flashlight. Billy lay still, stiff, with his eyes closed, then heard his grandfather pull the window down halfway and hook the screen. In about a half a minute he heard the porch door close and footsteps on the stairs. It was his mother, he could tell. He wondered where Tom was and why he didn't come in with his mother. She passed by the door of their room and started up the stairs to where her room was. She was crying very low, like she had a handkerchief to her mouth. Billy lay rigid, wondering what had happened. He heard a scratch and opened his eyes a little to see his grandfather light a cigarette and sit down on his bed. His grandfather said, in a whisper to himself, "One-thirty in the morning. A spectacle. One-thirty." Billy wished hard but he was afraid that everything was spoiled. As he was going back to sleep he heard a man's footsteps pass the door and start up the stairs. That must be Tom. Everything was *really* spoiled. He wanted to yell out curses but started to cry.

The next morning he saw that his mother's eyes were red and he knew that she had been crying. Things were very strange at the house when they all had breakfast, his grandfather seemed very loud and happy, and talked about how the weather was changing, fall was definitely in the air, almost time to get back to the old grind, but it would be a relief. He even spoke to Tom the same way, all smiles and jokes, but it gave Billy the creeps. His mother sat very quietly, picking at her breakfast and leaving her second cup of coffee half-drunk. For some reason, everybody else was as loud as his grandfather, but their voices were phony and reminded Billy of how the kids in school talked when they put on a pageant for Open School assembly. Mrs. Schmidt was even waving her arms around the way Wanita Whiteman did when she played Lady Freedom last term. Tom smiled and smiled but Billy didn't remember him saying a word except to excuse himself to go out on the porch and smoke his pipe. When breakfast was over, Tom wasn't on the porch. Billy wanted to go and look for him, not to ask him anything about his grandfather yelling, he just wanted to be with him, but then it was time for mass and they went to the white wooden church in Mr. Sapurty's car. Mrs. Schmidt usually went in Mr. Copan's car but she said that the weather was bothering her arthritis, and when they left she was sitting on the porch with his grandfather and Dave Warren, who wasn't a Catholic, at least he never went to mass. At mass, his mother didn't seem to be paying attention to anything and when they rang the bell she didn't even beat her chest or bow her head, just stared right in front of her so that he was afraid the priest even might say something to her.

When they got back, his mother changed into a pinafore and came downstairs and then she and his grandfather went across the road and sat together on the church steps and Billy was afraid that his grandfather was going to start yelling at her again. He was standing in front of her and a couple of steps lower and swinging his stick back and forth and talking and talking right into her face. His mother kept looking past him at the far fields where the cows were grazing, tiny black-and-white and brown-and-white dots, they looked like little toys in the hazy sunlight. His mother came across the road when the dinner bell rang and his grandfather followed, but she went upstairs and at the table he said that she had a headache and wanted to lie down for a while. Tom came in late and excused himself, saying that he'd taken a long walk, and then he started to talk to his grandfather about the wonderful collie that Mr. O'Neill down the road had, yes, he'd had a long talk with him that morning and did his grandfather know that Mr. O'Neill fed the dog a pint of heavy cream in the morning, a sirloin steak in the afternoon, and another pint of cream at night? That was all he got. His grandfather said that Mr. O'Neill was a wonderful man and had raised prize-winning collies all his life, he had one, a big dog named Harriet, that had been the most beautiful dog that he'd ever seen, but she was killed about five years ago by some damn fool in a coupe that took a curve on two wheels. Then they were silent and all that Billy heard was Mrs. Schmidt talking at the next table about her relatives in Germany and how happy they were that everything was beginning to be the way it was before the terrible war and how this Hitler was doing wonders and how he wanted only peace for the German people. Tom looked up at the ceiling with a little smile on his face, smoothing his moustache with his fingers. It wasn't a very nice smile but Tom didn't say a word.

In the afternoon, Tom took him and the Copan girls swimming—nobody else felt like going because it had clouded up and got a little chilly, and his mother was still up in her room with a headache. It *was* cold at the lake, and after about an hour or even less, Tom said that he thought they really ought to get home before they all came down with the chills. When they got back, Tom changed into a pair of slacks and a sweater and said that he had to go into Hackettstown to take care of some business matters and make some phone calls and probably wouldn't be back for supper. He told Mrs. Stellkamp that he was going to really try, though, because he didn't want to miss the bread pudding that she made for Sunday night dessert. She told him not to worry, she'd save him a good portion and he could have it any time he wanted. She sounded really polite, like a waitress.

After Tom left, Billy went up to his room and played with his China Clipper. The whole place was deathly silent and he wondered what everybody was doing. His grandfather wasn't playing croquet—nobody was—and Mrs. Schmidt and Mrs. Copan, who usually sat in the sun near the kitchen garden and crocheted, weren't there. Well, there was no sun to sit in. He walked upstairs and knocked at his mother's door and called to her, but she said that she really wanted to rest and would see him at supper. Her voice sounded really sad and tired and he was afraid that something really bad had happened while he had been at Budd Lake. Although last night had been bad enough. It was funny that nobody even mentioned it once.

Tom didn't come back for supper and his mother had something light, some poached eggs on toast that Eleanor took up to her room because she said that though she was feeling much better she thought it would be wise to stay in bed and rest. Mrs. Schmidt sat at *their* table for the first time, and in his mother's chair! He didn't like it much but his grandfather didn't seem to mind a bit, he even looked like he liked it. A lot. Mrs. Schmidt was talking about him finally drawing the line and his grandfather was smiling the way Billy hated to see him smile, with his false teeth hanging out of his mouth like someone had just glued them on the inside of his lips. He didn't want to listen to what they said because he knew it had something to do with all the yelling. They both seemed really happy about it.

After supper he hung around the church steps for a while, waiting for Tom to come back, but by nightfall he still hadn't returned. Billy went down to the barn but Louis had finished milking and so he came back and sat on the church steps again, listening to his grandfather and Mrs. Schmidt and the Sapurtys and Copans laughing on the porch. It was all sad and really rotten to him without his mother and Tom there and he knew that it would be like this the rest of the vacation. He wanted desperately to go back to the city. Now. By the time he had to go up to brush his teeth and wash, Tom still hadn't come back.

In the morning, Tom was at breakfast before anybody else, dressed in a suit and tie, and when everybody looked at him he said that he'd been on the phone with his boss last night and damn if the man didn't insist on him cutting his vacation short and coming back to close a sale. It was a big deal and the salesman who had got the contact just didn't have Tom's "expoit" touch, so the boss demanded that he come back in. Billy loved it when Tom said things like "expoit." He was the same Tom no matter what his grandfather did! The close would take a couple of days at the least, Tom said, and then at least a day in the office and, well, he shrugged, that just about puts the old kibosh on my vacation. Billy's mother was pale, and when Tom went out to his car with his valises she stood on the porch watching him while his grandfather sat in a rocker watching the both of them. And Mrs. Schmidt sat in another rocker watching all three of them. Billy wanted to cheer when his mother finally went across the road and she and Tom stood together a minute talking next to his car, then they shook hands and Tom started to get into the car. But then he stopped and waved at everybody, and called "Billy!" Billy jumped off the porch and ran across the road to him, and Tom gave him a hug and rubbed his head. He grinned at him and told him not to look so sad—that he'd see him in the city just like they'd agreed. Absolutely. Positively. Absotivolutely! He got in the car then and in a minute he was gone.

No matter what Tom said, Billy felt so bad that he thought he'd cry, so he ran from where he said goodbye to Tom straight down to the barnyard and stood watching Louis' pigs for a long time. Tom would have to be *invited* to come and see him in the city and his grandfather didn't like him—Tom was right about that. Tom would never be his father, not now. If his mother only hadn't gone to the WigWam with him maybe everything would still be all right. What was the matter with his grandfather? Maybe he yelled like that at his mother when she was still married and his father left and just never came back. Maybe, though, Tom would come, maybe.

After a time he returned to the house to get his slingshot, well, he had that. Everybody was on the lawn and he could hear the dull clack of the croquet balls being struck, and his grandfather said, *"Now* we'll see how you like the woods!"* The idea of them all just *playing* this game, just the idea of it made him angry and he went inside and into the deserted dining room. As he neared the stairs he trailed his fingers across the sideboard and they touched something. He stopped and saw that it was some kind of leather thing, a wallet or something, then he realized that it was Tom's tobacco pouch, he'd seen it a million times. He picked it up and unzipped it, yes, the rich smell of Tom's tobacco enveloped him. He forgot his pouch! He was rushing so much to get back to work that he just put it down and forgot it. Billy stood for a minute, then took the pouch and went upstairs to his mother's room, hoping that she was there. He knocked at the door, then knocked again, and his mother said, "Yes?" He said that he had something to show her and she told him to come in. He turned the knob, holding Tom's pouch before him in his other hand.

Penny arcade cigarette lighter that nobody ever filled.

Buddy was a pain in the ass but he didn't have to die because of that. In Jersey City it was always grey and rainy.

The funny white stone pipes in the drawer with green ribbons tied to them.

Gramp's fat guitar. Was that the kind of thing Tito Guizar played?

Uncle Joe talked funny and always gave him cold chicken to eat: "Boys gotta to eat."

For his birthday when he was little Margie gave him a rector set. She had a green dress on and smelled sweet. "Like the five-and-ten."

Daddy came in with one kind of suit on and went out with another one on right away.

Mrs. Herrick next door gave him and Dougie vanilla cookies and hot chocolate when the old hunkie's police dog scared them.

Daddy took the tail off the zeppelin when he cut his heinie. "God damn mockie bastards at Shiffman's!"

You could eat potatoes with big rats on your shoulder? How? They liked potatoes too? People could be anything!

"I'm *sure* you have to *work* tomorrow, don't you, Tony?"

Once Gramp saw men pull a dead man out of his coffin and try to make him drink whiskey. Granma said the ice would melt under the coffin sometimes and the dead person would roll over.

Snow halfway up the door and Daddy dug a path like a big tunnel.

Everybody would die, even him.

A bunch of things like blotters attached together with a leather cover that said LAKE HOPATCONG, N.J., and had an Indian in a canoe on a river.

"Matches her shanty-Irish teeth."

Buddy fell off a rope or something. He had a little backache and then he died.

The orange stuff on the salad was called French dressing Daddy wouldn't eat: "That's what makes the Americans all crazy."

His other gramp was blind and he couldn't understand what he said to him, they'd sit together in the backyard while the old man smoked licorice twists Uncle Angelo said were cigars. "Pop talks that damn Chinese to him all day long."

The tin pig had a sailor suit on and a sailor hat and a drum and when you wound him up he beat the drum and walked funny across the floor until he stopped and then he fell over. He always smiled in a kind of scary way.

Once an old witch talked to him from behind the door in the kitchen that went down to the cellar. "Your mother told me to tell you to stop untying your shoes." He ran around the house screaming and banging into the walls, the witch ate Mom!

"And I'm *sure* Miss Little Helper has to *work* tomorrow too?" Daddy pushed the salad away, "Give it to the pigs, O.K.?"

The dirty kid who smelled like coo-coo handed him a can of worms to eat. Cousin Katie told him to stay away from the filthy little dago.

A whole bunch of tiny little canes made out of blue glass tied together with a rubber band. Granma saw him looking in the drawer and hit him with her ·skinny belt: "Like your father! Just like your father! Oh, Jesus, Mary and Joseph!" Daddy maybe looked in the drawer and they made him leave home when they found out.

Mom worked at a steam table and got tired. It must have been hot, whatever you did there.

He told Mom the fat man on the corner outside the saloon smiled and tipped his hat, and she pinched his arm. "Sh! He's a bookmaker. I had enough of Italians to last me a lifetime."

Some kid who was a cousin or something, Frankie Caffrey, ate bananas all the time with sugar all over them. "My mother says that gives you pimples." "Shut your fuckin mouth, you greaseball!" He asked Mom about these funny words that pleased him and she told him that Frankie was nothing but a thick ignorant Mick.

Uncle Tom always took him to a park to have a catch with a

hardball and once showed him the guy who said "Call for Philip Morris!" playing softball. When they went back to Uncle Tom's house he'd make pizza in a stone oven in the backyard and talk to Aunt Marie like his other gramp did.

"You don't even have a father and that's why you can't go to Cathlick school. You're a Protestant." He spit in Pat's face and ran. "You're as Irish as *that* Mick!" Mom was really mad.

In the dark church with all the statues wrapped up in purple cloth they had to walk in line down the center aisle and then there was Jesus on the floor on a crucifix and they had to kneel down when the nun slapped her wooden clappers together and kiss Him on the mouth. His stomach turned over and he gagged.

Peggy Copan sat on the railing of the porch with her legs up and he saw her pink underpants.

Mrs. O'Neill asked Mom if she bought her fish from the guinea street peddler because he had the best. So guineas were dagos and wops and also greaseballs? He was a greaseball like Daddy and his other gramp! But he was also Irish like a thick Mick. A greaseball Mick?

"Is Margie a thick Mick?" Gramp laughed, shelling peas for Sunday dinner. "Between you me and the lamppost, not one of them that's not, if truth be told, Billy—save your mother."

When Helen Walsh kneeled down to kiss Jesus he saw her white underpants and so did Guido Pucci who made a hole with his left hand and moved his right finger in and out of it fast. Sister Francis de Sales saw him smiling and yanked him out of the line by his ear: "You committed a terrible sin laughing on Good Friday in Church!"

What Guido did meant fucking, because girls had a hole in their stomachs and you stuck your thing in it. Guido wore rubbers to school because his shoes had such big holes in them. He was a *real* greaseball because he was born in Italy. In the Christmas play Guido wore a black cardboard moustache and a gold earring and a shiny yellow shirt. His name was Happy Tony and he waved a little Italian flag: "I am Happy Tony, the fruitstand man. I love to sing and dance and my favorite dinner is spaghetti and meatballs! I come from sunny Italy's pleasant land where grapes and olives grow!"

Granma's corset stiff and monstrous on the chair, he smelled its

flowery perfume. Did that mean that Margie wore one of these things?
But her smell was different.

On 68th Street when they moved back from Jersey City he had a
fistfight with Angie Salvati his first day on the block. "Cockeyes!"
Then they were friends and then he was friends with everybody.

He couldn't judge a thrown or batted ball and so was admitted into
games out of pity. But nobody could run faster.

Mom at the kitchen sink in pink underpants and stockings with her
chest bare, drinking a glass of water. "Billy, go back to bed!" her arms
crossed over her breasts.

Granma hid the corset when Dr. Drescher came with his medicine
bag. He would listen to his chest with his ear thing, just like he did
with Granma. Bottles of dark-red and black medicine and sticky
spoons. "Port wine to build up the blood, ja."

He thought the Swedish Hospital would be all white and was
astounded to find it drab and ordinary. "Swedish ships are the clean-
est." "The Palmolive company buys all the filthy oil and grease in the
tanks after a voyage, that's what they make that soap from, why do
you think they color it *green?*"

He thought for sure Granma would open her eyes in the casket, her
cheeks were so pink and terrible.

If Tom Thebus got to be his father what would *his* boy do for a
father? White polo shirt and white shorts.

Peggy Copan told him that girls had to sit down to pee. Why was
that?

Helen Copan had to go and get dressed two hours before she went
dancing with the lifeguard. Two hours! It's because ladies have to put
on under their dresses all those things with straps and hooks and
metal things.

"But all Italian ships are white."

A whole pack of paper napkins: Chez Freddy, Manny's Rest, Hi-
Top, WigWam, Harry and Mary's, Bluebird, Seven Gables, Blue
Front, Red Apple Rest, Mom's. Granma's thin belt zipping around
in an arc to catch him behind the knees.

Charlie Taylor said his mother had hair all over her hole, he saw
it once. What did ladies have to have hair for? Not Mom! His birdie
felt itchy when he thought of it.

Guineas were all riffraff and so were the shanty Irish. He was both of them.

His other gramp gave him a funny-looking thing he picked off a tree and Mom told him it was a fig.

Uncle Joe walked back and forth in the living room with his hat on: "Goddamma crip' thinksa now he'sa the bigga boss!"

Kickie Delaney showed him a picture in a little book with Ella Cinders and she had a man's big birdie in her mouth and big drops of sweat were falling off her face and he felt weak and funny in his head. "Ladies like to suck off a man's cock." Cock was the real name for a birdie.

He and Mom visited some old lady cousin or something on a dark winter afternoon and sat in the kitchen in the dim light of a kerosene lamp. Tea and stale cookies. "My God! Nothing cheaper than an old skinflint of a shanty spinster." On the way home they stopped into Holsten's and had hot chocolate with whipped cream on it. He wasn't to tell Granma. That night on the couch in the dark front room he heard Mom say that she might have sure picked a winner but God knows what's right is right and she had the best when she had anything and that if she'd married some Pat or Mike she'd have lived in a coalbin as God was her judge. "That's right! Praise the greaseball mucky-muck to your own mother's face! Jesus, Mary and Joseph!"

A big cardboard box bulging with his toys, the zeppelin down at the bottom but he didn't play with it anymore.

On the first day of school, Miss Rush pulled him out of a line of children marching in a circle. He cried and didn't want to go back to school. "You marching goop! Now, sit down in the corner until you can be good!" He had only just been marching around in a circle. Mom said she was an old dried-up battle-ax. She hugged and kissed him and squeezed orange juice and the next day they put him in Miss O'Reilly's class instead.

The box had two smiling children on it and Mom told him the words said "The Gold Dust Twins." He learned to read right away.

Miss Rush was round all the way around her body but her legs were skinny and she wore big black shoes. She probably wore a corset like Granma.

Mrs. Schmidt had a big round shape. And her titties were really big, that was a really dirty word, like cock.

They took him in to see Granma at the hospital and she was all grey and took his hand. Her hand felt like a bunch of cold bones and she didn't have any teeth!

Jimmy Kenny came to the funeral parlor all dressed in his cop suit with a gun and everything. "She was a good woman, Marie. It's all for the best." Mom told Gramp it was a wonder the big gawm could spare the time. "Coming to pay his respects in his uniform! What riffraff!" Frankie Caffrey came in his blue serge Confirmation suit and said the Rosary, the thick ignorant Mick.

He got a new box, Super Suds, and threw his zeppelin away.

One summer evening while it was still light and Mom was talking on the front stoop he got up for water. "The Magrinos'll be around all smiles before you know it looking for your straight Democratic vote." On a chair he saw something pink with those straps with metal things hanging off it and flushed. But it was small and soft and stretched when you pulled it, so even with the straps and all it wasn't like Granma's.

Who made the world? God made the world.

Babies sucked their mothers' titties? Johnny McNamee said that all ladies had their titties full of milk, like cows. That was the funniest thing he ever heard.

Kickie Delaney was dirty and he felt like with those kids Cookie and Honey when they took him in the garage. "A lady's hole is a cunt." Cunt sounded like it had hair all over it.

He told Mom that the Alpine marquee said IF YOU COULD ONLY COOK. "Did you *read* that?" She bought him *Black Beauty* in the five-and-ten.

Tom Thebus told him that boys had to be strong and clean to grow up to be men so they shouldn't touch themselves. He didn't know what he meant.

At Steeplechase in the place where air from the floor blows ladies' dresses up he blushed and didn't know where to look. And those straps were to hold up a lady's stockings!

He finished *Black Beauty* in bed with the chicken pox and cried so that he had to wipe his glasses.

In Caught Caught Blackwell once, all the kids quit because they couldn't catch him, the last kid out.

Gramp got him an Army .45 cap gun for his ninth birthday right after they moved in with him and Granma.

Buttons that said something he couldn't understand, green ribbons attached, one had a tiny white stone pipe pinned to the ribbon.

Mom bought him *Skippy* by Percy Crosby for his ninth birthday and he read it four times in a row straight through. He didn't know any kids like that.

Granma shaking the *Brooklyn Eagle* at Mom: "Are you going to let this goddamned bimbo get away with this? Mrs. Recco? *Mrs. Recco?*"

After the lady from the Relief came to the house Mom cried and they moved in with Granma a few weeks later.

He heard Mom say that she had a crackerjack lawyer now, Aloysius Moran, "a black Irishman smart as a Jew."

He got to know the kids on Senator Street but it was the same thing all over again with playing ball. "This new four-eyed kid can't catch."

Mom stopped working at the steam table.

He saw Tom Thebus touch Mom low on her back, almost on the heinie, when everybody was going in to supper, she turned around quick all red in the face, and gave him a little push.

He joined the library and got a book about a caveman and one called *Penrod.* He didn't know any kids like that either.

"The son of a bitch is out on Gerritsen Avenue pretty as you please with that tramp!" Gramp was supposed to do something about it or something.

Kickie said that ladies had their holes between their legs, not in their *stomachs.*

He started crying in a movie about Tarzan and Daddy took him home and on the way bought him Charms.

The bookmaker asked Mom if he could help her through some slush at the corner and she made believe she didn't hear him.

Mom slapped him across the face so quick that nobody saw it when they left Granma's grave but he didn't remember what for.

Rhoda Sandgren wet herself right in her seat in school and all the pee ran down on the floor. He laughed like the other kids but he felt really sorry for her. Later he thought of what Kickie had told him about ladies' holes.

He kept missing the ball in a catch with Uncle Tom and wanted to cry.

Georgie Olsen told him in the schoolyard that his mother had to fuck to make him get born and he hit him on the head with his wooden pencil case and Georgie knocked his glasses off. They told Miss Lanchantin they were fooling around.

He'd never seen anything as white as the armband and tie he wore for his First Holy Communion. Blue serge suit from A&S. The host tasted like glue. "All the girls are so cunning, they look like little angels." Even the Mother Superior smiled.

As long as he was washed and in bed he could stay awake and listen to Lux Radio Theatre.

"Tito Guizar will sing for you."

Sister Andrew said that a boy once bit a host and it started to bleed, and some boy didn't tell all his sins in Confession and when the priest put the host on his tongue he dropped dead right at the altar rail. Jack Gannon asked if you by accident swallowed a drop of water when you were washing your face in the morning before Communion, could you receive? You couldn't.

Mrs. Schmidt sat down next to Gramp on a wooden lawn chair and started talking to him and Mom turned her head away and made a face.

He helped Louis bring the cows into the barn at night. They smelled delicious, like sweet hay and milk.

Max, the Russian barber who was Cousin Katie's friend, smoked long cardboard cigarettes and cut all his curls off. His hair grew in straight and Mom cried about it for almost three days. "He has to look like boy, not girl and sissy." Mom told Cousin Katie that as far as she was concerned he was a goddamn Polack greenhorn who had no business being in this country.

Vinnie Castigliano passed him a note in class and it had a stick-figure drawing of a girl and between her legs a big dark pencil scribble. Vinnie had written "Pat Christie's bush" and drawn an arrow pointing to the scribble. That was another word. Kickie said that Vinnie used to play with his own sister's cunt and she was *fourteen,* with a bush and all.

He won a Missal for getting the best mark on the Catechism test, the regular Catholic School kids got a Missal plus a comb in a little black cardboard case.

Mr. Bloom, the druggist, took a cinder out of his eye and gave him two Hershey kisses.

When he had the measles, Mom pulled down the shades and made him poached eggs and junket.

Tom Thebus made him laugh when he imitated Mrs. Schmidt: "Oh, ja, undt vor der lunsh ve haff it der Floadingk Islandt dessert, zo-oo-oo nize." Gramp said he was a goddamned overgrown horse's ass.

Mom saw a picture of Daddy and Margie in the *Eagle* with some other man and got so upset and mad that she started to cry. Daddy had a suit on with a bow tie like rich people wear, and Margie looked really fat.

He saw Gramp drinking whiskey right out of the bottle one day. Wilson's "That's All."

Mom had an argument with Gramp across on the old church steps one hot afternoon.

Uncle Charlie took him out of the funeral parlor and bought him a black-and-white in Holsten's.

Mom dried him after a bath in front of the kitchen stove at Cousin Katie's.

He had three pennies and lost one and threw the others in the snow because now they were no good.

As soon as he got a new Big Little Book he tore out all the pictures he didn't like.

A stack of cardboard things they called "coasters" right next to a ball of string. And the buttons said "Erin Go Bragh."

Bubbsy said that Mrs. Long caught one of the big kids feeling a girl up in the auditorium and he got sent to reform school. How did a girl feel? A bush.

He never wanted anything so bad as to smoke tobacco like Tom's in a pipe like his.

He saw Mom clap when Tom made a really good croquet shot and she looked like a girl.

When The Shadow laughed on the radio he would start to cry in fear.

The bookmaker gave him a nickel once and he was afraid to tell Mom.

Why did God make the world?

He played Alkali Ike in a school play and everybody said he should be a movie star, Dolores Marshall kissed him once in the middle of the play and her mouth tasted like orange Lifesavers.

To know Him and love Him in this world and to be happy with Him forever in the next.

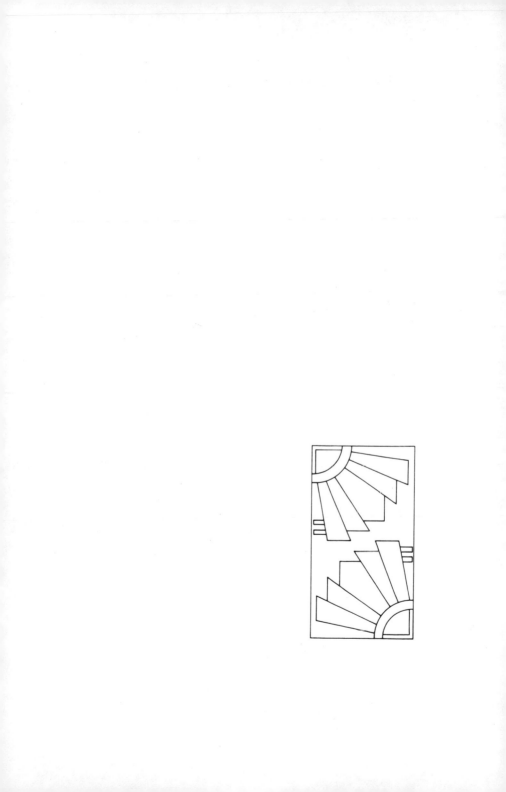

Surely she doesn't look like the mother of a ten-year-old boy. Perhaps the woman thinks this as she examines herself in the mirror in her small room. Her figure, in a flowered bathing suit, is trim and well-shaped, is what may be termed desirable. She does not think this word and has not thought of herself as such for years, six, seven?

The bathing suit is of one piece, rather too generously cut, and skirted: one cannot know whether out of modesty or a desire to conceal what she fears is a slight thickening of her thighs. She grasps the skirt at its hem and pulls it to either side in a flare, as if she is about to curtsy, looking at herself in the glass. Her face seems to disapprove. The bathing suit is, for a woman of her age, somewhat prim, much like the kind her mother wore the last time she wore a bathing suit. She has had this garment for four years, it is as it is, although she has done her best to ignore it or deny it to herself, because of her wish to preclude what would have been her mother's mocking laughter had she bought a suit that showed her figure to advantage. Her father, too,

would have laughed, desperate as usual to ingratiate himself with his
wife. He would have contributed the words "chippy," and "jane," the
phrase "like Astor's pet horse," and her mother would have repeated
it.

Do you want to go around looking like Astor's pet horse?

Sure. She wants to go around dolled up like Astor's pet horse. The
mother of a six-year-old boy!

She suddenly pulls at the skirt and wraps it closely around her
thighs, which are, despite her fears, still firm and smooth. They are
not the thighs of an old woman, not even those of a mother of a
ten-year-old boy, they might be the thighs of a, what do they call
them? career woman? A *mature* woman who just never married. She
knows, with absolute clarity, and in misery, that it is the bathing suit
that has filled her with doubts about her attractiveness. She is not her
mother! Damn it to hell, she is *not.* And her breasts are still firm.
Surely she might be childless, she might be in her late twenties.

She hears Mr. Thebus and her son on the lawn below, although she
cannot see them, her one window facing across the road to the old
white church. They are laughing together, having a catch with a beach
ball, while they wait for her to appear. Appear in this bathing suit,
that she now pulls at—the waist, the skirt, the bodice, the shoulder
straps—in frustration and embarrassment. She will soon be at Budd
Lake with her son and Mr. Thebus. The latter will be in his navy-blue
woolen trunks with the immaculate white web belt and its gleaming
brass buckle, and his white athletic top. She will be in her flowered
rag. Eleanor Stellkamp and her fiancé, Dave Warren, will be there,
with the Copan girls, Helen and Peggy. Eleanor will wear her white,
shiny, bathing-beauty suit; her flat breasts and oddly protruding belly
will be displayed to all, but she will be in her white, shiny, bathing-
beauty suit. Helen and Peggy will be the young, slim girls that they
are, oh, how they are! The blankets will be laid on the sand next to
each other, and she will sit, the heavy folds of this disgusting garment
encasing her in ugliness.

She is not her father's wife, she has a right to something, doesn't
she? She hears her son call: They're all ready and waiting for her, and
she pulls on her rubber bathing shoes and a flannel beach robe. She
tightens its sash, rolls two towels together and takes her change purse,

tightens the sash again. She will go downstairs now, the skirt of the bathing suit clinging to her thighs as if made of iron, out onto the lawn and into the sunlight and the appraising glance of Mr. Thebus. The beach ball will be under his arm, and he will smile, as he did that early afternoon five days ago when they got out of Louis' car, fresh from the station at Netcong, to find him waiting on the porch, to see him rising from the glider in his white ducks, puffing aromatic wisps of smoke from his pipe, his finger in the pages of *Gone With the Wind*. Her navy dress with the white polka dots seemed to her wondrously fashionable, incredibly flattering, held, as it was, in his bright glance.

Dear Katie,

Thanks for your lovely postcard. Atlantic City must be beautiful this time of the year and what a relief it must be to get out of the hot city for a few days. Poppa was saying last night that he wishes you would *think it over* about coming up here for a week in August or more, if you want. There's plenty of room and I know you'd enjoy it because you always have.

It's funny here without Momma God rest her soul and I think that Poppa really feels it but he won't say a word just plays his croquet as usual beating everybody. The Sapurty's are here and Grace is still the same accident looking for a place to happen that she always was, trying to look like a school girl. There's another family here through the second week of August a nice woman and her husband and, their two girls who are both Boy Crazy. Specially the oldest girl who makes a spectacle of herself at the lake with any thing that wears pants. Her father eats like a stevedore as he sure wants to get his moneys worth. You remember Helga Schmidt? Well, she is here too, the heart broken widow and it is pitifull to see how she is playing up to Poppa who doesn't even know she is alive.

Eleanor and Dave Warren will be married in the Fall. Eleanor is still homely as sin but Dave would not win any beauty contests either so, they seem to be a match. God love them. There is another man here and the gossip according to Grace Sapurty and her Big Mouth is that he just got a divorce. He seems to be a real gentleman to me and has taken a shine to Billy and they get along

together just like ham and eggs. He has a real sense of humor.
Next week he is going to drive us on an outing to High Point.
Remember going there when we were just girls? They were
happier days God knows.

Well that seems to be all the news for now. Write to me and let
me know how Leonard is doing with that back of his and drop a
line to Poppa too? And really think it over about coming up for a
week anyway. Say hello to Leonard and Arthur and Janet and
give them my love.

Marie

I haven't really had a chance to offer my sympathy to you, Helga.
I mean poor Otto. A wonderful man. It was such a shock
to us.[1]

Ja. For me too, Marie dear. But *you* can know about it with your
own poor mother passing away. Life is hard, hard. I was saying to
Otto last winter, just last winter, before he took sick. Ach, we thought
it was a bad cold, how Bridget was last summer not looking so good.
Peaked, you know, and so pale, not like her skin always was so nice
and fresh. Peaches with cream.[2]

Yes. She was sick a long time before we knew just how sick she
really was. The doctor, oh . . . the doctor said it was her blood was
just tired.[3]

Ah, ja! The *doctors.* They don't know nothing!

Momma was always so strong and full of fun, you know? It was just
terrible to watch her get weaker and weaker every day. But she was
a soldier.[4] Never a word of complaint out of her.

A swell regular sport she was. I remember like yesterday, right
here, watching her play croquet with your father. Ja. Always a good
sport she was. And ready for anything. Ach, life! Who would believe
that you and me—? Always she had, always, a nice smile on her for
everybody and a nice word.[5] A real lady. I'll miss her more and more.
None of us are getting any younger. Ah! Your poppa must be so sad

---

[1] Stale but mannerly.
[2] The voice of the Teuton is heard in the land. Undt zoon ve der peach pie vill steal,
ja, Fritz?
[3] "La science, la nouvelle noblesse! Le progrès."
[4] If a soldier, there was something about her.
[5] From fantasy to science-fiction.

but always a gentleman. You never see him telling his troubles to the world. Polite and nice. You're a lucky daughter, ja.

Poppa misses her so much, I know. Well, they'd be married thirty-six years this fall—October.[6] That's a lifetime.

Thirty-six years! Your poppa don't look a day over fifty![7] God bless him. The boy—he misses his granma?

Oh my God, yes. He *adored* his granma. Well, you know how grandmothers spoil their grandchildren. But he seems to have gotten over it, you know how kids are—especially boys.

To have such strength to forget. Well, God is good. We don't know how lucky we are when we are kids, ja? God makes it so they don't suffer like we do.[8]

Yes. God is good. If I didn't believe that . . .

Now now now. You shouldn't too much upset yourself. What's past is past. Maybe it's all for the best, poor Bridget and Otto, God bless him.

They say that God works in mysterious ways.

I believe this too. Very much. We got to go on living our lives no matter what, ja? You have your big handsome boy to make grow up to be a strong man, and to look after you have your poppa. Now more than ever your poppa needs you, ja?

Yes. Oh yes, we have to go on living. That's what life is about. But it's so hard.[9]

But you need to have some fun and relax a little too. We don't live on only bread, God said. I am starting again to play the piano.[10] It's nice and makes me peaceful. And you, I notice how nice it is you have a nice friend here for you.

A nice friend?

Ja. The nice gentleman with the moustache? And a pipe he smokes?[11] Mr. Teebus?[12]

---

[6] October banns punished their heir with frosty stinkers.

[7] Hark! The crackle of flattery off in the brush.

[8] "A gentle hand was laid upon. Fevered brow. Brimming eyes." God is hauled on stage. Oh yes, "credo, credo." Zut!

[9] It may be "hard" but nihil sine magno labore, no?

[10] Sports et Divertissements? Auf Wiedersehen? Euphonic Sounds? Heliotrope Bouquet?

[11] Forget not, O wife, the maddening aroma of same.

[12] This may be an Irani name.

Oh, Mr. *Thebus.*

Ja. Excuse me. Sometimes my English.

Well yes, but. Mr. Thebus is not really *my* friend, I mean my friend alone—I mean he always, you always see him playing croquet with Poppa. They're really serious about their game of croquet.[13]

Ah?

Yes. *Yes.* I mean, *you* watch Poppa play most of the time, don't you? It seems that way.[14] I mean, you see . . . him and Tom . . .

This is a game I love watching. A nice and calm gentleman's game. It is good for the nerves, ja? Better than a hundred *doctors.* And it, ah, it reminds me of Otto. God bless him.

Well. Otto. Well you know the old saying, six of one and half a dozen of the other.[15] Anyway, Mr. Thebus and Poppa really hit it off, I mean he's *our* friend. Poppa thinks the world of him.

Ah? Oh ja. A gentleman.

And Mr. Thebus has taken a great shine to Billy too, you know. So of course, we talk about *him*—Billy. And if we take a little walk once in a while it's no skin[16] off anyone's nose. Is it?

It is good to have this friend. What is so nice, so very very nice is what a good man and regular sport is your poppa. He don't mind it a bit to be left all al—to be, have his nice privacy for a few hours, ja? Dear, believe you me, your poppa knows you are still a young woman. Ja!

A young woman? I don't know really what . . . Tom and I have taken two walks, three, *three* walks. And one night we went to get clams for everybody at Harry and Mary's.[17] And Peggy Copan came along.

Ah, ja. How nice! How good to have nice friends your age—and one that your poppa *likes* so much, ja? A croquet player and everything.

I mean it's just, well. Well, God, *anybody* can make friends with Tom,[18] Helga.

---

[13] L. *croceo, crocere,* fr. Gr. κροκοσέω, to tear up the purple crocus with wooden mallets.

[14] Eros, in his usual slouch, enters.

[15] Old saw here used with a want of precision.

[16] Herr Noskin: Friend, Sport, and Man!

[17] Encumbered with bivalves by the score they were, so to speak, "clammed up."

[18] Dijo una mouthful.

Ja. With *Tom.* What a gentleman, so handsome. And so polite
and full of fun. And with his nice little shiny car. So sporty.[19]

Yes.

I don't want to tell tales but Frieda told me he had some unhappy
things at home? Some trouble, his wife? Ja?

He's . . . I think, he's divorced. He never mentions it. To *any* of
us. Has he ever mentioned it, ah, to you . . . ?

Ach! Me? I hardly know the gentleman except to say good morning
and once and a while watching him play croquet with your poppa. It
reminds me so of poor Otto to watch the men play croquet.[20] God
bless him. Mr. Thebus don't talk to *me.*

Yes, well, I don't know anything about his personal business. He's
just a good friend and that's fine with me, and that's that.

Ja. Dear Marie, listen to a piece of advice? Divorce, in this day
and age, so what?[21] Not one soul has ever spoke a word about yourself for instance. Ja! They haven't got anything for you but a good
word. Mr. Thebus nobody knows about but I don't ever hear a word
either.

I don't even know, Helga, *if* the gentleman is divorced.

Ah, I'm sorry, excuse me, I'm making you mad.[22] Who cares? is
what I'm saying. It's probably my English, ja? He is a fine gentleman,
always a smile and a joke and a nice word. Please don't think I'm a
busybody butting in, but a young and attractive woman like you
. . . You *need* to have some good clean fun, you need to stop worrying
and worrying about your poppa.

Worrying about him? What do you mean, worrying about him?

Marie. Dear. Please. You'll listen to a woman almost old enough
to be your mother. I'm not ashamed of my age. I know your poppa
for years now. He can take care of himself. He's the first, the *first*
person to say he wants you to be independent, to do what you like to
do. Ja! And he likes, *so* much, this Mr. Thebus anyway. He must be
happy to see you having a nice friend.[23] Ja?

[19] Here, "nice," "little," "shiny," and "sporty" are pejoratives.
[20] The author may intend this lawn game to stand as a symbol of lost mores.
[21] "Divorce is the sign of knowledge in our time."
[22] Blame it on her youth.
[23] The word "friend" commences to irritate.

That's fine, but that's not the same thing as, yes, I know Poppa really likes Tom, but I do worry about him being left alone even if I just take a little walk after supper to the Hi-Top.[24] Poppa needs me.

You are a good daughter, ja. But don't talk the nonsense to me, please. You think your poppa can't find people to chat with and pass along the time of day? What do you think your poppa does when you and the girls and all go swimming in the afternoon? What?[25] Dear Marie, your poppa knows me years and years. We have a million things to talk about.

Oh, *you*. Well.

Ja, me. And the other boarders and Frieda and Louis when he comes in for a glass of beer.[26] He has his cronies, your poppa. Thank God.

I know he has.

Marie, let me talk plain to you like the nose on your face. I know that you feel at wit ends, ja? A nice gentleman comes along, divorced, all right, all right, let's just make believe he is, he likes you. You find out he is a very nice and attractive man. He likes your young man of a son. You both have had terrible heartaches, ja? So what is wrong with a quiet stroll once and a while?[27] Maybe even he might ask you out in the evening? A dance or a movie date? Marie, dear, your poppa will be fine. He needs some privacy also.

You mean you'll look after him.

Well. Look *after* him . . .

What I mean is, I mean, as long as we're speaking plain, if you and Poppa, he's a widower and you . . . you see what I mean?

Ach, Marie! My God. Poor Otto is not in his grave a year, and your poor mother. God rest their soul. I am talking about chatting. A song on the piano.[28]

Of course, I'm sorry I mentioned it. And I'm thankful for your advice, Helga, but Poppa really comes first. A little walk after supper,

---

[24] In reality, the name of this "spot" was the Hi-Hat.
[25] Hangs around *in quadriviis et angiportis?* In Netcong?
[26] Undt den Looie says: "Vhere in tunderation iss der peaches pie?"
[27] Nozzing.
[28] Maybe this time Sports et Divertissements? Even Avalon?

well . . . But I'm not going to be, I'm not going to be going here and there, well, you know what I mean.

Of course, ja. But if you *want,* ja? If you *want.* An ice cream, a nice Tom Collins.[29] Everybody loves your poppa and he wouldn't be lonesome.

Thank you.

I mean it. I remember Otto used always to say, "Everybody thinks so high of Mr. McGrath." Otto always said that. "A real gentleman," he'd say.

Thank you. Otto used to tell me that, too, oh, many times, summers past. I remember he once told me sitting right here the way we are now. Poppa and you walked down to the far meadow to pick blackberries? Was it?[30]

I don't remember this, dear. I don't think so.

Or when you and Poppa went to get a pitcher of spring water from the old pump behind the church?[31] Oh yes, I think that was it, you and Poppa. With the spring water. I remember it. Very well. Momma had gone shopping in Hackettstown.

Well, I . . . it's hard to remember such things. So long ago. With Otto on my mind. And your poor momma. Brrr. It *is* chilly, I think I go in, ja?[32]

---

[29] Or liqueurs fortes comme du métal bouillant, if available.

[30] These remarks help prove that we cannot live in the country, for the country will bring us no peace.

[31] The chalky-white building that "broods" over our story.

[32] A las cinco de la tarde with the odor of pot roast and kohlrabi in the air.

Present a small verbal graph describing the Tom Thebus that existed in Marie's mind.

A modern Apollo in white ducks; the manly source of aromatic pipe smoke redolent of the exotic; bronzed limbs; a ready laugh; flashing white teeth; very smart; Ronald Colman; sweet on her; a magazine illustration; a small wheel turning; somewhat like the handsome and collegiate teller lost in the mists of time; a man with a secret hurt carefully buried but often apparent in his deepset and poetic eyes; strong and silent; a go-getter; absolute opposite of shanty Irish; possessor of a glamorous and mysterious name; the driver of a glittering and classy car; good family man fatefully thwarted by dark elements beyond his control; expansive personality; singing, head high, down the road of life; a real gentleman.

On what foundation was Marie's personality built?

The young daughter as white goddess; sudden onslaught on the ego with the arrival of maturity; subsequent decay of the invented whitegoddess state, also known as the gift that maims.

Who were the people most responsible for this subsequent decay of the role of white goddess given her to play in her childhood and adolescence?

John McGrath; Bridget McGrath; Anthony Recco; Billy Recco; Margie.

Note one semi-incantatory phrase that came to Marie, in whole or part, at odd times and unbidden.

O Lord I am not worthy that Thou shouldst enter under my roof; speak but the word and my soul shall be healed.

Was her soul ever healed?
It seems unlikely.
List some other literary fragments stored in her mind.

Pale hands I loved beside the Shalimar,
  Where are you now? Who lies beneath your spell?

Do you know you have asked for the costliest thing
Ever made by the Hand above?

Oh, where have you been, Billy boy, Billy boy?

My hand is lonely for your clasping, dear;
My ear is tired waiting for your call.

I am the master of my fate:
  I am the captain of my soul.

A cheer for the boy who says "No!"

The boy stood on the burning deck,
  Whence all but he had fled;
The flame that lit the battle's wreck
  Shone round him o'er the dead.

Crying, as I floated onward, "I am of the earth no more!
I have forfeited Life's blessings in the streets of Baltimore."

Chisel in hand stood a sculptor boy
  With his marble block before him.

The legend of Felix is ended, the toiling of Felix is done.

'Mid pleasures and palaces though we may roam,
Be it ever so humble, there's no place like home.

Backward, turn backward, O Time, in your flight,
Make me a child again, just for tonight!

Behold this ruin! 'Twas a skull
Once of ethereal spirit full.

Who fed me from her gentle breast

And hushed me in her arms to rest,
And on my cheek sweet kisses prest?
          My Mother.

It takes a heap o' livin' in a house t' make it home,
A heap o' sun an' shadder, an' ye sometimes have t' roam—
Afore ye really 'preciate the things ye lef' behind.

Suppose, my little lady,
     Your doll should break its head.

Tho' th' door wuz saggin' from its hinges
     An' th' rats wuz long as muh arm,
Still, I git those melancholy twinges
     When I think o' home on th' farm.

During periods of stress, were any of these remarkable lines of use to Marie?
Many of them.
Give the titles of some other poems that Marie had, in whole or fragments, by heart.
To My Unborn Son; Among the Beautiful Pictures; If—; Where There's a Will There's a Way; The Rose Still Grows Beyond the Wall; When Your Eyes Do Burn With Salty Flood; Lord, Make a Regular Man Out of Me; The Land of Beginning Again; The House By the Side of the Road; The Face Upon the Floor; The Humble Midgets Speak; Abou Ben Adhem; Curfew Must Not Ring Tonight; Even This Shall Pass Away; Recessional; Poor Lil' Brack Sheep; Roses in December; Somebody's Mother; Then His Hard, Stern Lip Did Tremble; Home Is Where There Is One to Love Us; Lullaby Town; Breathes There the Man; In Flanders Fields; 'Tis the Last Rose of Summer; Drifting Sands and A Caravan; 'Twas His Face on the Golden Shore; Barbara Frietchie.
The names of some of her favorite poets?
Ella Wheeler Wilcox; Blanche Shoemaker Wagstaff; Captain Cyril Morton Thorne; Burleson St. Charles MacVoute; Dinah Maria Mulock Craik; Edgar A. Guest; Josiah Gilbert Holland; Lorna Blakey Flambeaux; H. Antoine D'Arcy; Emma Simpere Furze; Alaric Alex-

ander Watts; Mary Artemisia Lathbury; Blanche Bane Kuder; Jean
Ingelow; Carruthers Sofa-Jeudi; Maltbie Davenport Babcock; Nixon
Waterman.

Was Marie afraid of men?

Sexually, yes.

How had Marie really felt about her mother?

She had feared and despised her and was relieved at her death. She
denied this last to herself and the subsequent emotional pressures
caused her to suffer excruciating gas pains, much like those at the time
she had ascertained, beyond all doubt, the illicit affair between her
husband and Margie. At that time she suspected that the "evil eye"
had been put on her or that ground glass was being mixed into her
food.

*Why did she not realize Margie's intentions toward Tony? And vice
versa?*

The idea of illicit sex, and indeed, of licit sex of certain kinds that
she refused to imagine, terrified her. She could conceive of no one that
she knew involved in any of these activities, certainly not her husband
and his secretary.

*What of Marie's feelings toward both Margie and Tony in terms of
their relationship with Billy?*

Their delight—especially Margie's—in Billy, a delight that Billy
returned, made their adulterous affair seem utterly monstrous and
perverted to Marie. Although there was no reason why they could not
carry on their affair and still love Billy, this combination, to Marie,
seemed hideous.

*Perhaps it sprang from their smiling betrayal of her affection for
them?*

Perhaps. But it seems deeper than that. She thought of Billy as
somehow soiled. Although the Tony-Margie affair was banal in the
extreme, Marie turned it, for her son, into a passage of spectacular
depravity. Her stories, for instance, of giant rats perching on Margie's
shoulders in her filthy cellar flat were, for Billy, the stuff of night-
mares.

How did Marie regard herself?

As a little girl with golden braids in a crisply starched, knife-pleated
dress with matching knee stockings and hair ribbons, crying bitterly

as her mother beat her Cousin Katie with a belt for some job left
undone; as a bride removing her wedding gown following the wedding
breakfast and blushing as she looked at the lingerie in her trousseau,
packed neatly in luggage not yet closed; as a young woman of seven-
teen in country tweeds and a sweater, sitting on a rock in a field, the
sky grey and lowering; as a strong woman, jaw set, mouth firm, head
high, standing behind her son, her hand on his shoulder, Facing Life;
as the bride of Tom Thebus, boarding a train with him for an extended
honeymoon trip on his fabled yacht at berth in some equally fabled
marina; as an old woman with carefully powdered silver hair and a
beautiful heirloom diamond brooch at her throat, surrounded by
loving and beautiful grandchildren, her dear husband in a rocker
puffing on his crusted old briar, its aroma still the same one of rum,
maple, and chocolate.

How did John McGrath exercise his hold on Marie?

Via sadness, as in "I'm not needed anymore." Via bitterness, as in
"I'm the butt in *this* family." Economically, as in his giving Marie
$1000 (in two installments of $500) after Bridget's death—enough not
to be thought of as cheap or heartless, but not enough to allow Marie
even the illusion of independence. Via lies, as in his not telling her that
her mother had left her $5000, which gift sheds a new and surprising
light on Bridget, although it may have been prompted by her final
feelings of guilt, remorse, and gratitude. (This seems unlikely.) Via
generosity, made to seem even more generous by its unexpectedness,
as in his giving Marie his wife's diamond dinner ring and offering to
pay for a new setting of its "three nice stones." Via veiled threats, as
in his references to the goodness, kindness, loneliness, and understanding of Helga Schmidt, fully aware of Marie's intense dislike of
this aggressively forward woman. Via suggestions of ill health, as in
his arrival at their apartment after work in the performance of one of
the following acts: heavy panting; heavy panting mixed with deep
groans; heavy panting, occasional deep groans, and a random "oh
Jesus" or "Jesus Christ"; heavy panting and exhausted "collapse"
against the wall of the hallway; a total lack of both panting and
groaning but an exhausted "collapse" with martyred look against the
wall of the hallway; heavy panting, deep groans, "Jesus Christs" plus
an exhausted "collapse" against wall, followed by deathly silence

ultimately shattered by a bone-deep groan, a slow and heavy stagger-
ing walk down the hallway into the living room, a trembling fall into
the nearest chair, hat and coat still on, a roll of the eyes to "heaven,"
a slow flutter of the eyelids followed by the closing of the eyes, and
the gentle placement of the right hand on the chest in what John took
to be the vicinity of the heart.

Is it possible to know a little of Marie's feelings toward her father?

They were wildly ambivalent. She despised him because she knew
that he had bent all his powers toward making her feel responsible for
him. Yet she loved him because, despite his cowardice in the face of
the fierce and bitter woman whom Bridget had gradually become, he
had done what he could to make her life and Billy's somewhat beara-
ble after her separation from Tony and Bridget's subsequent trium-
phant crowing over the marriage's failure.

What were her feelings toward Tom Thebus?

At this time they seemed to be love, admiration, attraction, fascination, and the old familiar sexual fear, the last courtesy of the Sisters
of Charity, especially one Sister Vincent.

What about her feelings toward the WigWam?

It evoked a bittersweet nostalgia and, like most, one but tenuously
attached to facts.

Dear "Ex" Tony,

I'm just writing to say "hello" and to tell you that I'm really sorry to see that you finally lost the little bit of hair you once had. If you are wondering how I know this it's because I am referring to a picture in the Brooklyn Eagle I saw with you and your fat floozie and I mean Fat, and some drunk mick of a crooked politician all posing together as sweet as you please at some affair in the St. George. What was it, the annual Ball of Alcoholic Anonymos or whatever they call it? Your new wife, ha ha, looked like she had a few stiff balls before she got there.

Or was it a meeting of that organization you made up, the Flo-Ral Society. Where all the relatives on your side and also the bimbo's side get together to kiss the great man's feet so some other deadbeat will get on the payroll. Or maybe you were just wining and dining that shanty harp mug next to you, my God, he looks crooked enough to be the next Mayor.

Maybe I'm wrong and that Fat lady next to you was the mick politician's wife. It could be. Those Fat Irish tramps all look the same to me but I guess it was Margie. My God, from the size of her it's easy to see that the rats don't steal the food from her plate any more like they did in the good old days. I wish I had the dress she is wearing though, because, it would make me a swell closet full of clothes. Where does she go for her clothes? Omar the tent maker? That dress would fit Finn MacCool. No kidding Tony, it is a knock out and you must be really proud of the slut.

A little bird told me that since that lovey dovey picture you and

Mrs. Trampo are breaking your necks to avoid each other. For instance, when you are in Miami she is up here and visa versa. I can't believe the honeymoon is over so soon. And all along I thought that you two would be like the Duke of Winsor and Wally Simpson. Such is life and you know the old saying, Time Wounds All Heels. It is *very true* and I am sure that you are finding it out if you get what I mean.

I heard another story from a little bird about two dogs that Mrs. Slutto had in Miami last year, I understand that they were twins. Of course the lady of the Manor never walked her mutts but it was the job of some poor greaseball who was also chief cook and bottle washer down there and who also drove the car and mowed the lawn. One day they fell in the ocean and drowned, I heard. I heard that they sank with all the lead that was in them. Mrs. Bimbo was very upset about it and fired the greaseball and drank a whole bottle of scotch. No rest for the weary is there, Tony? Can't you hire somebody who won't carry a pistol in his pocket?

As I am sure Florrie has told you if I know my Florrie, and probably Marianne and Bee as well, I have met a great number of very nice gentlemen over the past few months. And this summer one in particular, a man named Tom, who is a wonderful and refined gentleman. Had I an inkling that such refined men existed in the world when I accepted your proposal I would never have accepted your proposal. I was not much more than a school girl and you were an ignorant dago working on the docks covered with grease from head to foot. I must have been crazy. Probably I was crazy. Certainly you showed your true colors soon enough but that is all water under the bridge. Margie Fatso is the perfect wife for you even if you can still only call her your wife in Florida legally. As a matter of fact, poor Katie, after you left me and Billy even told me that this was a perfect match, she even said, Well this jane is a perfect match for Tony, God forgive me but that's how I feel. And now I can see that poor Katie was right. I was always too refined and too delicate for you and I soon found out what it was you wanted from a woman, all those disgusting things that I told you Father Donovan told me were

things animals do. Not good Catholic people. But you have your
shanty bimbo now and you can roll around like pigs in mud.

Tom can talk about all kinds of things and he is an Inventor.
He is very interesting and Poppa thinks that he is really a fine
man. Poppa really likes him a lot. He has a little moustache like
Joe used to have before he became the Vice president or whatever
he is at Neptune and a head of brown wavy hair. How is your
brother in law, the cripple? God bless the mark but when I
remember how Caesar told me that he made Julius clean out the
toilets in the old place on DeGraw Street and you let him do as
he pleased, I don't care how crippled he is, for that he should be
crippled in both legs, God forgive me. Julius is the oldest brother
of all of you and he should be shown some respect. Who did that
gimpy shanty Irish trash think he was to order him to do that
nigger work? You didn't do anything to stop him, Tony but you
let Julius work like a nigger. Your oldest brother. I should have
surmised then that Margie had your ear. But I was blind.

Well I'll close now since I am going for a drive with Tom and
Poppa for a pitcher of cold beer and some clams on the half shell.
Are you ever going to legally marry that Miss Fat Pig?

> Feeling sorry for you,
> Marie (Time Wounds all Heels)

P.S. I have half a mind to write a letter to the Eagle and tell them
that I am Mrs. Recco and God only knows who that fat tramp is,
maybe, one of the kitchen help. Maybe I will.

How hard it was to believe and how thrilling it was to know that Tom was famous! And she, as Mrs. Tom, as the newspapers called her, the queen bee of so many functions. And her furs. And her favorite recipes jotted down by goodness knows *how* many reporters! The after-theater cafés and bistros favored by the glittering couple for late suppers with champagne, of course, and tasty things that waiters set on fire. Of course, both boys were in the best prep schools but came home for summer vacations and the holidays, of *course*. And then Eton or Oxford or Princeton. How she looked forward to seeing them in their beanies.

How grand to have a second honeymoon just a year and a half after their first. The first had been really and truly heaven—especially since it was also a sort of celebration over her annulment—the church, the wonderful, wonderful Catholic church had decided that Tony had been so rotten and mean through and through that she was entitled to an annulment because her marriage was a marriage in name only and actually was a very special case of cruelty. And when she saw Tom's "little"—ha ha—surprise! That morning when he took her down to the dock to see the yacht she thought she'd die. What was most wonderful about it all? The name, "Tomarie"? The smiling Negro steward, George, always shuffling around with his silver tray of canapés and Orange Blossoms and Mint Juleps? Or was it the gruff, weatherbeaten, and red-bearded captain, Ole Olson? All white and gold and with a yellow-and-white striped awning over the aft poop. And Tom all in white! His strong white teeth twinkled in a boyish grin that lit up his mahogany face. And how the sun had bleached out his dark wavy hair and his little moustache, oh, that she loved so much because it tickled her when she swooned in his arms and made her feel so wicked!

Could the weather be any better? All the way down to the Bermudas the ocean was smooth as glass or as Tom said, like the fishpond back home when he was a boy. She had to laugh when she thought of the white ducks swimming around in it. The golden shores of Miami. And the gay casinos of old Habana! That's how you pronounced it, Tom said, he knew everything. But he shouldn't, should *not* have given her that double strand of pearls for her beautiful ivory neck, he called it, that must have cost him a king's ransom. He kissed her nose and threw back his head and laughed when she looked worried, his muscles twitching in his square jaw. Money to burn! he laughed. But exactly what *was* his invention? She had asked him a dozen times but he had gently caught her chin in his firm fingers and shaken it back and forth and told her to worry about her frocks—what a lovely word!

The boys hit it right off as she had prayed they would, like two peas in a pod, diving all day long for sea conchs or sponges and coral off the side of the "Tomarie," while George served tumblers of iced coffee and tiny watercress and cucumber sandwiches. Tom beamed, really happy for the first time in *so* long, the worry lines disappearing from his brow. I *am* Mr. *Lucky!* he said, lighting up his wonderful smelly old pipe that she really adored, only she wouldn't dare let on, his "skeeter chaser." How often he said that lately, for no reason than that he was so grandly happy, and his dark-brown eyes would melt into hers as he gazed at her face from far far away. And how he would laugh, puffing through his briar as he watched her learn to smoke her Virginia Rounds. She loved the feel of the long ivory holder between her fingers. And always in the background Skipper Olson seemed to be gruffly swearing in Norwegian at the flying fish that plopped on the deck by the dozens, their rainbow colors flashing in the moonlight. Tom would roll his eyes up when she asked him what the old salt was saying and never tell her. He could be so adorably *mean.*

That *hush* in the casino when she floated in on Tom's arm and all eyes turned to look at them! It was like being with Clark Gable or George Brent. But Tom was better-looking, yes he *was.* And how the lights of the Riviera winked behind them as they returned to the yacht in their dinghy, sipping champagne as the moon went in and out of the clouds like in poetry. Tom had such class when he tipped the sailor who helped them aboard God knows *how* many francs. Merci! the young tar said, all smiles, his little red pom-pom bobbing around as cute as a button.

The best time of all—oh, how could she decide? But the way they spooned like high-school sweethearts in the pink twilight! Watching the lights go on in the cute little white houses on the beach. And once in their private cabin that had real oil paintings of famous sailboats on the walls, how they would snuggle and cuddle while the ocean rocked them to sleep and they heard the soft clump-clump of Captain Olson's wooden leg above them on the deck and his warm safe voice swearing at the sailors to fix up the sails and yardarms and anchors. And then they would, more often than not, come out on deck when it was very late and watch the stars without saying a word. Tom's arm encircled her waist in his powerful grip. He had such a strong, trim figure—as slender as a boy's. *He* would never have to worry about getting a corporation or even about getting fat and flabby . . . behind.

And at those times, her small white hand—pale hands I love, Tom always said—nestled close in Tom's big brown one, she breathed a silent prayer of thanks that she had whispered "yes" to him before she knew one iota of his plans to patent and sell his invention. She had blushed and lowered her eyes in sweet surrender to what she thought was this dashing but gentle guy who was perfectly happy just being a crack salesman. And then after he had throatily whispered that now, *now* he knew that she loved him for himself, that he had seen into the bottom of her heart, he had kissed her so hard that she almost fainted in the overpowering manliness of the scent of bay rum and rose oil and tobacco that floated around him. And then as they had walked in the moonlight and the crickets and the fireflies down the road back to the Stellkamps', he had told her, quietly and proudly, with no swellheaded braggadocio about it: I am a rich man, sweetheart. Very —*very* rich. And I will be even *richer*. The sky's the limit! And it is all, all for you, my beautiful . . . bride. And how long they had then stood on the road looking into each other's hearts she couldn't imagine. They didn't even feel the mosquitoes! How they bragged about that afterward to their set.

Even her poppa was finally pleased. Pleased? *Happy* and *thrilled*
with the little cottage that Tom had bought for him in the woods that
he had always loved to look at from afar. And his every need taken
care of, a valet and butler and a chauffeur to take him into Hackettstown when he needed a haircut or some groceries or anything or even
home to Brooklyn when he felt like chewing the fat with his old
cronies and maybe even drive them back for a night playing Casino.
And Poppa was speechless when he saw the croquet lawn that Tom
had installed with grass so green and smooth that it looked like green
velvet. And though he hemmed and hawed, he was so pleased with
his hand-made mallets and balls that he used to carry a mallet around
with him wherever he went almost. Could she ever forget that spring
morning when the old man had given her away, so dignified in his
cutaway coat and striped pants, and his eyes full of tears behind his
pince-nez?

And Tom! Dear, dearest Tom, who had insisted that she wear
white: You are my *bride!* He had *almost* raised his voice, and so she
had worn Tom's mother's gown, and carried lily of the valley and
white roses. He was so adorable and precious when he fumbled, all
hot and red, with the ring, a simple gold band that looked so beautiful
next to the huge engagement ring he had given her, a band that she
had promised herself that she would never, *never* take off, no matter
what, they could kill her! Inside, and so small that you almost needed
a magnifying glass to read it, Tom had the date engraved in Roman
numerals and—just like the yacht—"Tomarie," because, he ex-
plained, it means we are joined forever, we are one flesh. How she had
blushed at the word! She would always remember how his breath
caught as he whispered it, as she picked rice out of his silky and
shining waves. But the most darling thing were the beautiful words
also inside the ring, "One Alone To Be My Own." And even now she
thrilled as she thought of those words pressed up against her flesh.

It was their secret and in the months of joy that followed it was to
be a secret that they shared everywhere. In crowded parties, amidst
the hullabaloo of restaurant dinners after board meetings, on week-
ends in Long Island where they went to hunt grouses and pheasant,
even crowded together with the hoi polloi and riffraff when they went,
for a lark, into the streets full of the common people to search for dear

little bargains that it was such fun to buy. They would look into each other's eyes and Tom's would get all crinkled and silently they knew that they were thinking, together, "One Alone To Be My Own." They started to call it the secret of the ring, and then just the secret, and drove everyone who knew them just *crazy.* And it was true, "one alone," and would be forever and ever!

Sometimes, crocheting or knitting or reading one of the serious thick good books from the library that Tom had insisted the yacht's designer put in, she would look up and take her reading glasses off—Tom said she looked like a schoolteacher with "It" with them on, he was terrible!—and see Tom clutching at the rigging booms or something, his finely chiseled profile against the sunset that was purple and red and gold like in the oil paintings in the cabin, his eyes peeled for sharks and tunas and dolphins, and blazing with amusement at the flying fish that thumped at his feet. Or he stared at the golden shores beyond with the lights going on and the orange trees on them. Or she would watch him quietly as he puzzled out some technical business problem he had taken along with him, his mouth twisted around like a boy's doing his homework, chewing on his pencil—and her heart would *stop!* Really stop for a minute and then surge up again, leaping with joy! And he would look quickly over at her and smile his deep deep smile so that she had to jump up and run to him and hug him, almost crying with happiness!

I don't *want,* John, do not *want,* do you understand, you crawling around that damn dago and begging him to come back, come back, come back to Marie. She's a damn sight better off without him. Good riddance to bad rubbish! Bridget flings her leg vulgarly over the arm of the Morris chair and slaps yesterday's *Sun* against her thigh. Marie sits, pale, at the dining-room table, looking out the front-room windows at the tar roofs of the buildings on the next street. How she despises them.

But Momma . . . Momma, I don't think he *wants* to leave me. I asked him and he looked at me like I was crazy. He comes home . . . he *does* come home.

To change his goddamned shirt! Bridget says. Now I'll *not* have your father on his hands and knees, kissing that dago's ass and begging . . . you'll leave well enough alone. Let him have his bog-trotter slut, they make a fine pair.

Just a minute, Bridget, her father says. Now just *wait one minute.* This is Skip's whole life you're talking about. Skip thinks I can do some good talking to Tony, man to man, about this—I don't give a damn about how I *look.* Skip wants me to call him and by God almighty I'll call him. Is he suddenly a stranger? Don't we know our own son-in-law anymore?

You'll do nothing of the kind! Bridget says, folding the *Sun,* her face red with anger. Let the girl and Billy move out of that cheap cheesebox he calls a house and let that guinea go to hell! I'm telling you, John, keep your nose out of it.

I'm sorry, Bridget, I'm going to call him and see if we can't talk this over. It's one of those things that can happen. The man is human . . .

What I'm doing is asking for your white, your dainty, your frag-ile, your soft and goilish hand in marriage, to wit: I am plighting my troth, so to speaketh, Lenny Polhemus says, his face handsome in the shadow of his soft grey fedora.

Oh, Lenny, Marie says. I don't think it's very nice to kid a girl about that. I really don't.

Kid, me proud beauty? Do not be ri-DIC-ulous! Marie, I'm just head over heels over you. And he begins to sing, in a comic imitation of Russ Columbo:

> Alone from night to night
> You'll find me,
> Too weak to break the chains
> That bind me . . .

Oh, Lenny. You're terrible, Marie laughs.
I've got it bad, kid, and that is *not* bush-wa.

You're Mrs. Recco? Tony's wife? Margie turns to Tony. Tone, you never told me that your wife was so beauty-ful! I'm really pleased to meet you, Mrs. Recco. I didn't know you'd be coming, I would have fixed up . . . cleaned up the office, a little. It's terrible, we been working all week on some bids . . .

It's quite all right, Margie. These furs certainly won't be hurt by a little *dust,* Marie says, flinging her silver-fox stole across Margie's desk. I'm really *so* delighted that Tony has a secretary. I hope now he'll have *someone* to talk business with . . . goodness knows, *I* haven't got *any* head for it at all.

Marie likes other . . . things, Tony says. Reading and culture and mental things.

Oh yeah, sure, Margie says. Geez, I hope you don't mind me chewing this gum? I know how it looks to some people? I always forget that, I . . .

Oh, ha ha ha, Marie laughs, lounging in Tony's chair and crossing her legs. Chew away, dear, chew, chew. Tony, you *devil,* I hope you don't have any splinters in this old desk that I'll ruin my stockings on. I am *always* telling him to get some decent office furniture.

Oh, no, God dear, Tony says, and rushes to the desk to inspect it. Real silk hose? Margie says. Oh say, Mrs. Recco, they're beauty-ful.

You may go back to your bidding and paperwork things now, Margie, Marie says. I'll have to take my husband away soon for the afternoon. Remember, dear?

You bet, honey. Chop suey and dancing? At Yung's? How does that sound?

You *love,* Marie says, opening her diamond-studded compact. Would you get my mink, Margie dear, like a good girl?

Oh Lenny, look at that sunset, Marie says. It's pretty as a picture. God, how beautiful it is here. Hollywood!

Nothing, but n-o, nothing, is too good for my perfect little wife.

It's all pink and purple and gold.

You're *my* gold, honey.

I can't believe we'll be back home in Brooklyn in just a little more than a week. This has been so perfect I hate it to end.

I hate the idea too, kid, but a bank officer has his responsibilities, ri-DIC-ulous as it may be. Oh, honey, I love your hair.

Oh Lenny. Oh. Oh.

You will do nothing of the kind, John. What if the greaseball brings his floozy along with him?

Oh, Momma . . . *please.*

God damn it to hell, Bridget! I'll do what I goddamn well please in this for Skip's sake. And you liked that *greaseball* well enough when they lived down the street.

What? What are you trying to say, John? The poor man is losing his mind *and* his memory.

I understand, Margie, that you have some ri-DIC-ulous idea about Tony, I mean about Tony and yourself, Marie says, tossing her sables at a huge rat that is crouching in the corner of Margie's basement flat.

He . . . he loves me, Mrs. Recco, Margie says, scurrying to pick up the fur. And I think—I think he's just, just *swell.*

Love? *Love?* Marie laughs. Leave that old rag of a coat *be,* darn it! Do you know what love is? Do you know what it is for a husband to go out for chow mein and come back with a little pair of red silk slippers, all hand embroidered by old Chinamen? And Chinese apples? Does Tony worship the ground you walk on? *Love!* Do you know how he likes to eat a tomato or a soft-boiled egg? Did you know him when he was the best dancer in the neighborhood, the life of the party, and had a little red Moon roadster just big enough for two? Of course not! We have things you can *never* share. Please don't make me laugh, Margie, please! Have you given him a beautiful son that he adores? Did you ever—*will* you stop fidgeting with that coat and whimpering?—did you ever have the head teller at the main branch of the Dime Savings Bank of Brooklyn, a college man from Holy Cross, ga-ga over you, ready to kiss the hem of your skirt? *Love?* Give me my coat, *please.* I warn you to stay away from Tony. What you think is my husband's "love" is an infatuation for someone whose life is a sad tragedy. Don't you think that my husband is affected by the fact that you live here in this damp, this *cellar,* with the rats perching on your skinny shoulders? Why, my dear girl, Tony merely feels pity for you. And seeing you like this—so do I.

Oh, oh, Mrs. Recco, I'm so sorry, so sorry. I'll leave my position with Neptune tomorrow. I didn't know. I wondered why he was sweet on someone so common, like me.

I'll see to it that you get another job, you poor child. Poor child. You can always work at the steam table in Bickford's. I happen to know *Mrs.* Bickford personally.

How can I ever thank you enough, Mrs. Recco?

Hush, hush, no tears now. Just get me my furs, all right?

Well, Tony. I went to see Margie yesterday. In her *cellar.* The rats were so bold that they were stealing the food off the table. The boiled potatoes, I mean, that seemed to be the only food she had.

Margie told me. Oh gee, kid. Will you ever forgive me? I don't know why I ever got mixed up with that floozy.

Maybe you felt sorry for her. You big baby.

Yeah. I thought I could do something for the kid. But I didn't know that it would ever come to—

Let's not ever, *ever* speak of it again. What's in the big box, honey?

Oh, this? It's just a new fur coat and muff to match. Ermine.

Oh, Tony! You fool! You wonderful wonderful fool.

I'm telling you, Bridget, and there's no two ways about it, I'm going to talk to Tony this afternoon.

You goddamned pigheaded fool! You can't talk to a greaseball. All he knows is his spaghetti and olive oil.

Oh, Momma!

I'm buying out Acme-Guarino Stevedoring, Marie. In a year, I'll have half the work in Erie Basin. The sky's the limit!

Tony! Can we . . . ?

That vacation in Miami? I've got the Pullman tickets right here.

Tony, Tony . . . and I thought I'd *lost* you.

Let's not talk about that jane anymore, darling, it's a closed book. You need some new clothes for the golden sands, by the way, don't you?

> On the golden sands
> Of old Miami shore . . .

While Dave Warren delivered the eggs to the Warren House where she said she would meet him in two hours, Marie walked around Hackettstown, thinking to buy a new dress—or a new something! In the window of Jerry's Variety Shoes she saw exactly what it was she would buy for the evening: a beautiful white openwork sandal with a high heel and a cunning little strap around the ankle, perfectly stunning. When the clerk told her that her foot was the smallest he'd ever seen on a woman, she was pleased, as she was always pleased when shoe clerks said this, as they almost invariably did. She was vain about her feet and ankles, and her legs as well, although she didn't often think about her *legs*. Her feet were beautiful in the new shoes, the clerk didn't have to tell her *that*. She tried both shoes on, walking the length of the store and back, stopping to look at her feet in the floor mirror, holding her skirt around her legs to see the line that they made with her feet, then letting it hang free, turning this way and that. The clerk was looking at her legs and she flushed. She bought the shoes and then walked to the five-and-ten, where she sat at the counter and had a root beer. There was plenty of time to kill and she tried to pretend that she had nothing to do that night except sit on the porch, as usual, or go to the Warren House for steamers and beer with her father, the Sapurtys, and the Stellkamps. As usual. It was useless, of course, there was no way that she could pretend *not* to think of Tom and dancing with Tom, alone with Tom, alone together at the Wig-Wam. She hoped that . . . she didn't exactly know *what* she hoped, but since the other night when she had walked with Tom, that beautiful beautiful night . . .

She hadn't been to the WigWam in years and years and thought of it, all that time, as a place to which she would never go again. When Tom mentioned going there, and asked her about it, she had told him, oh, how blasé she had tried to be, that she used to go there and that it was a nice place. It was, my God! the place, well, one of the places, that had served to convince her that she was really married and could do what she wanted—what Tony wanted anyway. Anyway, not what *Momma* wanted—or Poppa either, damn it! Tony had taken her there the summer after they were married, a year before Billy was born. She was *with* Tony! They stayed as long as they wanted, they had the car —the old Packard—and returned to the Stellkamps' *when* they wanted, and whoever didn't like it, he could look out for the horns, Tony would say, using a phrase she had taught him, and thumbing his nose. Grown up. She was finally all grown up. In subsequent summers it had not been so easy, after Billy was born, the summer after the next, yes, because the very next summer she was *really* expecting and didn't do any *dancing*. But then the summer after Momma and Poppa had to baby-sit and they acted like it was the end of the world if they came home even a minute after eleven. But that first summer of their marriage! And when they came home, no matter what time it was, they had *their* room to go to, they weren't beholden to anyone for anything. Momma didn't like it much but Tony told Marie she was *his* wife and he didn't marry her mother and if the old lady didn't like it she could lump it. And still, Marie was nervous when they got home after midnight.

Dave Warren looked over at her with his mouth half-open like the damn fool of a gawm he was when she said that she wasn't going to the Warren House that night, but that Mr. Thebus was taking her to the WigWam to hear Red Nichols and His Five Pennies. Not that it was any of his business but she had nothing to be ashamed of. She held her packages tight on her lap, the white shoes, an aeroplane for Billy and a bottle of that hair oil that Tom used and that Billy had been asking and asking for ever since Tom had given him a little bit for himself in a jar. And oh! how pleased she was, a new bathing suit, that old rag would be in the garbage can tomorrow. Vera's Fine Fashions had it in the window on sale, a navy-blue flat-knit suit without any *skirt* to flap around and make her look like something the cat dragged in. She didn't want to be in this old tin-can Ford, listening to Dave

go on and on about the new Hackettstown High gym! God help us!
She wanted to lock her door and try on her suit. God knows she knew
what Poppa would say, the first thing out of his mouth would be
something about Tom this or Tom that and he'd look at her in it like
she was some kind of chippy. She knew the suit would be tight and
show her, but women her age wore them, wore them all over the
beach, she'd be damned if she was going to walk around anymore
looking like Whistler's mother! She was a grown woman and had
always hated that flowered thing. How many years? She didn't even
want to think how many. There was no way she'd be able to see all
of her but she could stand on the bed and get a pretty good idea of
how the suit looked. Dave said that he heard that Red Nichols was
a good orchestra and she said that she and Mr. Thebus both liked to
dance and thought they'd just go and enjoy themselves for an hour
or two and Dave said they could always dance at the Warren House.
The damn fool! Jumping around to those polkas with the farmers and
their wives in their Sears, Roebuck outfits wasn't *dancing.* And their
clodhopper shoes, my God almighty. God *knows* who he thought she
was! She squeezed the shoebox in its paper bag.

Billy didn't know whether to go outside and play with the new
aeroplane first or put some rose oil on his hair, and when Marie told
him he was running around like a chicken with his head cut off, and
imitated him, they both laughed, and Billy sat down on her bed and
bounced on it, holding the plane out at arm's length. She took her
shoes out of the box and tried them on, turning her feet and admiring
how she looked. Billy said he thought they really looked swell and
asked her if she was going to wear them dancing with Tom. Before
she could compose her face to give him an answer, in came Poppa like
a bat out of hell, and he told Billy to go out and play, he wanted to
speak to his mother. Here it comes, she knew it. The usual sarcasms,
Tom this and Tom that and Tom the other thing, just what did she
think she was doing, the man was nothing but a little cock of the walk
with his moustache and his big talk, talk is cheap, butter wouldn't
melt, bejesus, in the man's mouth, nothing but a patch on a man's ass.
Oh, how he carried on. Marie had had enough of all this, somehow
the shoes—and the bathing suit, the bathing suit—gave her the cour-
age to tell him that she'd spent years, *years,* and well he knew it, as

the chief cook and bottle washer, the pot walloper, waiting on
Momma hand and foot and cleaning and scrubbing and doing laundry, ironing so he'd, *he'd* look presentable to go to the office, a slave
and he damn well knew it, and bringing up a fatherless boy into the
bargain with never a bit of help and never a word of complaint out
of her. And it was time she was entitled to a little life.

He simply ignored her and said that she'd probably paid a pretty
penny for those shoes to look like Astor's pet horse for that horse's
ass of a man, a man? and did she want to know a thing or two about
him? When he started in with Helga says, Marie looked up at the
ceiling and clasped her hands at her bosom, God help us all! Helga!
But the old man went on, oh yes, Poppa went on and on like a
Victrola, stubborn Irish mule! Helga says that her cousin knows the
family very well, Tom's wife's family, and it was no secret why his
wife packed up and left him. The man spent his whole life chasing
janes, the scum of the earth, any tramp that cocked her eye at him,
she even saw him one day with some skirt in a fleabag hotel, coming
out of it, in Newark, by God, the man looked like the wrath of God
and the floozie with him was painted up to her eyes and the hair on
her out of a bottle with the roots growing in black! And there they
were arm in arm just as nice as you please, oh yes, don't tell me about
Tom. Oh, Poppa, she said. Don't you know anything, after all these
years, about Helga Schmidt? Never mind about Helga Schmidt! Of
course, of course, what did she expect? She's a fine upstanding woman
and knows whereof she speaks. If the shoe, bejesus, fits! And besides,
there was talk, and a lot of talk, that he even tried to love up his own
brother's wife, yes, goddammit! His own sister-in-law. The man is a
mongrel and he's taking advantage of you because you're all alone and
he figures your father is too old to do anything about it. And, also,
and he's also, he's a pup! And then Poppa forbade her to go to the
WigWam tonight or any other night. Marie told him, her face white,
that she was a grown woman, and could go dancing with a man who
had been kind to her and to her son—*and* to him!—and showed
nothing but the highest respect to all of them since the moment they
laid eyes on him. I don't care what gutter stories you hear from Helga
Schmidt! I'm entitled to *some* life! I haven't spoken to chick nor child
but the butcher and the grocer for years and years. Is that life? And

then her father, shaking his head in anger and disgust, walked out. Little turd of a man, he turned and said at the door. The man doesn't even have an ass, what kind of a man is that? And Marie blushed and tears came to her eyes as she walked to the door and shut it, hard, behind Poppa. Oh my God, she said, the spite, Poppa, the spite!

She thought she looked stunning in the suit, and turned, standing on the bed, so that she could see her behind. It looked a little, not exactly fat, but heavy. Well, she wasn't getting any younger, but she knew, as well, that her figure was attractive, still, God knew she looked better than Eleanor, who had the nerve to wear a suit like this in *white,* and she was older by ten years too. If Tom looked at her tomorrow . . . She'd be nonchalant, take off her robe as she always did. She wasn't going to make a damn fool of herself, was she? She yanked at the suit, trying to make it cover more of her behind and felt a little panicky. She imagined Tom looking at her tugging and pulling, my God! She'd better not be doing that tomorrow like some frip without any breeding. The suit was perfectly respectable. Everybody wore them. It covered her perfectly, that's the way it's supposed to look. She was still *young.* That walk with Tom, suddenly veering off the road with him, behind a tree in the cool dark. The mosquitoes, she'd said, but he had embraced her, my God, and kissed her and kissed her, she'd opened her mouth and felt him down there big and hard pressing against her belly through her thin dress. He'd tried to pull her skirts up, I love you, I love you, Marie, but she'd pushed away his hands, still kissing and kissing, oh! she'd almost died with excitement. He stopped trying to put his hands under her clothes then and stepped back, she could see his eyes shine in the starlight, and he apologized, begged her forgiveness, and even kissed her hand. She felt so bad for him. You must think I'm some rotten egg, Marie. But I've dreamed so long of holding you . . . Oh no, no, my dear Tom, dearest, it's just that, it's just that I feel I'm not even me! Like a baby. And then they kissed again and she opened her mouth again. She said they ought to start back. She stepped out from behind the tree and started toward the road and he said that he had to tie his shoe but she knew he was fixing, adjusting himself. She could feel the impress of him still on her belly and thighs and almost felt dizzy, God forgive me.

At the supper table, it was a comedy of errors if she'd ever seen one.

Tom talked about the war that everybody who wasn't blind in one eye
and couldn't see out of the other knew was coming, and how Germany
had been preparing for it for years, they never got over the last one,
and Poppa, *when* he broke his heart to look at Tom, looked at him
so sarcastically, oh, how superior! But Marie knew what that was all
about, you couldn't fool her—it was on Helga's behalf, oh sure, the
dumpy little kraut with her hooks out for a widower with a nice little
nest egg. The bereaved widow with her Germany this and Germany
that. She probably had a picture of Hitler on the wall, Marie wouldn't
put it past her. Marie, whenever Poppa wasn't looking, smiled over
at Tom and he smiled back and once, she thought so anyway, he
accidentally stuck his foot out and touched her foot under the table.
And that finagling Helga was chewing the fat to beat the band at her
table, my God, she had Mrs. Copan's ear, the poor washed-out bag
of bones, it's a wonder Marie's ears didn't turn red as a beet, and every
once in a while the poor widow had the gall to look over at Poppa
and smile this poor-man, poor-put-upon-man smile, the nerve of her!
and she made damn sure that Poppa saw it too, you can bet your
bottom dollar on that! Tom saw it too and talked even more about
Germany and how they wouldn't be satisfied until they had another
war because the Germans were really very Prussian, it was a historical
fact. Marie got so mad at Helga and her playacting that she decided
to wait until she looked over at Poppa again and then smile her best
smile at Tom as bold as brass, and how do you like that, dutchie? You
busybody. It was almost as if Tom knew what she was thinking
because he smiled back at her and made some little jokes, just for her,
to make her laugh. Billy had his eyes on everything, the boy must
know something is going on, not exactly what, but little pitchers.
Well, she had nothing to be ashamed of, she could hold her head high
and if she wanted to show manners to a decent wonderful man with
a head on his shoulders, what *should* she have to be ashamed of? She
was entitled to a life, too, just like everybody else.

After supper, Marie had time to kill before she had to bathe, so she
sat in her room, away from all the relics and damn fools on the porch,
wondering if she would really look all right in that old white dress.
Well, it wasn't that old, and it had a nice cut to it and the belt made
her figure stand out, which was, she knew, her worry. She felt

ashamed of herself, worrying about that, my God, she'd been hiding from the world for so long—through no fault of her own!—that she'd actually begun to think of herself as some stick of an old woman. What else had made her wear that bathing suit for so— Oh, that *suit*. Good riddance! She got up from the bed and began to undress quickly, then, naked, reached under her slips and step-ins and stockings in the top drawer and took the new suit out, looking at her watch as she began to pull it on, she had a minute, she just wanted, again . . . She adjusted the shoulder straps to lift her bosom and looked in the dresser mirror, cocking her head, then climbed on the bed and turned so that she could see her body in half-profile. She put her hands on her hips and smiled the way Madeleine Carroll smiled. I'd *love* to take a dip, Tom, she said, and smiled again, half-closing her eyes, smoothing the suit over her hips to see how her breasts looked with her arms pulled back tautly. If anyone looked in the window! And she turned to see if anyone, by some miracle, might be there, then felt foolish. She got off the bed and pulled the suit off, threw it on the bed and put her robe on, then took soap and powder, rouge, lipstick, and her toothbrush and toothpaste and stepped into the corridor.

Well. Not bad. Not half-bad. She was pleased with herself, patting her hair, looking again in the mirror, listening to Tom's voice on the porch, his laughter. The white dress looked fine, she'd pulled the belt tight to accentuate her hips and bosom and felt smooth and trim underneath in the new two-way stretch she'd worn the day they left the city. The white shoes were, well, they were even more stunning now that she was all dressed. What else? Something just right, something a little classy. What? Oh yes, yes, her white beads. Tony. At least he had some class, he knew what to buy when, before, oh . . . of course, they were just the ticket. Matched her white ball earrings, white, all white. God, I look like a bride. She took her purse and a white crocheted shawl in case it got chilly and left the room, five after eight. Perfect.

What else did she expect of Tom? He was perfect, an eyeful, really. He looked over at her and smiled as she stepped out on the porch, oh, God help us, we're to be the sideshow tonight, Dave Warren and those two silly girls. Poppa? I'd think he'd . . . Just as well he wasn't there, casting a pall over everything. Oh, but there he came, speak of the

devil, with a face that would frighten horses on him, but Billy reached
to kiss her and he told her how swell she looked. Tom took a step
toward the edge of the porch, put his foot on the first step, and she
bent and kissed Billy, pleased to see the touch of lipstick left on his
cheek. Well, Poppa, you can stand there forever with your hands in
your pockets like a wooden Indian, goodbye, goodbye—and may God
forgive her but she wished it was goodbye forever, that she was
shaking the dust of the place off her feet for good and all. She and Tom
walked to his car and she started to blush, dammit to hell, dammit
dammit dammit. What a relief it was to get in the car, and how it
shone! and as Tom was backing out of his spot by the church, smiling
vaguely in the direction of the porch while she waved—you'd think
she was going to China, my God, the way everybody acted—she heard
him say, she could just hear him over the engine, You're beautiful.
You're such a knockout. She kept waving, still blushing, and she
couldn't see anything really, was Poppa waving? He *was!* Yes, that
was Poppa! Thank you, Poppa, thank you, Bye, bye, bye-bye, Poppa,
and then Tom had the car out on the road and they started off in the
blue dusk, such a lovely night. A perfect night.

Tom told her she was beautiful when she blushed, that she was the
best-looking woman in New Jersey, hell, anywhere, that her dress was
lovely, that he loved her shoes, that there was nothing like silk stockings to make a lady *look* like a lady, that he had all he could do to
keep from hugging and kissing her right on the porch, damn everybody! She laughed and felt like a girl. The luckiest summer of my life,
Tom said. And I've got my brother to thank. Hell, I'm going to buy
him a case of champagne when the summer is over. He reached over
calmly and casually and put his arm around Marie, and she could
smell his hair oil and tobacco, his bay rum. She felt hot under her
clothes. The last time she could remember feeling this way was when
Tony used to start unbuttoning her blouse or the back of her dress in
the dark of the porch while he was *supposed* to be opening the door,
and the baby-sitter, that nice girl from around the corner, probably
listening to them, getting some earful. The time he pulled her over to
the couch the sec the girl left and they didn't even take their clothes
off! Tony could be so—God! That was a million years ago. Then she
felt Tom's hand move down from her shoulder and touch the top of

her breast and she let him, she *let* him, she wanted him to caress and
squeeze her and open her dress and unhook her and she'd sit there
and let him, she'd let him do what he wanted to do. She told him that
he really shouldn't? Tom? Really. Tom, please? He moved his hand
up a little and said that he was only flesh and blood and apologized.
And may God forgive her, she looked down quickly at his pants to
see if . . . What was she doing? The mother of a ten-year-old boy! Still
married in the eyes of God.

The WigWam was everything she remembered, it was even better.
And she wasn't sad or nostalgic, not a bit, about Tony or anything,
the good old days, oh yeah? Good? Tom was a wonderful dancer, she
knew he would be, just knew it, and she felt her own abilities returning, he led so well, she loved a man who knew how to lead, and they
danced all the fox trots, fast and slow, and a two-step as well. We're
game for anything, honey, Tom said, that's the way it should be. We
make a great pair. She decided on a Tom Collins and Tom did too,
it was warm and they tasted good, she'd always liked a good Collins
anyway, not too sweet. When she looked at her watch it was eleven,
impossible, and she held it to her ear. Now, listen, I *command* you
to have a good time and stop worrying about the time, you're with
me, I'm a grown man, you're a grown woman, and we're out on a
Saturday night like everybody else in the world who's not dead from
the neck up. Your father is able to make his own hot milk and tuck
himself in. Something like that, the funny way Tom had of saying
things, smiling around the stem of his pipe. Billy, she said. But Tom
gave her one of his looks and she laughed and felt ashamed and looked
at the table. He was right, it was silly to worry, Poppa probably spent
the night with ach der Kaiser anyway, God knows she wouldn't miss
an opportunity like this to get her hooks in him a little more. She
could do her backbiting in peace the whole night, that terrible thing
about Tom—she was about to ask him about it but knew then that
it would be the wrong thing to say, and they danced again anyway.
This time it was a very slow fox trot, "Alone," what a lovely old song,
and from the very beginning of the dance she could feel him really
hard down there against her belly and inner thigh when she moved
against him and she pushed herself close to him and closed her eyes,
well, she had her girdle on. She could hear his breath in her ear, My

dear Marie, my sweet, I love you, I love you. She opened her eyes to look up at him and he smiled and held her tight in the small of the back and pushed himself against her so that she could feel him almost as if he, oh my God.

At twelve-thirty, she said that they really better go, it was almost an hour's drive back and there was no use in, well, she meant, you know. Let sleeping dogs lie. Tom agreed. He paid the check and left a nice tip and they walked out, the air was cool and still and she pulled the shawl around her shoulders and Tom helped her, then caught her by the arms and kissed her, kissed her again. She wanted to get in the car and go and go. Go away. No, first go and get Billy and go away anywhere. Tom drove fast, the roads were dark and almost deserted, the wind bubbled in the half-open butterfly windows and his arm was around her shoulder, his hand on her breast, squeezing it softly and persistently, almost as if she imagined it, oh, how wonderful it felt, her eyes closed, his thumb slid over her stiff nipple and revolved around it, sliding smoothly over the fabric. Then the car bounced once, hard, and then again, Tom? They were moving slowly down a small, grass-grown road under tall black trees, stars between their leaves and branches. Tom stopped the car and turned to her, pulled her close, oh, the time! the time! It must be one in the morning, even later. Tom! But he was kissing her and she opened her mouth, wide, wide, greedy, and she could taste Sen-Sen and then his tongue slid all the way into her mouth and she sucked on it delicately, oh Tom! His hands were opening her dress and then he had her breasts free of her brassiere and slip and was kissing them alternately, and licking her nipples, sucking them, he was moaning, and she moaned too, smiling crookedly into the dark, her face burning. He was pulling at her skirts, pulling them up around her hips and trying to get her step-ins down, get them off. No. No. Tom, no, Tom, no, no, no, please. Not now, Tom. Here. Please not here now. He stopped but continued to caress her breasts and suck her nipples and she lay back against the seat, dizzy and breathing hoarsely, aware her skirts were still bunched around her hips and her thighs open. He said, Marie, he said it again and again, he wanted her to look at him and she opened her eyes and turned. He had pulled his pants open and exposed himself, it was sticking out of his pants, so big and stiff, and he pulled her hand over

to it firmly. She grasped him tightly and he moaned and took one of
her breasts in his hand and sucked just the point of her nipple, his
other hand crammed in between her legs but she wouldn't open them
any further. She began to move her hand up and down, O love, love,
love, he whispered, Marie was whispering too, Tom my dearest, how
big he was. She felt filthy, like a slut and a tramp, and imagined how
she must look, with her clothes like they were and doing what she was
doing. But it made her more excited and she moved her hand faster
and faster and put her other hand into his open pants so she could
touch his . . . his balls. Then Tom sat up, suddenly, his thighs wide
open and he had his handkerchief over himself and she could feel him
spurting and spurting and he breathed and grunted through his grit-
ted teeth. Her hand was all wet and sticky and she kept moving it up
and down, doing it, doing it like a tramp, until he leaned his head back
on the seat and sighed, then reached over and held her wrist and she
stopped.

God knew what time it was when they pulled up next to the church,
maybe even two? Tom kissed her tenderly, Marie, I love you, I love
you. She smiled at him and asked him to say it again like some high
school girl with a crush when she saw a light slide across Tom's
shoulders and across the dashboard. Come up here! Come up here
right now, goddammit to hell! My God, it was Poppa! She looked over
at Tom in terror and he was smiling at her, bitter and angry and
surprised. You pup! You take my daughter for a tramp? Come *up,*
here, Skip! One-thirty in the morning! Suddenly Marie felt her stomach turn and she thought she'd throw up and put her handkerchief
to her mouth and swallowed and swallowed. Tom bent and kissed her
temple and forehead, Do you want me to come up with you, take the
bull by the horns and get this out in the open? Oh no, Marie didn't
want that, he didn't know Poppa, when he was like this . . . He had
forbade her to even go, and what she'd done . . . a light was on in the
house, Mr. Copan was looking out the window, she heard the porch
door open and somebody came out, the flashlight was shining steadily
on the car now and Poppa was still yelling. She adjusted her skirts and
checked her buttons and got out, holding Tom's hand tightly as she
stepped into the beam of light, looking at his face, My God, Tom, and
he squeezed her hand tight. She must look like death warmed over,

she even felt pale, felt as if somebody had walked in on her while she was on the toilet. She began to cry, hurrying to the porch, quickly past somebody there, damn busybody, damn damn rotten . . . weeping silently till she was on the stairs, then sobbing out once, loudly, but then she controlled herself, rushing up the stairs, past Poppa's room, God! and Billy's! He woke up Billy! In her room she lay down on the bed with all her clothes on and wept for an hour, forever, humiliated and wretched. How could she ever even *talk* to Tom again? How could he? He wouldn't even want to *look* at her. It was cruel and mean and rotten, she hated her father as much as she had ever hated her mother. You *should* have, Tom, she whispered, turning over, pushing her face into the bedspread, sobbing again, You should have *made* me do it. Made me fuck and *fuck* you. Oh, God, forgive me, what will I do?

When Marie heard Billy at the door, she put the letter Tom had left for her the night before under her pillow. She had read it at least a dozen times—it had no reality but it was his, his. Everything that had happened since that awful scene existed in a haze. Her father yelling! Shining a light on her! She couldn't believe that Tom had left, either, but he had. Standing at his car, ready to go, he had whispered that he loved her and would move heaven and earth to see her—he had his ways, he said, and then she watched his white smile and for a minute felt safe, thought that maybe her life would continue. When they shook hands she almost began to cry, she wanted him to do anything he wanted, take her, force her into the car and take her away. She was ashamed and angry with herself for not letting him Saturday, she wanted to turn back the clock and be there again with him in the car, take off every stitch of clothes and let him *see* her.

The night before, she had awakened at three in the morning to a slight whispering sound, and turned the lamp on to see an envelope on the floor just inside the door. She had read his letter, crying, again, oh God, again crying, crushed by loathing for her life, for her father, mean, mean as her mother. Worse.

My dearest Marie, darling,

I'm writing this note because tomorrow I'm going to leave and go back to the city. Don't worry, I'll make up some good excuse about business, I don't want to look like I'm running away and add fuel to the fire, they'd all love that. Believe you me my dearest, it is one of the hardest things I've ever done in my whole life but I cannot see my way clear to staying another week in this atmosphere, I know it would make your life Hell on earth. I know how mortified you were last night and I still really can't believe what happened, last night. And I don't want to say anything disrespectful about your father but between you and me it was a very mean thing to do the way everybody lives here like people in a goldfish bowl. And when I saw your sweet beautiful face this morning at breakfast so sad and I could tell you were crying all night I knew then and there staying here would make everything harder all around, so it is the best thing for me to go and not give the relics fuel for their gossip, they have got plenty already.

Trust me my dear, that I will come and see you in the city by hook or by crook. What I feel about you ever since the minute I laid eyes on you won't be forgotten, I am not one of your out of sight out of mind sort of men. Just because Fall comes does not mean that I will not think of you, always. I did not have a chance to tell you on Saturday night but, you have given me back a real sense of manhood that I have not had since long before my wife walked out on me. I cannot imagine anything more beautiful than to go on with our beautiful friendship back in the city, this Fall. Maybe your father will cool off a little back in the city and be willing to talk to me man to man and look me straight in the eye instead of treating me like something the cat dragged in and to wipe his feet on me. It might just be that way when he is not seeing *Helga Schmidt* every day. She sure put a bee in your father's bonnet about me although, I cannot prove it. And I think she has her own reasons for shining up to him this way but I'll let sleeping dogs lie if you know what I mean and I am sure you do. Anyhow, I would like to prove to him that I am not the wisenheimer he thinks I am and that I have your best interests in my heart.

My dearest Marie, I will never, never forget Saturday night however it all panned out in the end. That cannot spoil the rest of the evening. I hope and pray that you do not think that I ever planned to take advantage of your purity because I know that you are a good and pure lady, and I mean a real lady and I'm not fit to kiss your feet. Just because you are a good sport and like to have a little fun does not mean that a man can make a pass at you, I know that through and through. I have been worrying about my conduct Saturday night ever since. But you were so beautiful all in white, like an angel, I must have got carried away and I am really ashamed. I hope that you will forgive me and tomorrow when I say goodbye, short and sweet, if you will just shake my hand I will know that you forgive me. I have nothing but the highest respect for your purity.

And please trust me that I will manage to see you in the city some way, by hook or by crook. And also try and talk turkey to your father who thinks because of Mrs. Schmidt that I am some kind of Valentino or something. I promised Billy that I would take him to football games this Fall and maybe Coney Island. I am saying that this is not goodbye. But it is the best thing for me to do right now in this goldfish bowl with a lot of wagging tongues making life unbearable for you if I stayed to the bitter end. With me gone things will have a chance to simmer down.

> Your dear friend and admirer,
> Tom

Billy had—what? What was in his hand? Tom's tobacco pouch, oh, surely it was Tom's tobacco pouch, she could never mistake it. She even used to carry it in her bag sometimes when they went to the beach. She knew that Tom had left it for her. Not as a memento or a souvenir, but somehow on purpose. It was a sort of link between them, even better than his lovely lovely letter because it was *his.* But now, holding it, she felt enormously sad and exhausted and tears came up in her eyes. She hugged Billy and kissed him, thanked him for bringing her the pouch. Then she asked him to please go out and play, because she had to write some letters. Billy backed out of the room and just outside, before he closed the door, asked her if Tom would come back, maybe, for the tobacco pouch? Because he once told Billy that it was his favorite, his old reliable, and kept his tobacco really fresh. Marie shook her head and smiled, then shrugged, and Billy closed the door.

For a moment she thought that Tom really might return, but knew that it was impossible, a dream. She understood why he had to leave, it was kind and considerate, for her. But she was sure, *sure,* that he'd left the pouch on purpose. She unzipped it and smelled the rich, sweet blend, her eyes closed, felt his mouth wet and tender on her bare nipples. Jesus, Mary and Joseph, she whispered, and shivered, then got up and put the pouch in a drawer under her new bathing suit. He'd never see it now. She flushed suddenly with resentment and anger. Her father had mentioned it to her the day before. Mentioned it to her! He had been snooping in her room, looking at her private things, it was unnatural. He didn't want her to wear it, he said. It was time he put his foot down, well past time the way things were going, he should have done it long ago and maybe things wouldn't have come to this pretty pass. She looked past him at the fields and told him that she didn't think it was right for him to go rummaging through her private things without her knowledge, and he told her to keep a civil tongue in her head, since when did she have the right to tell her *father* what he should or shouldn't do? Rummaging! She had seriously thought of going swimming with Tom and the others that afternoon as if nothing had happened, *and* with her new suit on, but that was cutting it a bit thick. Not yet, she couldn't do anything like that, yet. As far as her ever wearing the suit, well, she'd see. She had a *right* to wear it and knew that her father had got on his high horse about it because he knew she'd bought it so that Tom could see her in it, see that she was still pretty and young and had a figure. Her father didn't want that, he didn't want anybody to see her, like she was his *wife.* How he always loved it when strangers thought she *was* his wife! Once or twice he hadn't even corrected them, just smiled as if he hadn't heard them right. Oh, God! This was no life.

She smoothed the suit over the tobacco pouch and closed the drawer. On the lawn Mr. Sapurty and her father were playing croquet, that goddamned croquet! She felt like putting her foot through the window, smashing it to smithereens, then putting her new bathing suit on and going down on the lawn to take a sun bath—give that damn fool of a relic Ralph an eyeful! Sweet Mother of God! Did anybody ever have such a cross to bear as this?

People could grind up light bulbs and sprinkle the glass all over her food. She'd be dying and think she had gas pains. One of the season's prettiest weddings. St. Rocco's Church. 1926. Just a girl. The only man who'd ever *really* kissed her. What was she supposed to do? Before he started losing his hair. Red Moon roadster with the wire-spoke wheels. Tom talked until he foamed at the mouth and was nice and Caesar always with his nose in a book at any kind of an affair, quiet and smoking a pipe. But Tony was the best dancer, full of fun. Extended trip to Washington, Maryland and Virginia. When he wore that beautiful white Borsalino and tropical suit, walking through that ship without getting a drop of grease or oil on him. Just a young girl. He took her aboard that first job of his own and the men looked down at the deck when she climbed the ladder so as not to see up her dress. Good decent men, took their caps off. Why not? her mother said. You're an American girl. White satin and duchess lace, veil entirely of Irish point lace in cap effect. Angelo as strong as a bull, drank a cup of fresh blood every morning at the slaughterhouse, worshiped the ground she walked on. She could have had any one of the brothers. Tony was the best dresser, snappy, and quick with a dollar. I don't want any goddamned guinea name for the boy, we'll call him William. Do I look like a greenhorn? Do I talk like my brother Joe? Joe had a little moustache then and wore snap-brim fedoras. He was a hand-some man, but his *accent.* Trimmed with orange blossoms. Carried white roses and lily of the valley. Caroline Esposito was maid of honor in a gown of Nile-green taffeta with hat to match and carried a bouquet of pink roses. The party for Joe the Ice when he got out of prison. Envelopes with cash thrown in a pillowcase like a wedding reception. She thought he'd been in the hospital. Just a girl. When he came into her class? She must have been seven in the second grade. He was at least ten or eleven. Black eyes and curly hair, boots up to his knees, wore a long cape. Couldn't speak a word of English. If anyone had told her! After Billy came he asked her to do terrible things. Dirty things, she didn't know the names of them even. She didn't even know people could imagine those things. Father Donovan said they were sinful and she had a right as a Catholic wife to refuse. "The animal side." Katie's Janet was the flower girl, adorable, and little Ralph Esposito was the ring bearer. All of Irish point lace. Extended trip. And then Margie. Margie. Came into her house like a snake, butter wouldn't melt in her mouth. Red hair and rotting teeth. Secretary! Down there on Wolcott Street with the rats sitting on her shoulder and her gimpy brother with his dese dose and dems, common shanty Irish trash. She couldn't fry a goddamned egg without burning it to a crisp and that sneaky little shyster Jew lawyer running around to do the dirty work, Seymour Goldberg. May he burn in hell. Rose Spoto in orchid georgette and Minnie Recco in flesh georgette and Florence Esposito in peach georgette and Florence Recco in maize georgette, all wearing hats to match and carrying tea roses. Trimmed with orange blossoms, extended trip. Irish point lace. What happened? When he saw her in their suite at the Hotel St. George. Alone together. Just a girl. The most beautiful trousseau, the lingerie. House of sin they lived in on Gerritsen Avenue and Avenue T. Mr. and Mrs. Recco. *She'd* do all the dirty moron things he asked. Now she's a fat drunk and her gimpy brother's got ulcers. God is good. Caesar and Tom were both sweet on her. Tony was the best dancer, full of fun. The red Moon. Charlie was too young. He was the best man and the ushers? Frank Lupo, Tom, Anthony Faicco, and Charlie Esposito. The best dresser, snappy. He never paid back the two thousand dollars Poppa loaned him to start the business. Neptune Ship Scaling and Contracting Company, Inc. Without that money he still wouldn't have a pot to piddle in. When those dagos get on their high horse, her mother said. Too goddamned good to work for a decent American. Your father's not too goddamned good to work for other people. He worshiped the ground she walked on. Went out for chow mein and came back with little red embroidered slippers. Chi-

nese apples. Bouquets of flowers. In January. Why not? her mother
said. You always looked like you stepped out of a bandbox. Where
did their kind ever see a girl with your looks and breeding? A blonde.
Blue eyes. Those dagos are almost black as niggers. Black greasy hair.
Trimmed with orange blossoms. In cap effect. A reception for 150
guests. And dear poor Katie cried, a lot to cry about. So it turned out,
God help her. Buddy dying after falling on his back in the high-school
gym. A handsome boy and a year later Leonard had a stroke. Her
cross. The priest told her she of course couldn't get a divorce even
though he wouldn't give her any money for the boy and in the middle
of the Depression. A good Catholic woman. "Animal side." And Billy
wasn't allowed in parochial school because *he* got a Florida divorce
that wasn't recognized anyway. The Mother Superior with a chin on
her sharp enough to cut cheese said the first grade was full. May God
have mercy on her. The fat hypocrite priests eating their roast beef
on Friday! She'd seen it with her own eyes. Thank God her faith was
strong. That slut of a tramp did the things he wanted. Taught him a
few too, if truth be known. Probably right in the office, she wouldn't
put a thing past the floozy. His white Borsalino. Immaculate. When
the bed slats broke and Billy came in with the noise. They were as
happy as larks in that little house in Flatbush. Margie came to Billy's
birthday party in a green dress. To match her teeth, her mother said.
All smiles and Tony and her were doing God knows what filth. She
loaned her a pair of her best black kid gloves to go to her father's
funeral. Never got them back. They can take something you own and
get some old witch to put the evil eye on you. Right after that she got
those stomach pains so bad she crawled on her hands and knees in
agony. They can grind up glass. She thought it was indigestion. Lived
on bicarbonate of soda and never a word of complaint out of her.
When his mother died he never spoke for a week. No tears. The day
of her funeral he collapsed and had to be put to bed. Fiorenza, a tall
and silent woman. Then Margie came. Red hair and stains on her
dress. Chain-smoked. The old man would never talk to him again. Sat
blind under his grapevines and fig trees in the backyard and waited
to die. Charlie played the violin. Julius raised his sixteen children
behind his shoemaker's shop. The church does not recognize any kind
of divorce, dear. Sitting down to his roast beef, fat hypocrite, North

of Ireland convert, the worst kind. An American girl. They looked at
the deck, she was in a white summer dress and a straw hat with a navy
bow. When he bought the cigar at the Milano with a thousand-dollar
bill. "A favor somebody did." They can grind up glass. Some old
strega with the evil eye. Billy with spaghetti and butter sauce. Three
packs of Juicy Fruit. A head all golden curls. Oh God. Fell down the
stairs in the new house and three days later his eye was crossed.
Orange blossoms. Extended trip. They all worshiped the ground she
walked on. Her mother said it was God's judgment on her for moving
so far away. Mother of God! Joe the Ice with his prison pallor, a nice
man but a *cafone*. He would take off his cap to talk to her. Look at
the floor. His Borsalino. Joe's son was born in prison. His wife did the
time for him. Morphine or cocaine. Katie made her work like a slave
in Jersey City, a charity case. Who could blame her really? Her own
rotten life. Leonard sitting staring in his chair and her beautiful
Buddy dead at sixteen. One of the season's prettiest weddings. The
Eye and Ear with those goddamned wooden clinic benches for the
charity patients. Waiting all day. Those charity wire-frame glasses on
his little face. Where was God? A head all golden curls. Your father
and I haven't got no money, her mother said. Where did you get that
idea? Your father works hard for his money. You want a fancy
doctor? Wish in one hand and you know what you can do in the other.
Head all golden curls. Trimmed with orange blossoms. Face to face
with her meanness. Angelo drank blood. Strong as a bull. Ripped his
shirt open at her wedding and sang opera. Her relatives all shanty
Irish gawked at the greaseball. Her father's relatives drinking their
Episcopalian ginger ale. Let that big-shot dago pay for a fancy specialist. She cried and cried. Those wire frames. Margie in the paper with
him and some crooked politician. Mr. and Mrs. Recco. Slut and
whore. Mouth full of store teeth made her look like a horse. Slut.
Whore. Crippled brother called it a "finished basement." Finished all
right. Crawling with rats. Cockroaches. Caroline in Nile green and
she got no bed of roses either. The slats broke that Sunday morning.
Billy laughing too. Pulled him into bed. Head all golden curls. Veil
entirely of Irish point lace. Her mother dying of leukemia that old
quack called "weak blood," gave her sugar pills. And guess who was
the chief cook and bottle washer then? Guess. A maid who didn't get

paid. Billy and she moved in so she could be the slave. Katie's was,
oh *sure,* all right before. Billy's eye was the judgment of God. Cruel
God. Roast beef. Fat Father Donovan. May God help him. "Animal
side." Her mother allowed it to happen. Jealous of their happiness,
their house, Billy, everything. "Oh, what a *little* house." Waited on
hand and foot. "Good riddance to the wop." Extended trip. Then all
of a sudden. What happened? She didn't even know the words for the
things he asked her to do. Margie with her green teeth, her Judas
smile. She prayed, God forgive me, but make her die. Make her die,
God. He is good. Mr. and Mrs. Recco of Gerritsen Avenue. Time
wounds all heels. The night she went into labor they were at the
Follies. What happened? Red silk slippers. Bouquets and boxes of
chocolate. Coming out of the hold of that ship like he just stepped out
of a bandbox. Her mother beat Katie with a wooden slat and a belt
because they stopped in the ice-cream parlor for a cone. Afraid she'd
get stains on her dress that Katie, the poor girl, had to launder and
then iron with the flatiron on the coal stove, oh God. Dresses with
starch and hundreds of pleats. Saw them out the window, laughing
and eating their ice cream. A wooden slat, the belt whistling and then
the crack. A charity case. Her mother made eyes at Tony. God help
her if it wasn't true. "Good riddance" to the dago guinea greaseball
wop. Jealous of her happiness. Her father silent behind his *News* or
Mirror. Oh, Poppa, you never said a word! You should have gone and
talked to Tony about that chippy. The red Moon outside the door.
Full of fun and quick with a dollar. When she gave her the black kid
gloves she stroked them and smelled the leather. Shanty ignorant Irish
pig with her dyed red hair. Snake coming to Billy's fourth birthday
party. And Tony drove her home. Oh yes. Oh yes, of *course* he did.
Place crawling with rats as long as your arm. Duke Ellington at the
Cotton Club. When she went into labor. That Jew shyster Seymour
telling her a Florida divorce was "perfectly legal." What happened?
The boy asked for his father. "Why are we in cousin Katie's?" One
bath a week if you were lucky and by God clean the tub and floor on
your hands and knees. For boiled spare ribs and cabbage. Beans and
lamb that was nothing but a mass of fat. Caesar would blush and stare
at his book. She could have had. They worshiped. White roses and lily
of the valley and for a minute she couldn't recognize her own

strangely sad face in the wedding pictures. No wonder. A lot of water
under the bridge. Chinese slippers and flowers, orange blossoms and
white roses and lily of the valley and then those green teeth and red
hair. The rats would sit on your shoulder they were so bold. Take the
greasy food right out of your mouth. What happened? That girl on
the rock in the field, was it so long ago, was it possible? And sitting
under the trellis crocheting? Julius wrote love letters to Rose every
day and away for just a week. Florrie Recco saying, "Oh, Marie, oh,
Margie?" Maize georgette and tea roses. Prettiest wedding. Katie
scrubbing the kitchen floor even on Sundays, God help Billy if he
didn't walk on the newspapers. Her mother's giggling and making
eyes at Tony. The Milano every Sunday with the boy's Juicy Fruit.
Him in the highchair. Giggling. Wearing all her rings and her pearls.
God knows she couldn't take them to the grave. Squeezed into her
corset so she could hardly breathe. Giggling, her gold tooth flashing
at Tony. Poppa behind his *Mirror.* Works hard all day. The bride was
given away by her father. Orange blossoms. Red slippers from Yung's.
And in all the snow. Katie can't be blamed, poor dear Katie. Slave
and maid and laundress and pot-walloper all rolled in one. Took her
off the streets after her mother died. Beating her black and blue if she
opened her mouth. *"My* daughter," her mother said. "Peaches and
cream." Her pale-yellow dress starched, hundreds of pleats, yellow
socks and hair ribbons, cunning little white shoes. Katie's hands and
arms all burns from the flatiron. Margie with that crooked shanty
Irish bog-trotter in the paper. Mr. and Mrs. Recco at a dinner given
in Mr. Recco's honor by his employees. Her store teeth. Rats and her
gimpy brother. That little Jew bastard Seymour. "Perfectly legal,
Marie." Tony so broke he buttoned his coat like a woman so nobody
could see it was all frayed. Came in late from Erie Basin and the Navy
Yard but all smiles. Cut the top off his tomato and scooped the meat
out with bits of buttered crust. Secretary! "A dollar down and a dollar
when you catch me," her mother said about his new Packard. But she
rode in it all right, all right, every Sunday. Filled her face at the
Milano. "A specialist? Do you think your poor father's made of
money?" Behind the *Mirror.* Oh God. A long cape, just off the boat,
couldn't speak a word of English. An extended trip after which they
will reside in Bay Ridge. Just a boy, his tall boots, working like a man.

Wouldn't be surprised if that mockie fixed it up with some crooked
judge to have it say he was born here. On the Fourth of July. Ziegfeld
Follies when she went into labor. Worked as a scaler when he was
twelve when it was an art. All done by hand hanging from a scaffold.
Full of fun. Angelo sang "Ciel' la lun'." Goddamned greaseball, Uncle
Mark said, and Uncle Michael, Kitty and Mary Caffrey agreed. Cups
of warm blood. Tom foaming at the mouth telling a story. Joe had a
moustache. Orange blossoms and they were *fresh*. Down in Miami
Beach with the tramp with her green teeth. "Match her dress." Not
even a card for Christmas. Not a cent. Not a word. May God damn
them both. Bought Billy a game in Woolworth's where you shot little
brown celluloid beans into the eyes and mouth of some grinning
gawm. And then he got a scarf and a pair of mittens from her mother
and father from Namm's. And Christmas dinner, don't forget Christmas dinner! One year a little tin pig that marched around the floor
beating a tin drum until he fell over. And another scarf, even cheaper,
another pair of mittens, cheaper, cheaper. His white Borsalino. Miami
Beach. Not a card. Not a word. Down there with his floozy doing
every filthy thing. Mr. and Mrs. Recco. It is all, believe me, Marie,
"perfectly legal." Couldn't get fifteen dollars a week for the both of
them. Katie's. Charity case. Still has the burn scars from that damn
iron. Those pleats, my God. Eight dollars a week at the steam table
at Bickford's. Left Billy every morning with a dime for lunch and told
him not to talk to strangers or go with people who said his father
wanted to see him. Evil eye. Margie with the kid gloves and she never
saw them again. Crawled around on her hands and knees with 'the
pain. That old horse's ass of a quack gave her sugar pills. A handsome
little boy with dark eyes and curly hair. Long cape and boots. Katie's
Arthur decorating the tree with blue balls and icicles and blue lights.
All day long, the little snob of a peacock. His fiancée, bucktoothed
schoolteacher, her chest so big she could hardly stand up straight.
Beautiful Buddy dead and Leonard sitting like a stick and little Janet
running wild. "Wash the tub!" White satin and duchess lace, what
became of it all. She wanted a daughter too. Thank God it didn't
happen. God is good. Things she didn't know the words for. That
bimbo invented half of them if the truth were known. Showed him
how. And poor Minnie Recco left at the church two years later by

some dumb Polack with clothes that would blind you and big enough to fit Finn MacCool. Fiorenza died, tall and dignified. He collapsed. Miami Beach. Orange blossoms and an extended trip. "When you leave New York you is just campin' out." Who was that barber with the long Russian cigarettes? Sweet on Katie but Leonard still alive if you can call it that. Driving a trolley for fifteen years for the Public Service, then the stroke nearly killed him. Bad teeth. Sat in a rocking chair all day long and Katie waited on him hand and foot. Poor girl could hardly read and write and no wonder. Washing and ironing and scrubbing and cleaning and shopping and cooking. "She should get down on her knees and thank God she's got someone to give her a roof over her head and three meals a day." Her father silent behind his newspaper. Given away. They never saw anybody like you. An American girl. Blond and blue-eyed. They're black as niggers, look where they are, right next to Africa. Billy told her Mommy and Daddy broke the bed and she wouldn't say a word to her for a month, filled with rage. With envy, if truth were told, God forgive her. Her father tried to help, pitiful. On the hottest nights he would give her a glass of beer when her mother went to the bathroom. Only if he had a "good pint." She caught him once and he had no peace for a week. Gave her away. Irish point lace. In cap effect. She was a stunning bride, even the photographer said so and he'd seen hundreds. White roses and lily of the valley. Red Moon with wire-spoke wheels. Red silk slippers. When he took her in his arms in the dim light of the hotel room. Flowers in January. Let the big-shot dago success pay for a big-shot kike specialist. What actually happened?

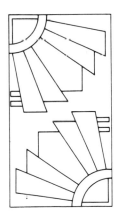

Tom Thebus is singing in a monotone under his breath, singing in the sunlight that turns the croquet lawn on which he stands into a dazzle of green. "I'll Never Smile Again." His mind is not on the game that he is playing with Ralph and Grace Sapurty, but he interrupts the whispered and only partly recollected lyric of the song again and again to look over the lie of the balls and the possible shots that he considers for them as well as for himself: he does this with a casual professionalism, an insouciance carefully kind and tinged with camaraderie and humility, so that neither of his opponents becomes annoyed, ever, at his advice. On the contrary, they are flattered by his attentions.

He glints an occasional smile across the lawn at the woman who sits on a canvas chair in the shade of the umbrella trees at the very edge of the lawn, just this side of the large and beautifully tended kitchen garden. His smile is easy and warm, a smile that he thinks of as one of his good points. He is, indeed, vain about it, as he is vain about his small, scrupulously trimmed moustache and his wavy

brown hair. She avoids his smile and his eyes, afraid, he knows, that
he will discover in *her* eyes her admiration for and delight in him. She
hides behind a copy of *Liberty.* But he knows that she admires him,
and his actions, although performed as if he is not aware that she is
considering each one of them with enormous care, are choreographed
for her pleasure. He crouches now, his hair softly gleaming with rose
oil, then stands straight, filling his briar from an old leather tobacco
pouch. Mr. Sapurty is gesturing with his mallet toward two balls that
lie close together on a slight incline beneath the heavy, powdery-blue
flowers of a giant hydrangea. Tom Thebus, lighting his pipe, nods, and
then gestures as well, using the stem of his pipe. It is a gesture that
he has seen made in countless movies, and he imitates it flawlessly.
Grace Sapurty shifts from one foot to another, smiling foolishly at
him, her fingers touching the pink and yellow embroidered flowers on
the bodice of her sundress.

Mr. Sapurty takes his shot. His ball hits the edge of the wicket
planted at the base of the hydrangea and rolls down the incline. Tom
Thebus smiles, not a smile of triumph, but one of good fellowship.
"Brothers in difficult straits," his smile says. "Tough luck," it says.

Tough luck, he says. That's a *hard* shot. He turns then and fires
a glance straight at the woman in the shade and this time their eyes
meet and she flushes, turns a page of her magazine, then another,
looking down blindly at her lap. Tom walks toward his ball, his mallet
on his shoulder, peering up with his eyes only toward a second-floor
window that overlooks the lawn. He sees behind the dotted-Swiss
curtain that hangs there the dark shape of the old man.

As he lines up his shot, his impeccably white shoes planted on either
side of his mallet, he begins to whisper again. "I'll never love again
until I smile at you." And then he sees, coming around the front of
the house, the heavy-thighed body of Helga Schmidt. She is smiling
a general greeting at all the figures on the lawn, her hand raised, but
her eyes are twisted upward and to the left, focusing on the flat white
of the dotted-Swiss curtain. Tom smiles as well, but not at Helga.

Dear Alex,

How are you doing little brother? I'm writing to you at Lake Ronkonkoma because I seem to remember that this is about the time that you take your two weeks from the salt mines. I hope the kids are okay and of course the ball and chain. I'm only kidding, Susan. You must have that damn palace just about paid off by now. What about your plans about living there all year round? I guess it's not so cheap to put in a cellar. And in times like these, oh boy.

I'm writing by the way, to thank you for finding out about this place for me at the office. It is, kid, just what the doctor ordered. It's about a mile and a half or two down a dirt road to the nearest main road and about ten miles from there to Hackettstown which is the Big City around here. Netcong is the other way, maybe fifteen miles. And very quiet and cool in the evenings. Some skeeters at night but what can you expect in Jersey? At least they don't wear shoes like people say. The people who run this place are your typical Germans, neat as a pin and run like clockwork. The meals they put on the table three times a day are enough to choke a horse. My table has five people plus yours truly and for breakfast for example there is always two platters of eggs, two dozen in all plus, ham and bacon and cereal and about ten gallons of fresh, and I mean fresh milk and coffee, not to mention bread and rolls and buns and biscuits, you name it. If you see me in the Fall and think you're looking at another Hindenburg, I won't be surprised, believe me.

I guess that Janet and little Tommy will be spending some time
with you later in the summer after they come back from my dear
sweet mother in law's in Connecticut. If she starts in on me kid,
do me a favor and take all her belly aching with a grain of salt,
okay? Janet has a tendency to paint me all black and what really
gets me is, she does it in front of the kid. Maybe you can get
Susan to ask her to take it easy on me for Tommy's sake. But for
God's sake don't tell Janet you heard a peep from me about this
because she'll do the exact opposite as sure as hell. God only
knows what she's been feeding the kid about me but it gets my
goat to be the villain of the piece. I know I have to bear a lot of
the blame for this mess but it takes two to make a marriage, am I
right! Gee how I envy you, kid. Susan is some peach.

Speaking of peaches, there is a gal up here who is in the same
boat as me, divorced, maybe about 34, 35 and she is quite a
looker. She's got a boy about Tommy's age and a nice kid too.
She has her father with her too. A widower and the old geezer
can't stand me. But Marie, which is her name, likes me a lot and
we get along fine. Don't get any ideas that romance is on my
mind. Once burned twice shy. It's just nice that there is somebody
my own age here and we can have some good clean fun and a few
laughs. The old man and I play a lot of croquet and kid, is the
old fart good? Oh brother. If I beat him once in a blue moon he
gets so sore that he snaps at everybody the rest of the day.

Alright, I'm stopping here before I write a book. Give my love
to Susan and tell her that I said you better be good to her because
she is pure gold. And love to the kids too,

Tom

P.S. Don't forget what I said about Janet and her tales. By the
way, you wanted to know the name of the lake up here. Budd
Lake is its name.

I never dreamed when I saw you get out of the car that day—I remember you were wearing a knockout polka-dot dress—that we, that I, would feel this way. I mean, feel the way about you, I do.

Poppa will definitely warm up to you. He's all discombobulated with Momma dead just six months. Don't worry, please Tom, about Poppa.

I'm embarrassed to say, but I've been having trouble sleeping since the other night we walked back from the Hi-Top.

Of *course* I can go out with you! What makes you think I can't go out with who I please, socially? My God, Tom, if you think Poppa's such a tyrant . . .

We really have a barrel of laughs, Billy and I. He's a swell kid. He reminds me so much, more and more, of my Tommy. I wish you could meet him.

Oh Tom, I feel like a high-school girl with her first crush. My first real crush was on a boy I worked with just out of high school. In a bank. He was full of fun. I feel just like that, but *more*.

But what about your father? My God, Marie, it's been almost three weeks you've been here and the old man's hardly spoken a civil word to me. When we play croquet even he won't talk unless he absotively has to. Can you maybe give him the lowdown that I'm not a deadbeat? He treats me like I'm contagious.

When you mention the other night, Tom . . . you make me blush. The mother of a ten-year-old boy. *Blushing.*

God, how I'd *love* to take you out stepping. You think you and me might go dancing this Saturday night? They've got Red Nichols and

His Five Pennies at the WigWam all weekend. You think you and me,
I mean, *us,* not a gang.

I've always loved that dress. I've been told it's very becoming on
me. But I've always looked good in blue. If I do say so myself.

Just some privacy! Some time together. And some privacy. Jesus H.
Christ. I feel like we're in a store window. Or a goldfish bowl.

I have to admit, Tom, when you came to the top of the porch steps
with your book and pipe, well . . .

I toss and turn. I get up and smoke. All I can think about is you
and the way, the other night . . .

I haven't been to the WigWam in years. It was always a swell place.
I'd love to go!

Really, Marie, really. Really, I never thought I'd ever feel this way
again. After all the misery and heartaches with my wife, well, let's
leave her out of this, but I never dreamed I'd ever look twice at
another woman. But you . . . you're special. You're just swell.

Tom. That's funny! That's so *funny.* The same thing crossed my
mind. The tricks life plays. Suppose *you* were that teller?

If you only knew how much I want, right this minute, to kiss you
and kiss you, oh, this is one hundred per cent *nuts.*

Yes, it would be lovely to meet him, he must be a little gentleman.
I'm afraid that Billy is no gentleman, but he *adores* you. He looks up
to you. I've done my best to try and breed *some* manners in him.

Good? You're an eyeful in that dress. You're an eyeful in anything.

Well then, let's make it definite for Saturday night. I'd love it!

I was thinking, Marie, how my life would have been if I only met
you twelve years ago. Oh, that kind of stuff is a lot of bushwa, I know,
but still . . .

The fields were so quiet with nothing but the crickets and the
fireflies. I felt like, this is silly, but I felt like we were in a movie.

The one thing I was hoping and praying was that you wouldn't
think I was just being a fresh guy. All hands. But you were so gorgeous.

I haven't been sleeping well either. I feel like I'm walking on air.

Even that first day when you came in from the station, your father
. . . if looks could kill!

I just hope that nobody notices how I, you know, look. I have the crazy idea that everybody can see right through me and how I feel. That Helga is the worst, what a busybody. If *she* gets Poppa's ear with her gossip!

He saw exactly how much I was admiring you and he didn't like it one little bit. Not a bit! I noticed it right away, more of a feeling. But it was right there. Still is right there.

It was like being on some road in a strange place. And I've been coming up here almost my whole life, long before I was married. *Years before.*

I got up that night and stood at the window like a damn fool for an hour at least, three o'clock in the morning. Thinking and thinking about you and knowing you were just down the hall. I swear to God, Marie, I almost went down and knocked on your door.

I can't remember the last time I was at the WigWam but it's always been a lovely place, a very nice class of people. They keep the riffraff out.

I guess you've been on that road with other people? I mean, your husband? I don't know why, but I feel so godawful *jealous* of him.

An eyeful in anything? Not in that old-maid's bathing suit from when Napoleon was a cadet. Don't say a word! You don't have to be polite.

I'll dust off the old perambulator and we'll pull up there like a couple of swells. Put on the ritz a little. I'll even wear my din-din coat.

I feel just as crazy as you. I want to do the same thing, but I don't think the Sapurtys over there would appreciate us spooning on the church steps, do you? They don't still say spooning, do they?

On you, on you you don't even notice it's old-fashioned.

What were a few of the salient qualities of Tom's "personality"?

An easy smile. An assertive but polite manner with women, a conspiratorial camaraderie with men. An ability to tailor off-color jokes for mixed company. A "look" that bespoke unending leisure and the genius to enjoy it. A curiously half-concealed aura of what many people (mostly women) took to be sadness and the attendant fascination this aura exerted. A gentlemanly ignoring of the jealousy felt by those who took him to be a fraud.

What were his "intentions" with regard to Marie McGrath Recco?

He would take things as they came. Our subject had an eye for the ladies, and Marie Recco, although in her thirties, was a decidedly attractive woman. She was also shy and vulnerable to attention and flattery, little of which she had experienced in years.

What were some of the things about Tom that made women admire and men distrust him?

To speak but of the moment, summer 1939: He swam too well, he owned a shining green Plymouth coupe (which word he pronounced, only half-jokingly, coo-pay), he often wore white and pale yellow to set off his deep tan, he owned a half-dozen pastel slack suits, he was divorced but did not speak of his former wife to his fellow guests except in mawkishly admiring terms, he smoked Rum and Maple pipe tobacco into which he shredded bitter chocolate, his hair was always perfectly cut and combed and gleamed with rose oil, he was a successful salesman for a meat-cutting-machine company and did much of his work by telephone, work which he somewhat speciously characterized as "stealing money."

Why did Billy Recco like him so much?

Billy thought that he would make a swell father. Billy, at this point in his life, thought that any man would make a swell father, except for his father, whom his mother had taught him to loathe and fear.

Would he make a "swell father"?

Perhaps to Billy Recco, yet he had paid and presently paid little attention to his own son, Tommy, a boy a year older than Billy. The boy had always seemed to him a mother's son. He had no other children.

Yet it is our understanding that he brought Tommy into many conversations that he had with Billy and Marie. Was this the case?

It was.

What was the nature of these references to his son?

To wit: my big boy; my Tommy; my dear little son; poor little Tommy; Tommy used to; you remind me of; I know you'd love; and etc. These remarks and many others of the same sort were often delivered with a sigh and what Marie thought of as "a faraway look" in his eyes, which look, it may be noted, made him seem to be a sensitive soul harboring a deep grief that begged to be assuaged.

Were these instances of what we may call manfully repressed pain legitimate? Or would they best be characterized as being adopted for effect?

It is known only that Marie Recco was moved to pity and admiration by them.

Did he speak of "little Tommy" to others?

Not during this summer sojourn at the Stellkamp farm.

What did he think of John McGrath, Marie's father?

As an obstacle to whatever "understanding" he might reach with Marie. He was correct in this thought.

What were some of the terms of opprobrium that Mr. McGrath used in regard to Tom?

At various times and in various circumstances, John McGrath is known to have said: little tin god, patch on a man's ass, phony as a three-dollar bill, Mr. High and Mighty, five-hundred-dollar millionaire, nigger rich, coo-pay?, guinea moustache, our conquering hero, couldn't keep a wife, skirt chaser, up to no good, goddamned fool of a ladies' man, a fart in a gale of wind, Lothario, another tale of woe, and nothing but bullshit and broken glass.

To return for a moment to Tom's coupe—or coo-pay: Why did this
mundane vehicle have the effect that it did indeed have upon people?

It spoke of independence and the devil-may-care, of freedom and
youthful rakishness. Thus it appealed to the feminine libido and awakened masculine envy and fear of cuckoldry.

Was Tom indeed a maker of cuckolds?

If rumor is to be given credence, the answer is "yes." Three men
putatively so served were: Lewis D. Fielding, a junkman of Ossining,
N.Y., through his wife, Barbara; Alfred Bennett Martinez, a plumber
of Ozone Park, N.Y., through his wife, Danielle; William V. Bell, a
shop teacher of Paterson, N.J., through his wife, Joanne. These are
not their real names.

We have been given certain intelligence concerning particular words
and phrases used by our subject, these serving to set him apart from
what he thought of as the hoi polloi. May we be enlightened as to the
nature of these distinguishing uses of the language?

He delighted in "ab-soid!"; "coozy" for "cozy"; "nook" as a term
for the female genitalia; he always "built" a drink; "sunny honeys"
was his name for fried eggs; he pronounced "croquet" "crocket," save
when he was losing; a navy-blue jacket that he wore on semiformal
occasions was his "din-din coat" or his "soup catcher"; his briar pipes
were, in winter, "mitt warmers" and in summer, "skeeter chasers";
his Plymouth coo-pay was affectionately dubbed his "perambulator";
and, among men whom he knew fairly well, he called his moustache
his "womb broom" or his "pussy bumper."

Was he in any way the injured party in the twelve-year marriage to
Janet Thebus née Baumholz of Passaic, New Jersey, a marriage that
ended in a bitter divorce?

Hardly. She had been a faithful and excellent wife and mother,
while Tom had been unfaithful whenever occasion presented itself,
said infidelity commencing but eight months after the couple's return
from a honeymoon trip to Asbury Park.

Was there one outstanding flaw in the otherwise carefully composed
whole that Tom presented to the world?

Yes, although considering our subject's amatory successes, the flaw
was apparently not an egregious one. Our subject's trousers hung
from his waist to his thighs with no readily distinguishable evidence

that he possessed buttocks. It was one of the few things that he was touchy about, and it is believed that he had, on several occasions, wept in self-pity over this physiological lack. A waitress in Weehawken, N.J., nettled by his rather broad and arrogant sexual innuendoes concerning the size of her bosom, once enjoined him: "Take a powder, you assless wonder!" It had taken a month after this incident before he would remove his overcoat when calling on clients employing female help.

Was he an absolute fraud regarding his relationship with Marie? Perhaps not an absolute fraud.

Dear Marie,

Dare I call you, Marie darling? Or should I address you, you swell thing, as Mrs. Recco, prostrating myself before your tiny feet in formality. Like a monkey in a tuxedo on a chain held by an old dago? And of course I beg you to forgive that terrible word knowing that you, dear princess and Queen of sweetness were once married to a dago and so got your name. But I don't hold that against you, not on your life, darling!

But feel that it was one of the nervous exesses of youth when the blood boils in its heat and has to be cooled even though the cooler is a dago. Don't I know of the furey of youth? My God. Did I ever tell you my ex, Janet was also of Italian blood and heritage. So believe me my lucious morsel of sugar when I tell you that I know whereof I speak when it comes to one, dago spouses and two, the fleshy reasons for marrying same. Or as they say, Any port in a storm.

No. God forbid I should ever hold it against you you married a ginzo. Who as I hinted, knows better than me what it is like trapped in a marriage with a greaseball! Didn't I tie the knot of conubial bliss, ha ha, with a ginzo myself? Or maybe that would be called a ginza.

But let me cease complaining and belly aching to you. Dear sweet Madam, my troubles must be extremely boring to you.

The purpose of this letter is what, I am sure, you are venturing a guess at. To whit. How come Tom Thebus, how I dream by the way that you call me Tom in your dreams and in private. How

come he is writing me a letter when he sees me every day from
morning till night and could certainly speak up concerning items
on his mind? Don't argue. I know that you are thinking
something like this, I just know it. I am a crackerjack when it
comes to female psycology. A man cannot be a salesman for years
without learning a thing or two about female psycology. The
receptionists and switchboard girls and so on that a drummer
meets and talks to every day teaches him more than he wants to
know, believe me. A drummer by the way, Dear, is a word for a
salesman in case you didn't know it.

Okay. The reason that I am writing you a letter is that I
haven't got the nerve to say to you face to face, your gorgeous
face, all the things I might find the intestinal fortitude to say here
on paper. For the truth of the matter is *I love you.* And I am
going ga-ga thinking about you and holding my tongue out of
sheer dumb embarrassment. I also have the feeling that you like
me! Maybe even more than like? I know that when our eyes
happen to meet you cast yours down and blush so sweetly. How I
hope and pray that it is the case that you do feel something truly
deep for me.

When I think of you in the lonesomeness of my room I am
embarrassed to spill the beans to you but, I must, I think of you
and I do *it.* My Honey Cake, you were a married woman for
years and even though I know that you are pure and clean as
newly fallen snow I know, that you know what *it* is. And my
deep deep shame is I wish that when I am in the throews of
passion that you are there with me! In the dark with your lips
blending with mine, the only girl in the world, with your sweet
body next to mine and your delicate and fragile hand like fine
China instead of my rough and callussed one doing *it* to me. And
I also dream that I am doing *it* to you. That is my shameful
dream. But I must tell you.

And that would be just a warm up, a prelim before the main
event, in my shameful dream. And Darling, you know what the
main event means. I tell you honestly and truly that I cannot
sleep a wink when I think of you shed of your clothing. I do not
count seeing you on the beach in the bathing suit that you like to

wear to the beach, however, I praise you to the skies for it and
displaying your sweet modesty to everybody. But my dream is to
see you a tigeress in the gloom of my lonely room. Not modest
but wild! Sort of tearing and ripping off your clothing and your
unmentionables and things to stand free and proud and noble. As
a lady wants to be forever and ever with her mate whoever he
may be.

And I trust and hope and pray on my hands and knees that
you might think that there isn't a man more worthy than Yours
Truly. I who worship from afar and fall down crying like a baby
on his bed every night in the silence of his lonely room, sobbing
to his God to let you love me as I love you!

Particularly after a day like last week when the wind blew your
skirt and lifted it up a little bit so that I almost fainted to see so
much of your gorgeous womanly charms. I almost bit the stem of
my old skeeter chaser in half. You remember that day don't you,
my Dear? I came down to supper late even though Mrs.
Stellkamp rang the bell so hard I thought it would break. I said I
had been napping, but I came down late because the vision of
your lower limbs drove me to the solitude of my lonely room and
I did *it* again, twice, and whispered Marie Marie. I was so
ashamed but I swear to you that I couldn't help it. And I thought
how I would like to be pulling your clothes off gently to gaze my
fill and feast my eyes on your womanly charms that I am driving
myself crazy thinking about. I think how they must measure up
against Janet's, my ex. She was kind of "small" down there if you
get what I am driving at?

Please again forgive me for this terrible letter but you can see
by now I could never say these things to you face to face. Can
you imagine me on the lawn or the porch telling you out of the
blue and by the way, for instance, that my ex had a very small
private organ. We would both die of shame and mortification. I
am blushing just writing this all down.

But you see, I can jot down such a fact and avoid the
mortification but still let you know what I must. And I can
imagine your sweet face burning with blushes as you read it and
maybe wonder how Tom rates with your ex when it comes to the

length department. How I hope that you are or maybe will be in
the future, thinking of me *that way.* I know that I think about
you that way always and watch you when you stand and walk
and cross your legs. I bet you did not know that I watched your
every move ever since that day you got out of the car from
Netcong. Even at Budd Lake and the Locks I watch you. And see
the Real You underneath that bathing suit that you always wear.
However I am not knocking your bathing suit. I love modesty in
a woman.

That was one of the troubles with Janet. I don't want to lay my
troubles at your beautiful little feet but Janet was not at all
modest, perhaps, it was the pure hot ginzo blood that ran through
her veins. As a matter of fact, she got involved with my sister in
law, Susan, who to look at her you would think was Miss Iceberg.
Janet and Susan would like to have some unnatural fun together
and one thing leading to another as it will, it was not too long
before Yours Truly also got mixed up and we would have *parties,*
if you get my drift? Believe me, my sweetest shyest violet, in such
cases modesty does not exist, not an iota. I am so ashamed to
write these filthy things to you because you are such a pure and
clean lady to your marrow. But I have to come clean.

But no matter how dirty and shameful those things were that I
was forced into doing by my dago wife and sister in law who, by
the way if I remember right is also pure blooded Italian on both
sides, I still kept a corner of myself clean and shining for the
Miracle of somebody like You, who I knew would come along
some day. Dear sweet Marie! And it is with that corner of me
that I yearn to hold you close and naked. And yearn also to do it
and do it and do it until we faint with exhaustion and happiness.

So if you think in your heart that there might be a chance that
we can get together some time in the near future when prying
eyes are closed or looking the other way, give me some kind of a
sign, a Lover's Sign. I am thrilled to write down those words.
Maybe lift your skirts slightly so that only I can see for a sec your
shapely limbs. Or cross your legs this way and that while you
read a magazine. Or touch me with your little hand as I pass you
by on the porch in the evening. Or chuck a hand full of sand at

me playfully at Budd Lake while you smile. Darling. Whatever
Sign you make I will know it. And I will act accordingly and we
will be One.

In the meantime darling, while I wait, can you manage to slip
me under the table, the expression goes, a keepsake of your feeling
for me if you have same? I know that you have. Perhaps a small
and intimate garment. You know what I mean? I am so nervous
writing this because I know that you are pure and fine and I am
afraid that such a request may shock you. A delicate hankie
would be nice except, hankies remind me too much of Janet my
ex, who used to make me do something very nerve wracking in
my marital duty and a hankie was mixed up in it. I'll tell you
more about it later if you insist but for now let sleeping dogs lie.
Anyway, hankies still have a funny effect on me. So I would
prefer something more intimate that has lived close to your sweet
pure skin. Something that a gentleman does not mention. But a
hankie would be swell if other items are embarrassing to you.

> I wait for a Sign, my dearest,
> Yours, Tom

I think that it is really a swell opportunity, a fine opportunity, for the two of us to get together over a glass of cold beer at the Bluebird on a quiet Sunday afternoon, and I say so. John McGrath agrees. We are both businessmen and despite the difference in age, God knows we understand each other. That is always the great thing about business, it brings you into contact with people of all types and breeds and from all walks of life and you get a chance to see a little of the world. Right? It is *damn* right.

Oh hell yes, the Depression, damn and double-damn the Depression, it has hurt business all across the board but if a fellow keeps his eyes open and his nose clean and isn't afraid of getting his hands dirty, hell, he'll make out all right. I'm making more money now than I have in years! I don't want to pat myself on the back too much, that *could* just mean that things are getting better all across the country. People beginning to talk a lot about defense contracts what with the European situation and all. Damned if you can make head or tail out of it.

The textile-factoring business, the whole credit game for that matter, goes along, day after day, come hell, high water, *or* Depression. Banking is banking whichever way you cut it. People always need somebody to stand behind them with the dollar when it comes to expansion and new materials and that sort of thing. It's an interesting business, that's all there is to it! Why, John has seen millionaires turn into paupers overnight. And vice versa! He tells me the wonderful story, wonderful, wonderful! about old Whitestone asking him to go into business with him, just the two of them, years ago, but how he preferred to work for a salary and not take all his headaches home.

By God though, they're still friends! Families exchange cards at Christmas and every other damn thing. Oh, absolutely! A prince of a man, old Whitestone.

I know, of course, who Whitestone is? I don't really *know* although certainly the name is a familiar one in business, a big name. A high mucky-muck all right. Well, old man Whitestone is just the President of the National Credit Office and you know what *that* is! There's Dun and Brad and the National Credit and that's it. A very very big man, but just as regular . . . A prince! Still good friends, yes indeedy.

I of course excuse John as he rises to go to the men's room just as I order two more beers. When he returns they have been paid for and John shows surprise and protests that it is *his* round but I wave it off and John sits. As far as business goes, John goes on, he has to see it as looking a damn sight better but mainly, *mainly,* at least that's what he surmises, because we damn well, yes indeed, damn well are getting ready to get into another goddamned war in Europe. God knows why! That's your damn Jew Roosevelt.

John lowers his voice and leans across the table and says that it is as usual a Jew war and that Helga—Mrs. Schmidt?—who was born and raised in Germany and still has a brother and lots of other relatives over there, have I got to know her? He thinks for sure I have, and certainly, hell, yes, I know her, a hell of a good sport, an honor to make her acquaintance. Well, anyway, it turns out that Helga says that nothing's the matter with Hitler as far as she can tell, he's been a godsend for Germany, and just what's the matter with the Germans getting their jobs back from the Jews? The damn Jews have run the country for years and the Germans are getting goddamn sick and tired of them. And if truth were told, they run *this* country too! It's for Christ's sake clear that every German you meet over here is clean and decent and hard-working. Can you blame them for how they feel about the kikes?

I mention that I've read some stories once in a while in the paper about how the Jews are being treated pretty bad but I admit that it's probably all propaganda. John says goddamn tootin it's all propaganda a yard wide and that Helga tells him all that crap in the paper, but Helga didn't say crap, is put in there by, who else? The Jews! By Christ, they *own* all the papers.

I am certain that surely if *anybody* knows what is going on in
Germany it is Mrs. Schmidt. You have to take her word before you
take the word of the papers. John nods and says that you have to go
a long way before you find a woman with a head on her shoulders like
Helga. I apologize, and then apologize again for putting my two cents'
worth in when I'm not asked but I think that they, John and Mrs.
Schmidt, make a handsome couple, a real match. I'm really sorry for
sticking my nose into somebody else's business. John nods and of
course, she *is* a fine, good woman and he's known her for years and
years, knew her husband, Otto, God rest his soul, he was a fine big
strapping man. John's late wife, Bridget, and Helga, had been the best
of friends. No need to apologize, certainly not. Between the two of us
and the lamppost and in strictest confidence, he and Helga haven't
actually talked *seriously* about it but they've put their cards on the
table and after the passing of time, for decency's sake, who knows?
She and John aren't relics, for God's sake, with one foot in the grave!

Of course, it must be obvious to me that John is not what anybody
could call lonely. There's Marie and Billy. And Marie is only too
happy to stay with him now that Bridget, God rest her soul, is gone.
But a man has no right to make his daughter a slave even though it's
her pleasure to cook and keep house for him—and for herself too of
course. Christ knows that Marie deserves *some* life! She hasn't been
given a fair deal, you know. Well, I don't really *know* but I had gotten
an idea . . . the "other woman"? I'm just guessing because Marie never
. . . I am one hundred per cent right, John lets me know, treated like
dirt by the man—*man!* An excuse for a man, by God. She's taken it
all in stride and kept her head high.

And then I have to excuse John, please, for talking out of turn, but
he thinks that it is something that has to be said . . . John suddenly
ducks under the table to tie the laces of his spectators as the waitress
comes over with two fresh beers and straightens up just as I'm paying
for them. He is annoyed, almost angry that he has again been pre-
vented from paying for the round and protests that it is his treat but
I smile and assure him that he can spring next time. John again
apologizes for talking out of turn but . . . he really thinks that I should
know that he thinks that Marie likes me an awful lot, as a matter of
fact, an old man who knows his daughter and has been with her

through thick and thin has a right to say, as far as he is concerned
and there's no two ways about it, that he thinks that Marie is sweet
on me. I protest, almost blushing, but John nods his head. He very
deliberately does his best to make it crystal clear to me that as far as
he is concerned and he damn well doesn't want me to think that he
is being common, God knows he hasn't spent his life working with
really good skates, and the girls who work at the office are, by and
large, fine decent girls, not a floozy in the bunch, so . . . He wants to
make it crystal clear to me that he is being as straight as a die with
me. That's maybe why he might sound a little rough saying that Marie
hasn't been *married* in the true sense of the word for six years and
six years is a hell of a long time for a young woman in the prime of
her life to go it alone. Is he being crystal clear? Alone, without a man
to look after her, or anything. To be as plain as the nose on your face,
Marie seems to John to look like she can use some companionship,
some manly companionship. It seems to John that she can *use* it. It
seems to John, as a matter of fact, that she needs it. John grants that
a woman is not like a man in that respect, but still. Still and all. She's
been kind of nervous the last year or so.

I wonder. I wonder and smile and blush. I bend my Trommer's
coaster in half. I wonder aloud, still smiling and blushing, if what
John is saying is what I *think* John is saying? Yes indeed. I am
absolutely right that what I think John is saying is what John *is*
saying. John is telling the God's honest truth to me because he thinks
I'm a crackerjack salesman, and he'd always admired a moustache on
a man, always admired a man who smokes a pipe, how he wishes he
could cut out the goddamned weeds! Always, *always* liked a go-getter
too. Not some goddamn milksop of a momma's boy crying about how
cruel the world is, can't make a dollar, thinks money grows on trees
for Christ's sake! A man's got to take the bull by the horns. John *likes*
me and wants me to know how *he* thinks Marie feels about me.

And certainly, let's call a spade a spade, John implies, it's perfectly
clear to him that the way he feels Skip, that's his pet name for her,
John says, the way he feels Skip feels about me is the way that I feel
about her. Do I think that John is, for the love of God, blind? That
he can't see us every day of the week mooning over each other and
making eyes morning, noon, and night? Pretending to just happen to

be in the same place at the same time? Going to Budd Lake and the Locks all the time, oh, perfectly respectable, with Billy along and Dave Warren and Eleanor? John wouldn't be surprised if even Dave, for God's sake, who was behind the door when the brains were passed out, it was no secret, has noticed our mooning around. And Dave Warren wouldn't know it if he smacked his thumb with a hammer, hasn't got the brains to button his fly. John considers that it wouldn't be a crime, far from it, if I should invite Marie out some evening soon, maybe dancing at the WigWam or the Seven Gables or the Hi-Top. Skip hasn't danced, to his knowledge, in years, but it used to be a treat to watch her on the floor. She could really step. And Billy! Why, Billy looks up to me the way he should have been able to look up to his father and was just the other day asking John how old he'd have to be before he could smoke a pipe, like Mr. Thebus. John got a kick out of that Mr. Thebus but Marie has drummed manners into him, and respect, she doesn't want him growing up like the goddamn hooligans and riffraff on the street corner.

I'm wondering and stammering, just a little, wondering if John wouldn't mind then, if I begin to, well, date Marie, act, that is, like her escort? I had indeed, there was no use trying to deny it, I had been hit by her like a ton of bricks ever since the day I'd first seen her get out of the car from the station. John is laughing as he rises and picks up his walking stick, God knows he wouldn't mind one iota if I begin to court Marie, and if the thing comes to naught, well, there's a lot of summer left for the two of us to have some good, clean fun together. We've *both* been married and know our p's and q's. John is a little worried about seeing Skip looking so drawn. She needs a real change. A woman in the prime of her life.

On the road with the sun low over the fields to our left as we stroll toward the farmhouse John mentions that he intends to settle some money on Marie when he dies. But hell, he thinks that's a hell of a note really, and he has now decided there is no reason in the world that she shouldn't get the bulk of the money right now if she decides to remarry, *to* the right man. And I am enough of a man of the world, it seems to John, to know what he means by the right man. If I get his drift?

I'm smiling into the glare of the sun, lopping the heads off black-eyed Susans with a switch and John brings up Helga Schmidt's name again and considers that if he does what we discussed in the Bluebird concerning that wonderful woman, a congenial and lovely *lady,* Marie would feel really free because she'd know that he'd be well taken care of in his old age after retirement, which is, let's call a spade a spade, not far off. And that might, it is John's considered opinion, *might* just make Skip a little more receptive to anything an, what can John call it, an *admirer,* might have to say concerning marriage.

Then John mentions the possibility of a double wedding, oh, certainly as a joke. But anyway, it seems to him that irregardless of what happens between him and Helga, that I should go ahead with his blessing. All that John wishes for Marie is her happiness and he doesn't want her worrying about *him.* But I should take my time and not rush into anything.

I clap John on the back, as happy as a clam. It's been one of the best Sundays! How swell that everything, as quick as a wink, should almost solve itself! God almighty, it has been a *crackerjack* talk. John laughs and says that it will be such a joy to him to see Marie's face when she tells him that I've asked her to go dancing and then, *then* her face when he says, why, of course, Skip, you'll *go,* won't you? God knows, he'll tell her, *I* have no objections to *Mr.* Thebus! Oh, it will be rich!

We hear the supper bell as we reach the fork in the road. I think that maybe I'll ask Marie to take a walk after supper and tell her, well, something about how I feel about her. If John doesn't mind? The rush? My God! Mind? He doesn't mind and thinks, as a matter of fact, that he just might take a leaf from my book and ask Helga to play the piano for him in the parlor. She used to all the time in years past, but of course poor Otto was alive then.

Just then, as we come around a curve in the road, we are face to face with, speak of the devil! Marie and Helga, who are arm in arm, laughing and talking to beat the band. And when they see us in front of them, they separate and rush to us, Marie stopping in front of me to look into my eyes, her cheeks slightly flushed, and Helga calmly and yet surely taking both of John's hands in hers, her eyes modestly on the ground. The four of us stand in the gorgeous light of the sunset, at a loss, just at a loss for words.

Susan had always been a terrific artist, and how. The way she could draw Mickey Mouse and Jiggs and the Katzenjammer Kids! Just exactly, exactly, like the real ones. Her flowers were also beautiful. Her trees.

She crossed her legs, the lamplight shining on her silk stockings, wow, concentrating on her sketch pad. And Janet looked just as good too. If Alex knew . . . but sure Alex knew what a knockout Susan was. Janet was giggling and, blushing? Hey, what's up, you two? They both looked over at him, Susan's mouth open a little and she was panting. Well, a little bit. He got up to build them all another highball. Janet was still, dammit, blushing. What in the *hell?*

Thanks for the lift, Tommy. You have to wait *hours* if you miss that trolley that comes around eleven. Thanks.

Any time, Susan.

Cigarette? Oh no, I forgot, the pipe. I like the way it smells. I wish that Alex would switch to a pipe and lay off those cigars. What's so funny?

Because Janet is always telling me how rotten my pipes smell.

Oh. God, it's a nice night.

Here . . . give me your coat if you're going to sit here awhile.

Just let me smoke this cigarette. Alex is asleep by now anyway.

That's a nice dress. I wish to God Janet would buy something stylish for herself, Christ. I'm making more money than I ever made in my life, Depression or no Depression. She acts like we're on relief.

Well, Janet . . . you do like this dress? When I saw it I really fell

in love with it. It buttons all the way . . . see? You can just . . . If you
want, of course.

Hey.

Susan! You can't just come into my office and, my God! Disrobe!

Oh God, oh God, oh God, I can't stand it Tom, oh Tommy,
Tommy, I'm nuts about you, burning up! This way? Do you like me
like this? Back like this with my legs up like this? Anything you want,
my love, my dearest. Oh just *tell* me what you want. What you like.

Jesus Christ, let me lock the goddamn fucking *door,* will you?

Here, you two nuts. Now what the hell are you up to? Oh oh.

Susan had almost completed a drawing in the pad on her lap, a man,
a man, a woman, a woman, and . . . another man? Yeah. They were
going at it hot and heavy, like nobody's business. Christ almighty!

Janet! So that's what you've been blushing at like a schoolgirl. Janet
put her highball down and handed Susan her cigarette, then suddenly
stood up and abruptly pulled her dress off, then her slip. Susan
reached over and touched her inner thigh. Jesus H. Christ! Am I going
crazy? Is this my wife? Is this my sister-in-law?

But we're right out in the *street,* Susan . . .

Shh. High-school kids do it all the time. We're in the pitch dark
under the tree and nobody is on the street around here, oh, ah, *there,*
after ten o'clock.

Oh my God, oh Jesus. *Susan.*

It feels good, right, Tommy, good. Good? Do you like it?

I'll get over here like . . .

Yeah, yes, oh yeah . . .

Pull down my . . . yes . . .

Oh! Hold on there, over *there,* and we can . . .

Oh, Tommy! Tomm-my! Slow . . .

Your blouse. Open your damn blouse . . .

Oh oh oh oh oh oh oh oh . . .

Jesus fucking H. Christ . . .

When Janet sat back down in nothing but her shoes and stockings, Susan leaned over and they began to kiss like the French do, you know? with their tongues and both their mouths open and for Christ sake you couldn't hear anything but them moaning and slobbering and they were both squirming, brother. Janet's hand was up Susan's skirt and Susan had her legs wide open, really wide open, oh Christ! Tom just took his goddamn pants off. He was almost crazy looking at them. Then he got busy on Susan's clothes and she was watching him with her eyes half-closed as she pushed and writhed against Janet's hand, wherever the hell *that* was. And my God, she didn't have any step-ins on at all. My sister-in-law?

I can't! I can't with the damn gear shift, *you* come over here.
    Susan, we can't . . .
    Then let's go in the back, oh Christ, Tommy, I *want* it! What the hell's the matter with you?
    O.K. We'll climb over. Here, come on, here. O.K.?
    Yes, ahh yes, oh baby, baby, I'm all ready . . . just sit back and I'll get right, like, like this? O.K.? OH.
    Ohh.

Like that, like that, yes baby yes, oh play with them, play with them, baby baby, ohh.
    Just. Push. It. Back. Push. Back. Back! Yeah.

Oh honey, look . . . look out, here comes a, here comes, Susan, a car! Here comes a car, ohh.
    I don't give a good God damn, don't stop, don't stop, hear? Don't stop please, please.
    It's so good. It's so fucking good. That son of a bitch Alex!
    Fuck me fuck me fuck me fuck me.

Bent over the desk with her beautiful behind in the air and her tweed skirt up around her waist and her slip too and her pink step-ins wrapped around one ankle and her jacket open and her blouse open and her breasts hanging out of her chemise. So that Tom could hold them one in each hand as he thrust into her. Her knees quivered and

she lay her head on the desk and bit her knuckle looking at a letter.
Dear Mr. Thebus: In reference to your letter of the 16th inst. inquiring
as to the feasibility of an all-purpose slicer being. She felt a flicker of
fire from her nipples down to her crotch. Go fast! she said very calmly
and conversationally. She began to throw her buttocks up in perfect
rhythm with his thrusts. Tom groaned and started to come.

Hold my skirt up! Jesus! OH!
 I'm coming! Susan, Susan? *Susan.*
 Hold my skirt *up,* dammit. OH! OH! OHH!
 Oh yeah that's. That's. It, baby.

Now Susan had everything off too but her shoes and stockings and
they were all three tangled together on the couch like some real
goddamn dirty picture. It's funny that Janet started all this. Not
really. But yes, really. She took her clothes off, just like that. Oh, Janet
said you can really screw, Tom, Susan said. She did? I just told her
you really liked it, you know? you liked to . . . you know? How? How
do I like it? I'm ashamed. Ashamed? They all laughed. I told her you
like it dog-style. Oh? Susan said. I didn't believe her but if you do,
and she immediately got on the floor on her hands and knees and
stuck her beautiful backside in the air, her cheek on the rug, looking
behind her. Tom knelt between her thighs and Janet massaged his
penis lasciviously, kissing him and bringing his right hand to her
breasts. Alex likes this too, Susan said. You men are all the same.
Then Tom leaned forward and pushed into her and took her breasts
in his hands and Janet's eyes got wide watching.

Somebody's at the door!
 Fuck me. *Fuck* me.
 There's a car! Oh, there's a goddamn car coming!
 Fuck me, fuck me. Fuck the car. Fuck *me.*
 The bell?
 The bell? At this hour?
 Oh, Jesus Christ, I bet it's Alex come to pick you up, Susan.
 I don't care. Don't stop, Tom! My God, you can really screw!
 But the car's stopping! It's my secretary I think and she's got a key

to the office and besides, she's shining a light right in here, maybe it's
a cop. I don't care if it's Mahatma Gandhi, fuck me! Oh baby, please
please please make me come off, oh Jesus, please?

Oh, hello Alex. Yes, Susan's in the living room but she says you
should wait a minute, she's got a surprise for you. The robe? Yes, Tom
and I *were* going to bed early but we all got to talking. Ha ha. Susan
meant to leave *ages* ago. You know your brother, once he gets started.

Let's do it in the front seat too!

It *is* my secretary and she . . . uh, Miss Thompson, uh. Ha ha. Miss
Thompson? Why are you, uh, undressing?

Alex! I wouldn't go in there if I were . . . Susan is standing in the
middle of the room, her bare breasts just visible under her open blouse
and jacket, her hair in disarray, sweat running down her face. Her
tweed skirt is over the back of a chair. She is struggling to pull her
step-ins on but they have caught on one of her high heels. She leans
against Tom, who is completely naked. What in the *God* damn *hell?*
Alex says. Janet shrugs and opens her bathrobe, slips it off, and lets
it fall to the floor. The doorbell rings again. The doorbell? Now what?
Susan sees her husband and gives up the struggle with her underwear.
Tom shrugs and grins. They all look at the door as it opens slowly
to reveal Miss Thompson. She closes the door behind her and begins
to pull her clothes off, whimpering. Oh, Mr. Thebus! she says, I can't
stand it! Tom looks modestly at the floor as Miss Thompson advances
on him, scattering her garments. And who's this *other* handsome
man, she says, looking at Alex and licking her lips.

Then, through the still-open door enter, in various stages of undress, Tom's eighth-grade English teacher, Greta Garbo, a typist
currently employed by Uneek Metal Parts, Inc., a woman in powdered wig and domino, and Tillie the Toiler. Their eyes are bright with
sexual frenzy.

Marie went into town with that simp, Dave Warren, and wouldn't tell Tom why, and he went along with her little mystery, asking her twice, hell, three or four times, her reason. As if he didn't know anything about women! But with a dame like Marie it was best to play dumb, she'd get a kick out of it and he'd score a few more points, the attentive beau. He even made some sappy cracks about being jealous of Dave, as if that rube even knew what to do with it. What in hell *wouldn't* he do to get her drawers off? Not that he didn't like her a lot, really, she was swell. Tom could easy see that she'd be a great girl friend, but the way she was acting ever since that night he French-kissed her on the road, Christ, she was hell-bent for the altar, anyway that's how it looked to him. Jesus, she almost fainted—a hell of a long time between drinks! If he played his cards right, just right, he could get into her before the time came for him to go back to the city, what? ten days more, nine. She kept telling him about Catholic this and Catholic that but if he asked her to marry him she'd chuck the whole goddamn thing. They're all the same. Billy thought he was God almighty Himself, he was a nice kid, a little too nosy and under your damn feet all the time, but he was a great information service. Nothing to be done with that old bastard John, though, *he* knew what Tom was after, all the fucking castor-oil smiles in the world wouldn't soften him up. He had half a mind to cross the old fart up and ask Marie to marry him, just to see his face.

He finished shaving and patted some after-shave on, thinking that he'd want to shave again after supper, smooth as a baby's ass and heavy on the bay rum too, that always got the janes in the mood. Marie wasn't really a jane, or just *another* jane, she had class. Besides, it had been a hell of a long time since he'd had a shot at a doll with such a shape on her—Jesus, even that ugly rag of a bathing suit couldn't hide her build, she must have been *something* at eighteen, but who knows? She's probably better now, a little more meat on her and her behind had just a little bit of a spread, my God, the way it felt when he was pulling her skirt up, he could feel the soft cheeks right now in his hands. He began to clip his moustache.

She was going to buy something special in Hackettstown, of course. If she wasn't who he goddamn well knew she was, he'd lay odds it was some new underwear, but not with her, brother, not with her. She wasn't the kind who thought that anybody else would ever see it, what would it be then? Maybe earrings or a bracelet. Something nice for a nice lady. She looked damn good dressed up, the day she got out of Stellkamp's car in that polka-dot dress, wow. The cunt her old man ran out on her for must have been some lay, that's all he had to say, and no two ways about it. Probably played the old skin flute for him to beat the band. If the old lady had looked like Marie, hell, who knows? Maybe he wouldn't have spent so much time chasing all those skirts. *Maybe.* It's funny you get used to a dame and then she just don't get you hot anymore, same old crap, stick it in, drop your load, good night sweetheart. Might as well hump a piece of liver. A guy could probably get tired of fucking Jean Harlow—well, nobody had to worry about who was or wasn't screwing *her* anymore, a shame. In his room, Tom put on a pair of shorts, anklets, sandals, and a pale-blue polo shirt. He'd maybe take a little walk for himself to the Bluebird and have a Coca-Cola. He would have got a kick driving Marie into Hackettstown but that was laying it on a bit thick, yowza. The old bastard had his Irish mug down to his shoes already about tonight, got to be a goddamn prize sap to rub it in. It was a miracle she even said she'd go, the way the sour old geezer had her at his beck and call, you'd think she was his wife the way he gives her all that guff, do this and do that and do the other thing. His wife was probably a battle-ax who led him around by the nose. Now *he's* the big shot, huh, don't forget to dot the "i."

Not that he *wouldn't* consider marrying her, it wasn't so hot after all those years to be a bachelor again, harder every day to get the old ashes hauled. And he missed a nice coozy home to come back to, let's

face it, after busting his ass all day long buttering up some goddamn
hunkie or dutchman to make him spring for an order. Giving them
all that bullshit about the wife and kids, pulling out the old snapshots.
Jesus Christ! Well, Susan was his downfall, even now thinking about
that bitch cockteasing him—probably every other man she ever met
—to death, got him all hot and bothered. And that goddamn fool Alex
thought he'd married the Virgin Mary. Christ, every time she crossed
her legs she made damn sure you got an eyeful of the promised land.
Must have driven the goddamn iceman crazy. Marie'd probably get
some moolah from the old man too, maybe enough for them to go
down to Florida and take it easy, maybe do some part-time selling,
straight commission, for some rube outfit? Ah, all pipe dreams. If
Tom succeeded in seducing Marie, any ideas he had of marriage
would fly right out the window. Just stick it in that sweet little nook
of hers, Jesus, after all those years of the straight and narrow, it must
be tight as a bride's! But he'd like to have it more than once, bang-
bang, so it was best to play it close to the chest and keep a proposal
back like an ace in the hole.

Halfway to the Bluebird, he decided to turn back, go the other way
to the Hi-Top, and have himself a club sandwich. Old lady Stellkamp
didn't take it too well if you didn't show up for meals, but he didn't
want to be sitting at that damn table with John McGrath, listening
to all his hot air about all the big shots he knew in business. Some big
shot he was, a pair of white shoes he must have bought in the year
one. He'd have himself a nice quiet lunch and a few beers, get back
in time to run a rag over the old perambulator a little and clean out
the glove compartment, maybe have a game of crocket with that poor
fish Sapurty. Kill some time and then play it nice and easy at supper,
o-ho, Mr. Nonchalant. He'd maybe shoot a look over at Marie once
in a while, give her that Clark Gable grin, and let the old son of a bitch
make of it what he would. She was a swell-looking woman, really, the
dumb greaseball that married her didn't know when he was well off.
Well, like he figured, the floozy he started carrying on with must have
had a snapping pussy or some goddamn thing. Maybe she liked it in
the backyard entrance. A lot of guys go for that.

The Hi-Top was almost empty, a couple of high-school girls sitting
at a table eating hot fudge sundaes. They weren't bad-looking, one had

a nice pair of headlights, probably gave every poor kid in the class a hard-on all term long, no lie. And these kids didn't mind showing them either—like those two Copan sisters, jailbait if he ever saw any, the younger one sitting on the porch railing with her legs up just as calm as you please, a man could look right up her skirt, one day she caught him looking at her and she just stared at him, fresh little bitch didn't move a muscle. And her sister with that dumb ox of a lifeguard, parked out by the churchyard, she was learning fast, oh Christ, was she! It's a wonder the kid had the strength to even show up at the beach, let alone swim. The little chippy must have whacked him off till he was cross-eyed. He looked over at one of the girls and she saw him and started to giggle and whisper to her friend, and Tom turned his chair a little so they couldn't see his rear end, Christ almighty knew why he should care what a couple of small-town sluts thought about how he looked! But he waited until they had gone to leave.

Billy was beating the piss out of Sapurty in a game of crocket when he got back to the house and Tom went up to his room so he wouldn't mortify the poor dope. When the game was over, he came downstairs and sat in the shade and Sapurty took a powder, with some lame excuse so he wouldn't have to play the kid another game. God knows what he and Billy talked about, the kid went on and on about everything, Jesus, he could talk you to death, he could be a pain in the ass. He had some kind of a toy plane he started to run around with, making aeroplane noises. Well, his mother was probably back then, trying on all the fancy lace undies she bought in town, ha ha and ha again. You just *might* be able to get drawers made out of burlap in that burg if you were lucky, but she wouldn't get even them. The kid was really excited, God only knew what his mother had been telling them about their date, you'd think it was the Fourth of July and Christmas all rolled in one the way he carried on. When Tom told him he was going to wear a tie, Billy started clapping his hands, Jesus, you had to feel sorry for the kid, cockeyed and under that old bastard's thumb for years. Strike two and he was only ten. What was that thing he'd told him about the lighter he won in Coney Island? Tom forgot, but it was enough to break your heart. Tom said that it was too bad Ralph Sapurty had to leave, he wanted to see him teach Billy a few tricks of the trade in crocket. The kid was smart as a whip and just

looked over at him with his plane held up in the air and started to
laugh, pleased as punch. Tom did his best to keep a straight face but
then he started to laugh too. The sun was starting to get low and Tom
told the kid he wanted to shine up the perambulator a little and then
make himself presentable for supper and that Billy should go in and
wash his hands and face too. "Cleanliness is next to Godliness," Tom
said in his fake deep voice like he used with clients on the phone, and
stretched his hands out like they did in movies about the Romans in
olden days. Then he started over to the old coo-pay, looking up at
John's window out of the corner of his eye. He knew the old man had
been watching him all the time. And oh brother, if looks could kill!

He went out of his way, all right, let's admit it, at supper, to get
John's goat, talking about the Germans itching for another war. He
got a kick out of watching his face when he laid it on thick about the
Nazis and what was happening in Europe—oh, he had a soft spot in
his heart for that kraut Helga, all right all right, the old reprobate.
He wouldn't be surprised if he was humping her already. But all the
time Tom was cool as a cucumber, his voice nice and calm, a smile
on his face, just a gentlemanly difference of opinion. Marie would look
up at him once in a while, blushing to beat the band when he caught
her eye, my God, she looked like a peach! Frau Schmidt was as busy
as a goddamn bee, Christ only knew what baloney she was giving that
long drink of water, Mrs. Copan, the poor bag of bones was drinking
it all in, the old man of course at the food hammer and tongs, as usual.
And then Helga would shake her head and look over at John, full of
pity for the poor martyr. And making sure he got the full benefit of
her shitface smile. God, how he hated that woman! At one point, Tom
moved his foot and by accident touched Marie's under the table—
you'd have thought he'd ripped her dress off the way she jumped and
pulled her foot away. Maybe he was just wasting his time after all, and
all those sloppy kisses were just a fluke. Wasting time or not, she was
the best-looking dish in this neck of the woods and even if they just
danced a little bit and chewed the rag like brother and sister, well, it
was laying the groundwork anyway. What he really got a kick out of
was when Marie got wise to Helga's fake grinning over at the old man,
it was rich, she all of a sudden started to smile over at Tom to beat
the band, making sure her father got an eyeful, you had to give her

credit. It was like something in the movies, hell, you see it all the time.

Tom lay down for a while after supper and thought of Marie, amusing himself by imagining how she'd look in the raw, even better, in just a few little frilly things, and got an erection, there's life in the old horse yet! Now let's make sure that happens tonight if the time is ripe and opportunity knocks. You've always been a strong closer, kid! He'd bathed before supper so he just gave himself a whore's bath and brushed his teeth, rubbed just the right touch of rose oil in his hair and while it was working in, shaved again—bay rum time, kiddo! Acts like Spanish Fly with some dolls. He dressed with care, nice, serious, but also sporty, and thank God it was cool so the goddamn tie wouldn't choke him. Ah, last but not least, a Trojan in the watch pocket—Christ only knew why some guys stuck them in their wallets, can't think of anything dumber than having some jane with her skirt up and her legs spread from here to there while you tear through all the shit in your wallet looking for a goddamn scumbag. Whatever else he might be he wasn't a dumb cluck when it came to cashing in—a dame in that position in your car somewhere sometimes changes her mind if she imagines even for a second how she looks, no matter how dark and coozy it is. When you see that open pussy, brother, you got to jump right the hell in, don't give them a second to catch their breath. O.K. He looked, if he did say so himself, like the cat's meow.

Billy was on the porch, and those two little whores, and sappo Dave Warren, his mouth open like he was catching flies. Christ, this place was really the squirrel cage! He only had to wait a minute, thank God for small favors, when Marie came out, and she was something to see. Ah! it was shoes she bought, white, a few little strips of leather and high heels—they made her calves swell out so luscious in silk stockings that he could almost feel their warm meat, Christ almighty, she *was* a looker! Now, he thought, just a word of polite conversation and then let's vamoose! And where was the old reprobate tonight? Not even going to show up to give Tom the fish eye and see his little girl go off with the big bad wolf? Oh, there's the old bastard, his face like stone, let's go. Let's go! McGrath standing there like a little tin god with his hands in his pockets, he wasn't even going to say goodbye to her! Now that is a low-life bastard! A mean, rotten thing to do. Tom started down the steps, Marie next to him, looking down at the ground as red as a beet, God only knew whether she was embarrassed at being made a spectacle of or mortified by her father, probably both, but hell, Billy was making up for the old stick, calling out goodbye and waving so that you'd think his arm would fall off. They got in the car and her skirts slid up a little above her knees and Tom got an eyeful of her legs and she pretended she didn't know it, she's like a kid for Christ sake, pure as the driven snow, just my luck. He looked over at her as he started the car, "You're really a knockout," he said, "just beautiful," and he pulled the old perambulator out on the road, there they all were, still waving, Jesus, it looked like even old lady Stellkamp deserted her pies and came out of the kitchen for the big show! What a bunch of hicks. But that old bastard of a father of hers still stood there like a statue, well, how about this, mister? and Tom tapped the horn twice, thinking, that says Fuck You.

He drove nice and easy, it was a perfect evening, just getting dark, and God only knows what he told her about what a beauty she was, then, what the hell, he took a chance and put his arm around her and slowly, oh yes indeedy, slow-a-ly, let his hand slide down the front of her dress so that his fingers touched the top of her breast, just a few inches away from the nipple, and by God, from the look on her face, oh yeah, he'd lay odds that her nipples were as hard as rocks. Jesus, she was ripe for plucking, but he knew that she'd have something to say and she did, please stop, the old line, Christ, they all went to the same fucking school, these skirts, and he moved his hand up, but. But he kept his fingers lightly just where her breast sloped and started to swell. He was always a fast talker, give me credit, hell, and he started in on the old tried-and-true flesh-and-blood line, what the hell, it usually had some effect and it was a damn sight better than lame excuses or begging or waiting for the jane to pull your hand away. This way, you admitted your weakness and still got a little tittie anyway. He had a bone-on too, too bad it's not like the fuck books where the girl just tears your pants open while you're driving and sucks you off. Ah. But he'd bet Marie never even sucked her old man off, though you never could tell with these quiet, shy dames. She was relaxed now and didn't make another peep about his hand and he played it nice and easy and didn't try to grab at her, just let his hand lay there like it was natural as hell and he didn't even realize what he was doing.

A nice atmosphere in the WigWam, lots of young couples who looked like they were going to go in for a little action later on—all these young guys looked like they were gash hounds but why not? Some of the girls were pretty nifty dishes. Marie had a Tom Collins and another one right after and he knew they went to her head because dancing she could feel his boner poking her in the belly and thighs and by Jesus if she didn't, he could swear it unless he was going crazy, push up against him and rub herself good against it. She was wearing a goddamn girdle but he had experience with those, the trick was not to try and take it off but just unhook the garters from the stockings and pull the thing up a couple of inches or roll it up if it was one of those boneless ones, hell! he was getting way ahead of himself. But it wasn't a fairy tale that she was glued up against him in the slow numbers and he gave her a nice soft nuzzle against her hair over her ear, "I love you," and every time he whispered it she squeezed his hand and let the inside of her thigh slide against his rod. Jesus Christ! They had another Tom Collins and danced some more, and he was so hot that he was getting himself a real Grade-A case of lover's nuts. Marie was flushed, and he knew that it wasn't just the gin, God, he wanted to get her back in the car, but he didn't want to push too hard and blow it. She was some dish, Christ knew what she was game for but he sure as hell wasn't going to find out here. And just a minute later, when he was trying to figure out how to suggest they skedaddle, she looked at her watch and, God bless her, said they'd better go, it was twelve-thirty.

Out in the air he could suddenly feel the gin, so he knew that she must have a good buzz on. Besides, he'd always heard that gin was like a love potion, hell, the niggers drank it like water and didn't they fuck like rabbits? He turned and took her by the arms and kissed her just before they got in the car and she was ready, willing, and able, brother. He must have stuck a yard of tongue down her throat and when he stopped she stuck hers out just a little, but she stuck it out. She didn't know a goddamn thing but she was itchy and that was half the battle right there, kiddo. His balls were really aching now and he

helped her into the car and her skirts slid up again to the middle of
her thighs. This time she let Tom get a good look at her pins before
she pulled the dress down. When he got into the coo-pay he sat down
nice and easy, his nuts were killing him and his pants were all stuck
out in front with his stiff, Jesus, it was as hard as a rock and Marie
got herself an eyeful but she looked away as quick as a wink and
started to fool with her purse clasp and then her earrings. Well, he
sure as hell wasn't going to let the gin she had in her go to waste, by
Christ he wasn't. Before they'd gone a mile he had his arm around
her like before and this time he didn't waste any time, he got his hand
right over her whole sweet knocker, squeezing and stroking it and
then he let his thumb slide nice and easy down over the nipple that
stood up like a little button under her clothes. She didn't say a word,
just put her head back on the seat and let him play with her, the
sweetheart. She had a little smile on her face and he could see her
teeth.

Tom knew a great little place he'd seen a million times, a sort of
little cowpath between where you turn off the main road at the Hi-Top
and the dirt road turnoff that you took to the farm. Just wide enough
for a little car and you could turn then into some tall grass right under
and behind some big trees. Must be pitch black at night. He drove a
little faster, sweet Christ! he could swear he was going to get some
nookie, he'd moved his hand across her chest to her other tittie and
she squirmed a little and said, "Oh Tom, you shouldn't," but she
didn't, thanks be to God, do a goddamn thing to stop him. What a
piece she must be! He always loved it when some dame kept saying
no-no-no while you were humping her cross-eyed. He saw the Hi-Top
and turned off and a minute later was turning off down the cowpath,
nice and slow, driving behind the trees and parking. Sweet baby! he
said, or something, Christ knows what, and he was grabbing her
almost before he had the goddamn ignition off. She came to him,
pressed her tits into his chest and they kissed and kept on kissing.
Come on, kid, Tom said to himself, do your stuff, and he opened the
front of her dress one-two-three and put his hands inside her slip and
brassiere and just eased her knockers out, my God! He caught his
breath, they were beautiful, just right, a handful each, with her nipples
dark and stiff poking straight up. He bent over and started to lick and

suck her nipples, Marie was panting and stroking his hair and he could hardly believe it, he could hardly believe it, he was sure as shit going to screw her in a minute. He got the hem of her skirts in his hand and pulled them up to her hips, oh God help me! the way her legs looked slightly open and the whiteness of her thighs against the dark stocking tops stretched so tight by her garters. He started to pull her step-ins down, don't forget, don't forget, you son of a bitch, about unfastening the garters, and all the while he kept lunging at her breasts, his tongue stabbing at the two hard nipples. But then she said no. She said, goddammit, no! Marie closed her thighs and started to pull her skirts down. What the fuck is this? Christ knows what she was saying, something about some other time, not now, not here— the same old shit, they're all the same, think the goddamn thing is made of gold. She was leaning back on the seat though, her breasts still hanging out of her clothes, Christ! He pulled his fly open and yanked his hard-on out of his pants, then grabbed her hand and told her to look at him, for God's sake, my darling, my dear one, look at him! I love you I love you I love you I love you. Marie opened her eyes and saw him exposed, let him guide her hand to his dick, then she grabbed it, I mean really got a handful of it, and started to frig him jerkily and erratically while he sucked at her nipples again, running his hands over her thighs and hips under her skirt, sliding his hands under her garter straps, working her thighs open to jam his hand into her crotch. Jesus Christ! She doesn't, does *not,* know how to jerk a guy off! She was whispering something, smiling, her eyes closed, rubbing him up and down, allowing him just enough room to move his hand barely, just barely, between her legs. Dumb as a goddamn post when it came to . . . he thought of that usherette who would frig him with one hand and tickle his hole with the other. Then he felt Marie's other hand caressing his nuts, Oh baby, oh my darling, and now! Now! He was going to! He sat up straight, his back pressed against the seat, and pulled his handkerchief out of his breast pocket, pushed it against her moving hand, but she didn't take it and he clamped it over his rod and her hand himself just as he began to come, don't know shit-all about anything, but oh oh oh baby baby. He thought he'd never stop coming and when he did she just kept frigging away, holding his balls for dear life and staring at his dick with her

mouth open. He put his hand on her wrist to stop her. Then she took
her hands off him and looked away as he cleaned himself up and
adjusted his pants. She was covering herself up too, smoothing her
dress down, and buttoning up. "I love you," he whispered, smiling,
and they kissed again, chastely, but she was trembling, he knew, lay
seven to five, that she wanted to fuck him all night. Give her a chance,
kid, plenty of time. Am I complaining? He wasn't complaining, hell
no. A hand job from a doll who's almost a nun on the first date? Tom
had no beef, kiddo.

Now what in the name of hell? Some dumb bastard was shining a
light on the car almost as soon as he'd pulled into his spot and yanked
the emergency. Oh, o-ho! It was the wrathful father! Right out of some
goddamn burlesque, John was yelling, by Christ, he was yelling out
the window, can you beat it? He'd wake the fucking dead! Marie, my
God, the poor kid was sitting bolt upright like she'd been shot, looking
over at Tom with tears in her eyes, her hankie pressed to her mouth.
Was she going to get sick? The lousy rotten old bastard. Tom wanted
to know if he could come up with her, the old harp had his flash held
steady on the car now and some lights were coming on in the house.
Nice going, you old son of a bitch! The floor show. Let all those old
bastards embarrass her gawking. No, Marie didn't want him to come
up with her, he didn't know Poppa . . . Now some nosy Parker was
out on the porch, probably Saputy, sticking his two cents in. Marie
got out of the car and that mean old fart held her in the beam of light
till she was right on the porch. Then he heard the door open and bang
shut.

Tom filled his pipe and lit it, take it nice and easy, that old son of
a bitch hasn't got the right . . . he sat there, smoking, figuring he'd
blown it getting her home so late. If he'd been smart . . . Well, if the
summer was shot to hell he'd figure out some scheme for the fall back
in the city. She *was* a dish, my God, all innocence, but hot as a pistol.
My God, how he wanted to put it in her! And he *liked* her too, she
was really a lady. Didn't even know how to do it! Oh, brother,
tomorrow! Tomorrow would be one hundred per cent Barnum and
Bailey. He wondered what that poor cockeyed kid thought about all
this, the old bastard must have scared him out of his wits.

He was pleased with himself. The idea of leaving the tobacco pouch was absolutely the cat's meow! There was no question that John McGrath had beaten him, but the game wasn't over, not by a long shot. Still, the scene had been upsetting to him, because he didn't expect anything like it. Oh, he'd thought that the old bastard would bawl Marie out, sure, and he'd expected a lot of hard looks and a lot of frost for the next week, but never in a million years anything like that flashlight—and that godawful yelling! Christ almighty. The man was unpredictable, that was certain, sour old paddy. Tom was annoyed that he'd lost the chance to get Marie alone one more time, maybe way out in the fields somewhere, or in his coo-pay. *Somewhere.* It was a dead cinch that he'd have plowed her good and proper with just a little trouble, just a few don'ts—he could hear her now—a few blushes and sighs. But he would have done it, if he didn't know a damn thing else he knew dames, and Marie was ripe for picking. Even Saturday night—if she'd had just one more Tom Collins . . . No use crying over spilt milk.

But there had been no percentage in staying on. The atmosphere was so strained that he wouldn't even have been able to ask her anywhere with other people along, let alone by herself. The old man had humiliated her in front of all the boarders and the proof that she was innocent of doing anything wrong rested right on her. And the next day, Sunday, when she'd spent the whole day avoiding him—and everybody else, for that matter—well, that was the handwriting on the wall, big as life, brother. His letter to her was just right, just exactly what the doctor ordered, and how nicely he had said he loved her without saying that he loved her. Beautiful! Slipping it under the door

—that was nice too. They did it in some movie, and a goddamn swell idea too. So now, the next step, the good old tobacco pouch, left right on the sideboard where somebody would find it, somebody had probably found it already. The beautiful feature of it was that it didn't matter a good goddamn *who* found it, it would be found, it would be there—nobody would throw it away. And somebody would have to do something about it. It was like a business letter. He remembered Cliff Tengelsen, years ago, when he'd been as green as grass, giving him that tip. "If you got a minute to write a letter about some beef, write it, kid. They can yes you to death on the phone, but no business-man ever just throws a letter away. He's got to answer the damn thing some way, and if he don't, well, you write him another one reminding him of the first one. You get right under his goddamn skin." Well, the pouch was right there, he was the only one who smoked a pipe, even that clown Dave Warren would know it was his.

So when Tom got back to the city, he waited a day, then dropped a line to Marie. Christ, what a masterpiece, if he did say so himself. Better than the first one. Taking into consideration that she'd probably show it to the old man, or even that the old son of a bitch would get the letter first and open it—he wouldn't put a damn thing past him!—he'd written a letter that was as pure as the driven goddamn snow. Christ knows, he wasn't a crackerjack salesman all those years for nothing, hell no. A perfect pitch, nice and easy, take your time.

Dear Marie,

Sorry to disturb you, turning up like a bad penny after saying goodbye to all of you just a few days ago. But when I got back to the old grind here I realized that I must have left my old leather tobacco pouch up there. God knows it's old and seen better days but it's my favorite pouch and I've grown attached to it. I might have left it on the bureau in my room and I'd really be thankful if you'd ask Mrs. Stellkamp about it. Or maybe even in the dining room or on the porch. I was in such a rush when I left I'm lucky I didn't forget my head.

Anyhow if you find it, would you do me a favor and hold onto it for me and bring it back to the city with you. I don't want to put you to all the trouble of wrapping it up and walking to the post office so I thought that after Labor Day I will call and drop in one evening to pick it up and say hello to Billy and your pop.

I'm sorry your father got so mad the other night and I hope that he knows that it's all my fault keeping you out so late. I wish that I wasn't forced to come back to the city so quick as I really wanted to have a chance to chat with him and tell him that I am sorry for giving him so much worry on my account. Well I'll be able to mend some fences when I see him in the city. You know how much I respect your pop and how highly I think of him.

> Sincerely,
> Tom

Beautiful? Beautiful! The old tyrant could read it upside down and backwards and not find a thing in it. But at the same time Marie would know what's what! If she found the pouch she might even know already that I forgot it accidentally on purpose. McGrath would never just ignore the pouch, he'd never just leave it at the house, never. And God knows he'd never just throw it away and say the hell with it. Maybe he'll swallow the business about apologizing. If I can get my foot in the door—there's more than one way to skin a cat.

Tom mailed the letter as soon as he'd finished writing it a second time. His first letter had the phrase "a chance to talk to him and tell him" in the last paragraph and he changed it. The original phrase seemed too pushy and was the kind of thing the old fart would bristle at. He could almost hear him: "He's going to talk *to* me, is he? The pup!" No, this was the way. Friendly, humble. He'd maybe get over to see them about the middle of September, happen to be in the neighborhood, stay a half an hour, not to wear out his welcome, then about a week later ask them all to dinner, hell yes, all of them. It would take maybe another couple months to get Marie alone, mean-time he'd eat humble pie, but. But he'd do it. Take her to his place, a little drink before dinner, hell! He'd have her in the raw in an hour if he put his mind to it. Plenty of time, Tom had all the trumps now.

After he'd mailed the letter he thought he'd give that little Italian beautician out in East New York a ring. That goddamn Marie had got him pretty itchy. He was goddamned if he was going to start dating Mary Fist with all the easy ass he knew around.

Grates bitter chocolate into his Rum and Maple pipe tobacco. It is his elite trademark, the idea hauled from the back pages of some pulp. *Flying Aces.* Sweetish air surrounding him. All his pipes go sour.

When Susan crosses her legs and leans back on the couch. The way her dress rides up. Creamy swirl of her slip and her firm legs in silk stockings gleaming hazily metallic.

Janet's annoying looks of dismay when he gets home late, supper over and the dishes washed. Tommy in bed. The predictable blubbering that he cannot stomach.

The day of Tommy's birth he can't find a place to park and Janet clawing at the seat. Odd dim light of the waiting room and a nurse comes out with her clothes in a pile, her high-heeled shoes on top.

Woolworth's rose oil shimmering in his hair. Its aroma mixed with the rum, the maple, the chocolate. Gets used to the sour taste.

Flirts like a goddamn fool with Susan, hearty brother-in-law act. Pulls her to him roughly and rests his thumbs at the sides of her breasts. Flash of her peach slip.

The waitress in the diner just a few months after his marriage. Oh, she *loves* the smell of a pipe! He puffs and puffs, touching lightly his moustache. Parks out in Elmhurst in his salesman's Nash.

Her clothes in a bag on the bar before him, he has a few rye Presbyterians, a faint odor of perfume and soap from the paper bag in which he has put them. A sudden fear that she will die. The three other men in Reilly's do not know him.

His white Panama. What's the name of that big-shot guinea hat? Maybe he'll buy one in the fall.

Janet puts her mouth tentatively around his penis. Her eyes are closed and she is blushing, or maybe just flushed with excitement. He can feel her hot tongue slow and soft. Thank you, oh darling, thank you. My wife, my wife, my beautiful bride. Her breasts are brushing his thighs. Suck, oh suck, my sweet cunt baby. Like she was born for it.

She knows about his desire for Susan. Your own brother's *wife!* My God, haven't you got any pride, or anything? He shakes his head to show patient amazement at her accusations.

Calls the hospital at six in the morning and it is a boy. The cigars. Now comes the hard part, the boys say. Better get in touch with that old girl friend, Tom. What? Girl friend? You know—Mary Fist. Blushes. Nine out of ten do it and the tenth's a liar. That's how it goes, that old joke.

Buys her a nightgown and a peignoir to match, a pale maize. I'm sure your wife will like this, the salesgirl is pretty but flat-chested. But has good legs. But has faint acne scars. But has a perfect bottom. Sees *her* in the ensemble.

She *loves* the smell of a pipe! Rather gross face with big blue round eyes and bobbed blond hair. A tramp kewpie doll. As she smiles at him in the faint light beneath the trees she massages his erection with both hands. Jesus, *she* wasn't born yesterday! You married guys! Says tsk-tsk the way it is spelled.

He doesn't get the promotion to head salesman despite the baby. Nor the juicy territory in Long Island City. All untouched out there. Comes in the next day with a new pipe and hat. Fuck you all. Brings white roses home to Janet. Thought they'd make the place look coozy.

Janet has a good mind to talk to Alex about it. Making a spectacle of himself every time he gets a few drinks in him. Oh for Christ sake, Janet! You talk to Alex and *you'll* be the one making a spectacle! God, Tom, don't you like what I give, what I do for . . . ? You have to stare at everything in skirts? His eyes roll to heaven.

The day she comes out of the hospital with the baby it is cold and rainy. He forgets a coat and sweater for her even though she reminded him the day before. It's easy to see what you think of me! Not a thought in your head about me *or* your son! Oh Christ, just wait inside and I'll bring the car around to the goddamn entrance. Throws his raincoat over her shoulders.

The kewpie doll thrusts her wad of Juicy Fruit into his open mouth with her tongue as he rubs her breasts. She is pulling open the buttons of his fly when he begins to come. Jesus Goddammit Christ! Oh, you married *guys*. Fucking thing is ab-soid! He sits in wet sticky misery while she puts on fresh lipstick.

He and Alex and Susan drink Orange Blossoms. So tomorrow is the big day when your son and heir comes home! He is drinking too much gin too fast. Impressing her. She snuggles next to Alex and he plays with the hem of her skirt. The lucky bastard. Janet is one crackerjack of a wife, Tom. Don't deserve her. He has another Orange Blossom. Let's call it just a plain Blossom, he says. The orange's just a gleam in its eye—your eye. Mud in your eye.

There's always another time, baby. You know where I work. Don't eat any oysters but, O.K.? Flat azure stare directed at him from some dim corner past the last trolley stop. Pulls his pants and shorts away from his crotch with one hand and blows a kiss with the other.

What *do* you have under that kimono? Aha! Why, me proud beauty, you *are* a dainty morsel! Janet drops the red silk around her ankles and stands in the soft bedroom light in red pom-pom mules and white step-ins. Reaches over and pulls her into bed, a-ha! Sh, the baby. Sucks voluptuously at her nipples, her half-smile aims at the shadows on the ceiling. Sweetie, sweetie sugar nook. Clutches her between the legs softly. Thin scent of Juicy Fruit and gin on her breath.

Alex's false teeth bright and horrible. Maybe *I'll* grow a moustache. The old womb broom. I hear the janes go crazy? Don't ask *me,* Alex. I'm a married man.

He is transfixed by Janet's loveliness in her wedding gown. The taste of the warm Manhattans at the reception. Throws her bouquet of tea roses and her cousin Margaret catches it. Nice-looking girl but her nose is too big.

He is really polluted by now. Somehow he is blurting things out through the gin haze. About how Janet loves to, you know, do certain *things. Looks* like a schoolteacher, but brother! Alex is angry and embarrassed. Oh, have another drink, for Christ sake. I'll even build one for you. Susie?

A hundred, a hundred and fifty miles on the old perambulator every day and he outsells all those other deadbeats. And in crap territory, too. Day after day and calls in the evening too. Depression or no Depression, they got to cut meat.

Babs with the soiled drawers. What the hell. Dotty—no, Dolly—who cries and curses like a trooper. How about the hash-slinger with the big tits thought you could get pregnant going down? Christ, what tramps.

Your own brother's wife, looking right through her clothes. How would you like it if I stared at Alex that way? Or Alex at me? And the way you talk, all those double meanings. By the way, what did you tell Alex when I was in the hospital with Tommy? He looks up at heaven with a patient smile. Would you for Christ sake *please* tell me what you're *talking* about?

Oh, Alex likes it, too, don't you, honey? Alex gets up to get matches. Take it easy, Susan. And other things too, like—ahem!—you know what I mean? Bow-wow? If you get me? Tom's erection is painful as he imagines her on her hands and knees, her luscious buttocks in the air.

Janet is striking at the Annual Dinner in a new flesh-colored dress. He gets the Hundred Club Plaque, presented by Mr. Lawless. He wants to do it standing up with their clothes on in the kitchen but she says she has the curse.

That dumb bitch slut of a waitress makes that crack about his ass. He sits in the Nash and imagines how Janet must think of him too. Why, goddammit! He's just a clown to her even though she never said anything. Can he help it? Dear God, can I help it?

One day in the waiting room of A-Better Manufacturing this perfect sentence clicks into his mind: My wife is a cocksucker. He glances at the switchboard operator and she smiles back. Dingy greenish teeth. Who was that other cunt with the teeth? Joyce, out in Passaic. What the hell was he doing out there?

This must be some kind of a gag. A handkerchief? She is not kidding. You don't want to use a cundrum and I don't want another kid and neither do *you,* mister. This *must* be a gag! No gag, Tom. Of course, she's in that goddamn orchid nightgown, bad luck. Her not-tonight outfit. He wonders if she knows that's what it means to him.

Tommy cries with a bottle, without a bottle, all night, every night. Colic. He pushes the old perambulator till eight, nine o'clock every

night. Go home? Listen to all that and *her* bullshit too? If you think
you're getting supper at this hour you've got another think coming.
Stick the supper where it'll do you the most good, you bitch. Tommy
is crying.

What kind of a cluck do you think I am? Now that I got the
territory developed you're giving it to Disch? What am I? The work-
horse around here? I don't give a good goddamn if times are hard! He
gets another job, straight commission, no draw, and outsells everybody in a year's time.

One New Year's Eve just the four of them at Alex's new house in
Rego Park. Susan dances with him and says something off-color about
his moustache. What? Mr. Innocent, she says. But what is that big
hard thing in your pocket, Mr. Innocent? He presses his hand against
her bottom for a second. Why, brother-in-law! Janet and Alex talk on
the couch, examining snapshots of the children. The son of a bitch
would like to screw Janet, that holier-than-thou act can't fool me.

The bartender buys him one back and he tells him that his wife is
having a baby. Well, well, the man says. He looks at the paper bag.
Tom cannot tell him that her clothes are in there. He feels ashamed
—carrying around a woman's clothes! Good luck! The bartender raps
the bar with his knuckles.

Janet takes Tommy and goes to her mother's house in Connecticut.
Enough! Enough of your bimbos and tramps. You can't take Tommy
away! You wait and see who can or who can't. She returns after six
weeks. He embraces her and they cry and make love on the floor
outside the bathroom.

One girl he picks up on a corner under the El takes him to her place
near Erie Basin. Scrabbling and scratching in the walls. Just the fuckin
rats. They don't bother nobody. He cannot maintain an erection in his
fright and horror. A big strong guy like you? He gives her a fin.

So I'm batty because I want you to leave your stockings and shoes
on? What about you, hah? What about *you*, Janet? Didn't you ever
notice that all you really like to do is suck? Every goddamn thing
winds up with you going down and I'm sick of it. And *I'm* crazy!
Janet sits still on the edge of the bed in her slip, her face pale but for
a flush across her cheekbones. I'm going downstairs now to read, she
says. Oh, Janet! Janet? Janet, I'm sorry, I didn't mean to say . . . I

didn't mean to say anything like that. Really. She lies down on the bed and closes her eyes with her fingertips. You *are* rotten, Tom. You are a mean, rotten man.

Tells what's her name? Ruth? That he wants to be engaged to her. The perfect wife. He has always admired nurses. She masturbates him, sitting straight up with her eyes directly in front of her in the Fortway one Thursday night. That's that. Now she can get fucking lost. Three weeks of coffee for a hand job.

He runs into Susan in downtown Brooklyn. She is coming out of the Williamsburgh Savings Bank in a Nile-green tweed suit and a little hat to match, small dotted veil over her face, green pumps. O-ho! Spending the old man's money while he sweats in the salt mines? Chinese restaurant where there is luncheon dancing. She moves her belly gently, almost modestly, against his erection. Smiles right into his face. What a nervy bitch! Her terrific smell, my God! Jesus, kid, you are absotively the tops, whoo. Now, dear Tom, if you had a little place that we could go? I got the old perambulator parked down near Court Street. In a car? I'm a married woman, shame on you. He pushes against her belly, clenches his teeth. Besides, you don't really take me seriously? I really love Alex. Store teeth and all? You *are* a son of a bitch. But with a heart of gold, right? Oh sure, and a gold something else, too, in *your* opinion.

The sales conference in Washington at which he botches his presentation: "Selling the Second Unit." Keeps saying "depresson," though cold sober. The city terrifies and saddens him. In a hotel bar some old, really old slut gives him the cold shoulder. Masturbates in his room. On the train home he sees a girl, remote, in the sunny haze of a field, sitting placidly on a rock. He starts, it's Janet! Exactly like Janet when he first met her. What in the name of Jesus? He feels a chill.

The four of them pretty well looped by now. Alex and Susan go into the kitchen to make sandwiches. Their giggling, then silence, then whispers, and Alex breathing hoarsely. Why not us too? he asks Janet. He pulls her dress up and sits her, laughing, on the couch. Don't come in for a few minutes! he calls, yanking her step-ins down. Why, what *ever* can you be doing? Susan laughs. This is terrible, Janet says, putting her heels up on the couch, her hands on her knees.

When she goes this time she stays away for three months.

Ruth? Ruth? He has been away—the Midwest. Big business pressure. Big deals. Really. Take a walk, my phony friend. You ugly bitch!

I can't see Tommy? Again? What the hell do I give a good God damn about your fucking father and his fucking country fair? He's *my* son!

Buys three new pipes. In a month they have the familiar sour taste. His new Borsalino and a Studebaker. Can sell a meat-cutting machine to a vegetarian. Crackerjack. Crack-er-*jack!*

Alex and his new moustache. Hey! Ronald Colman! You like it too, Susan? She smiles what he takes to be a dirty smile.

Get the goddamn divorce any time you goddamn well want it, yes, yes, I don't give a damn, I won't contest a thing. Say hello to your *dee-*lightful mother, Carrie Nation, O.K.? And you can go to hell too, hear? *And* you can also go fuck yourself too! Mrs. Cocksucker! Tell your mother *that*.

He's still a young man, everything will work out fine. Meet somebody who knows the score. Touch of grey in his hair. Distinguished.

Listen Alex, I don't want to impose on you. You didn't expect a guest for supper, for Christ sake. Susan looks at him, same old lying come-hither smile. How he'd like to stick his dick right into that smile. Maybe *she's* got false choppers too. We've got plenty to eat, Tom, I'm roasting a chicken. Crosses her legs. Leans back in the chair. The way her dress rides up, the creamy lace at the edge of her slip, legs stretching the silk stockings tight, sheen of metal. That son of a bitch Alex. Don't even know what to do with that piece.

Maybe some nice mature divorcee. Knows the score. No illusions.

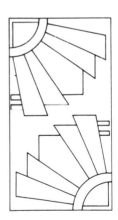

He barely hears the soft whispering, the sighing, of the tall sweet grass of the churchyard as the twilight comes down and the first fireflies begin their slow erratic scribbling on the blue air. Should he come to mind, one sees him on the crumbling stone steps of the church across the road from the farmhouse, a curiously elegant figure in that decidedly inelegant boarding-house world, dressed in rumpled summer whites and old black-and-white spectators, luminous against the softer, chalky white of the wooden building. He is tapping a stick against the edge of the step on which he sits.

His head is slightly inclined toward the churchyard as if he is listening for the sound of women's laughter as it was, faint and musical, during the Sunday evening church fairs of years before; swept now nervously away and up, into the dark leaves of the old elms, by a sudden damp gust that bursts out from behind the faded red of the farm buildings sprawled in thin gloom beyond the white house, so that there is left again but the sighing of the grass, of which he now becomes cognizant. He places his stick across his lap and he too sighs.

He is uncomfortably afflicted by an odd loneliness for his recently dead wife, yet he knows that he is better off without her and her claustrophobic oppression of him. That spirit which he still possesses within him is cruelly mangled; the rest rots in the ground of Holy Cross with Bridget. In a sense he is indeed but a white figure, nothing more, perfectly two-dimensional. He stands now, leaning his weight on his stick, looking past the farm buildings and across the fields rolling toward the smudged bluish foothills over which summer lightning shivers: Louis Stellkamp is driving the cows in, he hears their faint lowing and the barking of the mangy herd dog. His grandson is out there in the fields, running behind the cows, clapping his hands and grunting in imitation of Louis.

His daughter sits on the porch with three other guests in the soft mixed light of the evening and the lampglow from the dining room. Frieda and Eleanor are clearing the supper dishes from the tables. He looks across the road at his daughter, also in white, his chin up in reproach, but she does not see him, or she pretends not to see him. He bangs his stick sharply against a step, twice, then another time, the cracks sudden and decisive in the quiet. She still does not look at him, or, in any case, he cannot see whether she does or not. Ralph Sapurty, rocking slowly and smoking a cigar, raises his arm and waves, then lets it drop; the old man does not acknowledge him. The fool in his Weber and Fields plus fours talks so much he spits, and his wife with a face that would stop a clock! Grace Sapurty is there too, he knows, although he has left his pince-nez in his room: he can make out the bilious pink of one of her flouncy, silly dresses, and hear her high laughter as she tells another story about her wonderful son and his hardware store in Elizabeth. The fourth figure leans against the porch railing, half sitting; it is, of course, that of Tom Thebus. The old man feels a rush of helpless anxiety and anger and sits again. The mosquitoes will eat you alive over there! he hears Grace Sapurty call to him, and he waves toward the porch, dismissing her concern. The thin bitter sweetness of citronella is now apparent to him, the scent of summer, Bridget in her shapeless white dresses, the flash of her gold tooth.

He reaches into his breast pocket for a cigarette, but at that moment sees the flare of a match on the rapidly darkening porch and watches as Tom Thebus lights his pipe, the flame wavering and shifting, and he pushes the Camels back into his pocket. He imagines the heavy, false smell of his tobacco lacing the odor of citronella. How he loathes men who smoke pipes! He does not, or will not remember that he, as a young man, occasionally smoked one, but he refuses to remember almost anything of his youth—it seems a vast turmoil of sadness, wreckage, and waste. Bridget, her gold tooth, her white dresses, her false girlish voice when she was trying to make an impression.

The lightning shimmers again over the distant fields and hills, indistinct in the rain that pours down upon them, and the thunder booms closer. The wind is steady now in his face, the elms thrashing, and he rises to cross the road to the porch. Tom Thebus, he knows, will greet him with a pleasantry, and his daughter will avoid his eyes. Grace Sapurty will make a joke about sugar melting in the rain, as she has made the joke for eleven summers now, her fat arms a shocking white against the pink ribbons and pink bows and pink pleats. He descends the church steps as the first heavy, warm drops pock the dust of the road, his spectators raising little puffs of dust, there, and there, there, they hang in the air as if they might hang so forever.

My dear Bud,

I meant to write and thank you and Herb and the fellows for the first rate supper you arranged just before I left for Jersey. What with packing and this and that I haven't had the time. So consider this a bread and butter note in all sincerity to you and Herb and Davy and even old man Neumiller.

The old Stellkamp place is the same as ever. It is strange to be here without my wife, God rest her soul, and to be staying six weeks. I feel like Rockefeller. But between you me and the lamppost I can't wait to get back to the old routine. You can't teach an old dog new tricks.

The Sapurtys are here. I think you met Ralph Sapurty two or three years ago when you and your wife drove over one Sunday after visiting your grandchildren, and the three of us walked to the Bluebird for a glass of beer. Well he's still the same horse's ass but there's not a mean bone in his body. Did you meet Mr. and Mrs. Schmidt that day? A prince of a man who passed away last winter just about the same time as Bridget. Never sick a day in his life. Mrs. Schmidt is here as a guest of the owners. It makes it easier for me knowing that she has her own cross to bear. She's a fine woman with never a complaint out of her and happy as the day is long.

The fly in the ointment here is that there is a wise acre here this summer, a divorced man with no shame to him at all. A real five-hundred-dollar millionaire with a little greaseball moustache and a coupe with a rumble seat. Butter wouldn't melt in his mouth and he is nothing but soft soap. You know the sort of article I mean. I take him down a peg or two when we play croquet although right is right, to tell you the truth he's better than poor Sapurty by a damn sight. I'd rather play with my ten-year-old grandson than with him. It's just like taking candy from a baby.

All right, Bud, time to close and wishing you good health and best regards to everyone in the office. I'll see you all soon.

Regards,
John McGrath

You'll do as you damn well please. That's what you're telling me, Skip?

I've got a right to *some* life, Poppa.

Life? This is the *life* you're talking about?

Oh, Poppa.

Walking around here like the fifth wheel, I'm no more goddamn use than a fart in a gale of wind.

You have your friends. It's not as if you . . .

My friends. That's fine for you to say, making a spectacle of yourself. You're so busy you can't see out of one eye and you're blind in the other. *Friends.* Baggy-drawers Sapurty. Ach der Kaiser Louis. Can't get the smell of manure off him. My friends? This article Copan? My God, it's a miracle the man doesn't eat the plates and all.

But, Poppa, what good does it do if I *don't* go to Budd Lake or go, or don't go, I mean, anywhere? You at least have your croquet, and things. What about Helga Schmidt?

Leave Helga Schmidt out of the picture. What is all this sudden interest in her? Am I supposed to trot after a woman to hold my hand and tell me it's all right for my daughter to fall all over herself over a nigger-rich Romeo? In a pig's ass!

I don't mean you should go *running* after anybody. I'm saying there's a lot of people you can talk to, you don't need a nursemaid.

And you don't remember a goddamn thing you don't want to remember. Doctor Drescher? All right, he's a horse doctor but give the man credit where credit is due. You conveniently forget he says I'm not supposed to get aggravated after your mother passed away?

How do I aggravate you, taking your grandson bathing? Is he

supposed to sit here and stare at the four walls like these other relics?
He's not even eleven years old.

Bathing. *Bathing.* What a sweet innocent you can be, God in
heaven. I see right through all your playacting, don't make me laugh.
I haven't been alive all these years and not learned *something.* You,
with that Thebus article, like some chippy. You think you're pulling
the wool over my eyes with the boy tagging along? And Eleanor and
that damn mutt Dave Warren? I wasn't born yesterday, thank God.

I am *not* going to sit here and twiddle my thumbs every day and
wait for the dinner bell and then twiddle my thumbs some more and
wait for the supper bell. The other day when you had a face down to
your shoes dragging along like a lost soul I stayed here. I felt sorry
for you. If that's what you wanted you got your wish. Do you know
what Billy did that day? Do you? He spent the whole day down at
the barn killing flies. Killing flies! Why the boy is mad with boredom.
And you can come along anytime you want. When Momma was alive,
o-ho, you were the life of the party, not a place you wouldn't go. Lake
Hopatcong, Delaware Water Gap, High Point . . . Many's the day and
night when you could have let Tony and I go somewhere if you
minded the baby, but did you? Oh no. Do you want me to beg you
to come bathing? Get down on my hands and knees? Oh, how things
have changed *so much* since Momma died. *Changed?* Don't make me
laugh. The same old thing, the same old rigmarole. Nothing ever
changes with us. I can talk myself blue in the face, you yes me to
death. But the next day you forget all about it.

You want a change? Fine by me, just fine. You've got a roof over
your head and food on the table, all the clothes you want. Here you
are in the country on a vacation any girl would give her right arm for.
Change? That's jake with me. Just tell me when and we'll see how you
like it.

Oh, that's it. The roof over my head. And *Billy's* head. Don't you
ever get sick of throwing that in my face? My God, I thought you'd
be sick of that one by now. I had to listen to it day in and day out
from Momma, how grateful I should be, how thankful, even when I
was working like a slave, waiting on her hand and foot before she went
in the hospital. When Billy was six years old she even told *him* how
grateful he should be to her that he wasn't in the streets or in a home

or an orphanage. What a thing to say to a little boy! Talking about
an orphanage! And when we lived on 68th Street before Momma
ordered you—yes, yes, don't shake your head, *ordered,* I remember
it like yesterday—ordered, *ordered,* as God is my judge, ordered you
to stop paying the rent on that little apartment and took us in like two
charity cases. When we lived on 68th Street do you think I'll ever
forget that breakfast we got from her on Sunday morning after mass?
Two eggs and two pieces of bacon in a paper bag? We weren't to be
trusted to eat with you, Billy might ask her for another piece of bacon.
Is it ever going to end, the roof? When I think of my life. If I'd known
ten years ago I'd have to thank my own father for the roof over my
head! God help us.

I'm not going to talk about your mother. I had *my* cross too. I'm
talking about one thing and it's not two things, this Thebus article.
He's a sneaky-looking gazabo to me and what is it he wants with you?
A woman with a ten-year-old son. Oh, I'm just an old fart and I can't
see what's right in front of my eyes.

I'm entitled to *some* life, Poppa.

Well, you *have* your life, but I won't be all smiles at this mous-
tached article of a divorced man. The blind leading the blind, I say.
I saw the whole thing from the start when the man jumped up from
the porch dressed up like Astor's pet horse and a book under his oxter
to say hello to you. The minute we got here. We didn't get out of the
road when he was there all smiles and his pipe stuck in his mouth.

He said hello to you, too, Poppa. You've forgotten *that.*

To me! Ah, and I wonder why he'd do that? Something else the old
geezer can't see through.

But you didn't see through anything when you let him carry, oh
yes, let him carry all the valises upstairs. Oh no, I don't remember a
word out of you except Mister Thebus this and Mister Thebus that.
Jesus, Mary and Joseph!

That's before he showed his true colors. If I knew, I wouldn't have
given him the sweat off an ice pitcher. I don't like the man one iota,
just like I didn't like that greaseball you married.

You? You were against my marrying Tony? You?

You know goddamn well!

Oh *Poppa.* My God, what short memories we have. My God.

I never liked that damn dago and your mother told you what she thought too, but you wouldn't listen to anybody, you knew better.

Momma? Momma thought Tony was the most wonderful thing that ever came down the pike! At first. At *first* until she saw how happy we were and we moved away from Senator Street to that little house in Flatbush. That stuck in her craw, she was green with jealousy, God forgive me. *Please,* Poppa. Don't tell me about Momma and Tony.

You should show some respect for your mother, she not in her grave a year.

Oh Poppa. I've thrown away my whole life on my mother.

And on me too?

Oh Poppa.

I'm telling you one thing, Skip. This Thebus pup is two-faced and up to no good. You mark my words.

Poppa, I'm not doing anything wrong. He's full of fun. And he's got his own cross to bear. Believe it or not.

Did it himself or I'm no judge.

Oh Poppa, can't you have some feeling for somebody else, somebody outside of—God almighty.

Outside of what? Me? Oh yes, sure, certainly, it's your selfish father again, your egotistical father who puts the roof over your head, pays for everything, drops for the boy's eyes, glasses, everything.

I'm going in, Poppa. I want to take a nap.

Mm-hm, sure. Take your beauty rest to make sure you look like a girl. Go ahead. Go, go. Worked my fingers to the bone for all of you and this is the thanks I get. For all of you.

What was John's most treasured possession?

A letter from William X. Whitestone, the text of which follows:

Dear McGrath:

Bill Sutton has called to my attention your work on the Roseville Dress account. As you know, we have had no end of trouble here at National, in establishing the right line to take with Roseville and Ben Gelbstein. Dun & Bradstreet has been of some help, of course, Ed Murray in particular. But in looking over the careful file you have kept on the account in its business dealings with Textile over the years, as well as your notes and recommendations therein, it is clear that your attention to this difficult account has smoothed our path immeasurably.

You know, John, in what esteem I have always held your work as a credit investigator. This Roseville job reinforces my opinion of your skill and dedication to your accounts. Let me say that I and the National Credit Office as well as the entire credit business in New York is in your debt for this expert work.

My sincere good wishes,
Bill Whitestone

What were Bridget's last words to John?

"The reason you come to the hospital every night is because you're afraid what the goddamn neighbors will think, you can't fool me."

Name a few of the things that John came to loathe as he grew older.

The kitchen utensils; the metal clothes hamper outside the bathroom door; the bathroom door that refused to close all the way; the insurance man, Mr. Levine; the laundryman, Phil, of Crescent Laundry; the dank and rusty-colored shower curtain; the broken Morris chair; head cheese and boiled potatoes; Woolworth's sugar cookies; the artificial Christmas tree; boiled spareribs and cabbage; Bud Halloran; Bridget's corsets; Billy's crossed eye; Fibber McGee and Molly; turkey stuffing; rush hour on the Sea Beach Express; mandolin music; the Irish; Jimmy Kenny's mouth; Mr. Svenson, the landlord; the front room in which he and Billy slept after Bridget's death; any crèche anywhere; the dining room table; the revealing clothing of young women; Dr. Drescher; all of Bridget's relatives; the movies; all holidays.

What did he think of Bridget's dream books?

He thought that they were foolish items for foolish people.

Did he ever consult them?

Once. He consulted *What Your Dreams Mean, 1000 Dreams and Their Meanings,* and *Find Out What Your DREAMS Mean.*

As to?

The meaning of the following dream: Jean Whiting is dressed in the clothing in which he first saw Bridget. Bridget is outside the door of their apartment, but the interior of the apartment is that of a cottage that he and Bridget once rented in the Rockaways. Bridget is playing his mandolin. She opens the door and, smiling, says, "She's got a nice pussy, hasn't she?" He turns to see Jean Whiting naked and has an orgasm. It might be noted that the dream books did not assist him in the interpretation of this dream.

What tradition did he keep with religious devotion?

On New Year's Day, he visited all his surviving relatives to wish them the joy of the new year; at home, he made certain that he had on hand a supply of ladyfingers (bought at Ebinger's Bakery) and a bottle of sherry with which to refresh any guests who dropped in to wish him and the family the joy of the new year.

What did Bridget think of this tradition?

That it was an Orange Church of Ireland affectation.

What did John think of Roman Catholicism?

That it was shanty Irish hocus-pocus to keep the thick Micks ignorant.

Speaking of shanty Irish, what were some of the opinions expressed
by Bridget's relatives at her wake?

That she looked wonderful; that she looked beautiful; that she
looked better than she did alive; that she looked as pretty as she did
when she was a girl; that she looked alive; that she looked as if she'd
open her eyes and talk bejesus; that it was all for the best; that she
was with God in heaven; that she had gone to a better place; that she
was spared a lot of suffering going when she did; that she didn't suffer
at all thanks be to God; that she smiled like an angel after she took
communion, the Father said; that Marie's eyes were red as a beet from
crying; that poor John looked as if he'd be next, worn out with grief
as he was; that what John needed was a ball or two to buck him up,
it never hurt any man; that Bridget was so young a woman; that the
good always die young; that poor Marie was motherless too now; that
the poor grandson didn't know what to make of it all, God save the
poor little cockeyed runt of a thing; that the prayer cards were bejesus
works of art; that the undertaker's eldest son was a sissy; that begod
who could blame the boy growing up in an atmosphere like that; that
the flowers were the most beautiful anybody had ever seen anywhere;
that the casket must have cost a pretty penny; that the white Missal
and white rosary that Bridget clasped in her hands were for certain
the very same her mother God bless her gave her for her First Communion; that she was to be buried next to her mother in Holy Cross
as was only right; that poor John, being an Orangeman, was now
surely separated from her forever, saving of course in heaven if God
was good.

When John mentioned favorably some neighbors, the Mertises, what
were Bridget's invariable remarks anent same? Anent the Huckles? the
Svensons? the Astrups? the Phillipses? the Looneys? the Golds? the
Finneys? the Finks? the O'Neills? the Loftuses?

The Mertises: One's arse is fatter than the other. If they ever all got
on a trolley at once they'd sink it right through the pavement.

The Huckles: The old man's benny would fit Finn MacCool; the
wife was a frightened bird, God bless her, she's too homely to look
in a mirror for fear of scaring herself to death; the son, Georgie, was
a gawm, by God he was behind the door when they passed out the
chins, God bless the mark.

The Svensons: The old Swede bastard can't understand a word of English when you want a little steam heat but he's a genius when the first of the month rolls around.

The Astrups: There must be a law against cracking a smile where they come from in Scandihoovia, the greenhorn riffraff.

The Phillipses: They last drew a sober breath when Napoleon was a cadet.

The Looneys: When the poor little stunted rat of a man stands on the street you could drive a coal truck between his knees; the oldest daughter Philomena is a respectable girl but it's a misfortune that she looks like Ben Turpin.

The Golds: Pushy kikes. Do you see the cigar always stuck in the man's mouth like some Jew shyster?

The Finneys: If Thelma Finney puts any more lipstick and rouge on that potato mug of hers they'll take her for a stoplight. Ah well, you can't blame the woman with Jack crawling home on his hands and knees every night from Flynn's with the raving horrors.

The Finks: There's more than meets the eye over there with His Nibs a master tool-and-die maker and sits on the porch all day reading his red newspapers and his wife scrubbing floors like a nigger.

The O'Neills: Not that I mean any disrespect to the church but with the pie faces those two children have stuck on them they're good for a priest or a nun. For who would have them but God Himself? Mrs. O'Neill is holier than thou and well she should be as everyone knows that she drove her husband to drink and he died amidst a gang of bums and greaseballs in a charity ward in Kings County and nobody there to see the poor man draw his last breath.

The Loftuses: It's because the father and mother are in their sixties at least that poor Jackie looks to be turning into a moron and well on the high road to being a morphodite.

What were some of John's great disappointments in life?

The almost uncanny change that occurred in Bridget after the death of their second daughter. His decision not to go into the suggested partnership with William X. Whitestone. His failure to convince Bridget to allow him to see her in the nude. His son-in-law's abandoning Marie for Margie, a quintessential shanty-Irish slut; it seemed somehow a horrifying judgment on his own life's failure. His slöw transformation into a miser.

How did he feel about his grandson?

Billy frightened and saddened him. In him he saw but another boy poised on the edge of life's meaninglessness.

What misadventure befell John at Lake Hopatcong some ten years before Bridget's death?

Walking down a wooden boat dock in the pitch dark, John stepped off its edge into six feet of water, much to the surprise, fright, and subsequent hilarity of Bridget, Marie, Tony, Ralph Sapurty, a certain Mr. and Mrs. Rydstrom of Bethpage, and Cornelius A. Ryan, an alcoholic attorney.

Detail some oddities springing from this mishap.

Later that night, after a hot bath and three ounces of the Christian Brothers brandy, John thought over this accidental plunge into the lake and felt suddenly young. He remembered a girl who lived across the street from him when he was a boy of thirteen or fourteen, remembered walking her to the bakery one Saturday afternoon in the fall and buying her hot chocolate in Otten's ice-cream parlor, over which she told him that she wanted to be a nurse. It was at precisely this moment that he realized how magically lovely girls could be and he fell in love. Two months later, she and her mother and two sisters moved away after her father hanged himself in their backyard privy. Ten years after his marriage to Bridget, he mentioned this girl and discovered that Bridget had gone to school with her—had been, in fact, in her class—and that Bridget despised her for being a "dumb Polack who thought she was God's gift to the world, oh yes, a regular little prima donna."

Give John McGrath's opinions on any and all movies.

"A bunch of horse's asses." "A bunch of goddamn fools."

Give two conflicting reasons for the total apathy he felt toward the cinema.

His life and its problems were so present to him that he could not spare any of himself for the celluloid dramas of others. His life and its problems had worn him so thin that he found no parallels whatsoever in celluloid dramas.

What was the one truth in his life that he would not face?

That he had energetically conspired in his own defeat.

List a few of John's memories of his brother Bill.

His Trilby hat. His silk foulards. The brilliance with which he danced the Peabody. His endless stock of dirty jokes. The odd fact that all his girl friends seemed to blush constantly. The lecherous eye he always cast on Bridget. His monumental capacity for whiskey. His hangover cure—two ounces of whiskey, an ounce of port, two or three dashes each of Worcestershire sauce and Tabasco, a slice of onion chopped fine, and a raw egg: "It builds up the red blood, my lad," he'd say. His adoration of their mother and hatred of their father. The unearthly sweetness of his tenor voice before alcohol and cigars had wrecked it. The cornflower boutonnieres he wore on his summer suits. His amused tolerance of Bridget's relatives: "One must be kind to the lame and the halt," he'd say. The wry joke he made moments before his death. His long and womanly eyelashes.

What were, and had been, John's feelings about Helga Schmidt?

Desire and lust, against which he fought.

Why did he fight against these feelings?

He fought against these feelings when Bridget was alive because Bridget was alive. He now fought against these feelings for far more subtle reasons: He asked himself that if he, at fifty-seven, could feel these sexual urges toward a woman of almost fifty, how then did Tom Thebus, a man in the prime of life, feel about Marie? The idea of Marie, involved in sexuality of any kind, troubled him more than he could understand. So he curiously reasoned that if he "really" didn't feel anything toward Helga, Tom "really" didn't feel anything toward Marie. An admission of the reality of his own lusts would allow the admission of the reality of Tom's.

Had Bridget ever spoken to him of Helga Schmidt?

She had called her, in private, "Dutchie." She seemed to like her and referred to her often as a "decent woman." She regularly said that she had legs as strong as a horse. This latter image troubled and heated John, since he invariably thought of those legs wrapped around his back in coitus, in the position he had once seen a naked (but for stockings, shoes, and mask) woman in in a pornographic photograph Bud Halloran had shown around at the office.

What did Marie think of Helga Schmidt?

She was mildly hostile and openly contemptuous toward her. She poked fun at her accent, which she called "put on." She often made references to her "setting her cap" for a good man.

How did John think of Marie's attitude toward Helga?

He saw it as rude and self-serving. He thought that one, she wanted to marry him off to this Dutchwoman to get rid of him so that she could do whatever the goddamn hell she pleased; two, she wanted him married to this Dutchwoman so that he would be, if she proved right in her antipathy toward her, miserable for the rest of his life; three, she wanted to deny him any happiness he might possibly find with this Dutchwoman in his declining years by setting herself adamantly against any idea, however vague, of marriage. There was no way that he could reconcile these three theories.

What, essentially, was his deep, his irrational objection to Tom Thebus as suitor or friend to Marie?

His moustache was exactly the same as the one worn by the man in the already mentioned pornographic photograph. And if Tom was the man in the photograph, the masked woman was, of course, his own daughter.

Dear Mrs. Schmidt,

Right off the bat I hope you will excuse me saying Dear Mrs. Schmidt. Although I call you Helga when we are in conversation, when I wrote Helga down, dear Helga, is what I wrote at first, it looked too familiar and I tore it up and began again, but believe you me, Helga, the Dear Mrs. Schmidt as above does not by a long shot mean that I think of you less warmly than ever, and please do believe me.

You might find it a funny thing that I am writing this letter to you instead of just talking to you face to face. The truth is, that some things are hard to say right out and, much easier to write. You are the only one I can turn to with hopes of understanding, on your part. I am a lonely man and growing old and nobody at all seems to understand me. It seems as if I am the butt for everybody. It was once much different, believe it or not. First off I have to mention something that might surprise you.

You thought you knew Bridget, my wife. God rest her soul. But what if I told you that my life with Bridget was almost 30 years of Hell on earth. When I was a young fellow and first wedded I was full of fun. Believe it or not. I even used to play the mandolin and was pretty fair at it believe it or not. I still have my old mandolin at home in the closet but I can hardly bear to look at it, it makes me so sad to do so. I was also a regular Beaux Brummel. Bridget made everything turn sour and rotten. She put the kibosh on anything that I wanted to do that looked as if it might cost a

few dollars. She was really a miser, and I mean that and may God
forgive me for saying so. I could of now been a very big man in
the Credit Business if I had of gone into partnership with Bill
Whitestone. Maybe you heard of this gentleman. I think I once
mentioned his name. I could of been partners with him and he
was a brick of a fellow and I would now, without the least doubt
be a millionaire. Bridget threw cold water all over that idea
because I had to put up 1000 dollars with his 1000 dollars to get
us off the ground in a little office. That little business of 30 odd
years ago is now, the National Credit Office. Well, I can thank
Bridget for that, because of being such a tightwad. And what
good was it in the long run? Just 1000 dollars and it ruined my
whole future, a man of my age still doing what I was doing 30
years ago. Believe me Helga you did not know the half of it. You
know the jokes about how Scotchmen save string. Well, Bridget
saved even string with knots in it and even saved pieces that were
an inch or two long. She even saved pieces of glass from broken
bottles too, as God is my judge. Maybe some day I will tell you
all the other terrible things about our life together as man and
wife, how our conjagal bed was a mockery almost from our
wedding day.

And now at last, after I am starting to get a little peace and
quiet after poor Bridget's passing away, and by the way her
hospital bill cost almost 2000 dollars in the Swedish Hospital,
Marie is giving me neither peace nor quiet. There is no rest for
the weary as the old saying goes. I was always the best father I
could be to Marie, who is you know my only child and when that
pup of a dago husband of hers ran off with a little chippy tramp I
took her and my grandson off the street and gave them a roof
over their heads and fed them and bought them clothes. And
never asked for a dime in return. Now Marie is making a damn
fool of herself shining up to this Thebus article, who I don't trust
as far as I can throw him. You have eyes to see how she has
neglected me this summer, not that I need a nursemaid, but, ever
since the day we got here Marie has been more interested in
buttering up this man than in me, it has been Tom this and Tom

that and Tom the other thing. And this is supposed to be a
vacation where I can relax and sort things out. Instead I have
nothing but headaches. Also it is embarrassing to explain to that
damn fool Ralph Sapurty and this Copan article why I am always
moping around like a lost soul and why I hardly ever go to the
lake anymore. A man damn well knows when he is not wanted.

Billy has taken a cue from Marie and falls all over this man,
I'm sure you have noticed. Between you me and the lamppost I
know why the man acts like a damn fool and pays attention to
Billy's foolishness. Our fine friend with the perfume all over his
hair has got a method to his madness and knows that you can
catch more flies with honey than you can with vinegar. To get on
the good side of Marie he butters up Billy. There is never a cross
word out of his mouth to the boy, no matter what his shenanigans
are. God knows, Marie lets that boy walk all over her, she spoils
him rotten. There is no lack of damn fools in the world and I am
afraid that Marie is one of them.

I remember you asking me just the other day why I was sitting
over on the church steps all alone. I was so ashamed that I almost
got red as a beet that you noticed. But now you know why I am
alone so much, as if you could not see for yourself. I know that
you are a very smart woman. Thank you from the bottom of my
heart for not saying right out, that you knew why.

Between you and I, I can't see one iota of good coming out of
this business with Marie and this man. Marie is a good skate at
heart and I am deathly afraid that this man has nothing good in
mind. I think that he wants to take advantage of Marie and make
her do something that she will be ashamed of and I also think
that he might try to get her to marry him. I don't know if she
would ever do that because she is a good Catholic and you know
that the Catholic Church does not allow you to remarry if you are
divorced. They do not recognize divorce at all. But you never
know when you are dealing with a creature like this man.
Anything is liable to happen. This man strikes me all wrong and I
wouldn't put anything past him.

What I am afraid of is that she will do something that she will regret and then say the hell with the whole thing and marry him, figuring why should she cry over spilt milk, what's done is done and she may as well be hanged for a sheep as a lamb. That is this article's scheme I think. I hope that you will pardon my French when I say that this man is really just a patch on a man's a—. I'm sure that he thinks I have plenty of sponduliks and that my daughter will get it all when I am in the grave. I know his type like a book.

The little nest egg that I have left after Bridget's hospital bills and funeral expenses I would like to spend on some peace and happiness for myself and some good woman. Somebody who is not just a dizzy jane and who has had her share of troubles like me, somebody who is lonely and who would understand that my marriage was 30 years of a living Hell and would like to give a man getting on in years some comfort. But do you think that there is a woman like that anywhere?

I have watched and watched you for years now in the summer and you know how much I respect you and your love for music and such things. When you were married to Otto, God rest his Soul, I was green with envy of him when I thought of my marriage to Bridget and how we were living a lie. I am ashamed to admit this to you but I have to. That is why I am putting this in writing. Everything is going from bad to worse for me and my own daughter doesn't want to have anything to do with me and is almost ashamed to be seen in her father's company, so I have to tell somebody. And I have to tell you although I feel strange doing same that I have always admired from afar your looks, your womanly bust and limbs.

I must close now, but please if this letter makes you feel as if you wish to speak with me further about my tale of woe, let's have a quiet chat together, just the two of us. God knows we are both alone and not beholden to anybody.

Excuse me for being so bold and writing bust and etc., above. But I had to let you know how I feel about such a wonderful, wonderful person. You are a person who should be comfortable as she grows older without having to be alone looking at the four walls. You are a person who deserves a little nest egg and somebody to look after you. You are still a young and attractive woman with many a good year ahead of you with the right man. Let us have a nice talk soon.

Your old friend,
John McGrath

Tom Thebus has come to his door and opened it. By the sweet Christ, his moustache doesn't look half-bad, he don't look too much like a frog or a pansy floorwalker.

Hello, John. Heard you had a few tall Tom Collins with Sapurty. Ha ha.

Didn't sit too well with me, Thebus, you know I like my glass of beer. By the way, I thought you'd be teaching that poor little greaser a thing or two about croquet this hour of the day. You can go through the poor unfortunate lump like a dose of salts.

Ha ha. No, no. No need. Your grandson *Billy* can beat him without half-trying. Easy to see that he's *your* grandson. He's got a good head on his shoulders, that boy.

Marie down there? Sitting in the shade over by the raspberries with her crocheting and making goo-goo eyes at you? And did you have a nice time at Budd Lake this afternoon? Go ahead, go ahead, shake your head, but I know all about it and I'd like an explanation. You know my daughter's a good Catholic woman, don't you, young fellow?

Wh-what? What are you talking about, John, you old dog? Marie and . . . Marie and *I?* My God! Ha ha ha!

What's so goddamn funny, Romeo? The minute I laid eyes on you with your excuse for a moustache, jumping up from the porch the day we got here, that pipe stuck in your gob and a fat book under your oxter, I knew you were giving my Marie the once-over. I'm not blind *yet.*

No need to be abusive to a fellow, old man. I admit, cross my heart, true blue, and as God is my judge, that Marie is attractive and well-bred, a real lady, but to think that I— Oh, it's just a wow!

A wow? There's no call for you to mock her, you pup! She has recently gotten over a broken heart, but I suppose you know all about her marriage to that dago greaseball who is the father of that cockeyed boy, God bless the mark. Did she tell you how he shamed her running after that shanty-Irish chippy that called herself his secretary? A wow? I'll have you know that she's had *her* cross to bear.

You can come down from your high horse, John. I have nothing but the greatest respect for your daughter and mockery is not in my line. Scout's honor.

Respect for her? In a pig's ass, and you'll pardon my French.

How long have you known Mrs. Schmidt?

Helga? Oh God, five years, six years, longer. Years. I met her when she first started coming up here, with Otto, God rest his soul. They always came in July then, the first three weeks. What does *she* have to do with this?

And what do you think of her? Man to man.

She's warm and wonderful, full of fun. So was Otto. For a Dutchman, he had some real breeding. But you know how those Dutchmen are educated in the old country. But what has this got to do with the price of beans?

Ha ha! I love your colorful and racy way of talking, John. It's manly, like saloons and free lunch. The reason I inquire about Mrs. Schmidt—may I call her Helga?—is that I'm afraid that I am head over heels in love with her. Ga-ga. The lady was already here when I arrived, as you know, and we had a very charming and fine, a high-minded friendship, our first week together. All good clean fun, like stringing colored popcorn on the Christmas tree when I was a boy back in Illinois. And then, one evening, when Helga was playing the piano and singing "Auf Wiedersehen," I fell for her like a ton of bricks.

I didn't know Helga could play the piano.

Oh? Yes, like a regular angel. She . . . oh, ha ha! John, you *are* a great kidder! Didn't know! Anyhow, I was smitten. The next day we were out blackberrying down below the meadow where Stellkamp throws the chickens that die of disease? and I told her: Mrs. Schmidt, Helga, I said, I must tell you that your person, your smile, your

bewitching European accent, your strapping figure and deep bosom
—if I may use such a word in your presence—have made, I said, a
deep impression on me and I would very much like to have the honor
of paying you attendance while we sojourn here.

My God! Helga? You and Helga? Not you and Marie? Who also
plays and sings, you know, "Auf Wiedersehen."

Yes, me and Mrs. Schmidt, Helga and I. However, ah . . . unfortu-
nately . . .

You are not *her* dish.

You've hit the nail on the head, old man. In a manner of speaking,
she thinks I'm just a patch on a man's ass. When I unburdened myself
to the lady, she smiled and blushed and said: Ja, jawohl, but Chon
McGrath und hiss family, dey iss comink up here next veek, und
Chon, Mr. McGrath, he iss mein dream, ja? To see her blush drove
me half-wild, I don't mind admitting it.

Me? Helga Schmidt? By God, Thebus, that's just the way she talks,
too. You should be on Major Bowes. But . . . me? Don't make me
laugh!

That is it in a nutshell, old fellow, believe it or not. My attentions
to your daughter are a poor way of making Helga jealous. Just my
luck, it's not working. Just yesterday, Helga told me that she prays
to "Gott" every night that you will eat steamers and polka the night
away with her this Saturday at the Warren House. She is mad about
you, sir. She is even hoping, if I am any judge of women, for a
proposal.

You *are* giving me this straight from the shoulder, Thebus. Really?
Be square with me now!

I swear by all that is holy to me, by my father's insurance business
back in Illinois. I have no intentions of any kind toward your daughter
outside of friendship, although she is an attractive and well-bred
young lady, as I have already said.

She is not so "young." Look at the bathing suit she wears.

I had wondered about that . . .

Well. Hmm. Helga thinks that, you say, she and I . . . ?

Exactly. That is straight from the horse's mouth. And now, I think
I've overstayed my welcome. I have to go and beat poor Ralph to a
frazzle.

Thank—thank . . . you, Thebus. I'm sorry if I misjudged you.

Ha ha! Don't concern yourself an iota, John. I have nothing but the highest respect for you wanting to protect your daughter. You are a lucky lucky man. O.K., I'd better take a powder. Toodle-oo.

Thanks again. Tom.

One night he dreams of Bridget. Rather, he dreams of himself and Bridget together as if he is a third person watching them. They are in the country, here in New Jersey, for that matter, in any event the softly tinted landscape is familiar. She is sitting on a split-log fence, one that no longer exists, but that he recognizes as one that used to fence off the field of timothy wherein Stellkamp now pastures his two old and blind horses. Bridget is in a new gingham dress of white with pale-yellow stripes and a stiff white collar, and is half turned toward him standing next to her, smiling down at his hands, which are clasped on her knee. Her small feet are shod in black kid boots with tiny mother-of-pearl buttons and between the top of her right boot and the white cotton petticoats thickly swirling from beneath her dress can be seen—he sees—an inch or so of dully gleaming black silk stocking. He is also smiling in a curiously secretive way, smiling, or so it seems, into himself. He appears to be tremendously pleased, natty in a light-grey tropical worsted suit, a boater with a red-and-blue-striped band, a dark-blue four-in-hand, and gleaming white French-toed shoes. Behind them the fields are luminous green. Bridget slowly reaches toward him, still smiling, and touches lightly his clasped hands, then presses upon them to increase their weight upon her knee. He watches himself turn his head toward her and then up so that he is looking into her face, and he is not at all surprised to find that he is looking into the face of Jean Whiting, Bud Halloran's secretary of some ten years back. Jean smiles at him, her lips full, swollen, shining with lip rouge as her eyes shine with lust. She leans back on the top rail of the fence with both hands and opens her thighs and he looks to discover that she is naked from the waist down, her pink sex wet and open to him. Still smiling, he reaches for it, his fingers trembling, and as he wakes he hears her low laughter transformed to the laughter of Helen Copan on the moonlit road below, saying good night to her lifeguard.

He starts to reach under the bed in the dark for his bottle of Wilson's but then thinks better of it and lies back, still. The dream has upset him. He considers the wife who appeared in it, her gentle smile, so perfect that he almost believes that she always smiled that way. And his own contented and secret smile? That young man, he? The elegant angle of his boater. The crispness of his summer suit. He seemed so absolutely at ease with that young and adoring wife. Why did she turn into Jean Whiting?

Tears of self-pity come to his eyes as he realizes that he was indeed that young once, that Bridget had once, many times, many times, smiled at him that way—a girlish smile of acquiescence, surrender. Her surrender might have been, what? More complete? More abandoned. But it was as it was, and sweet, nonetheless. His face burns as he strikes against a fantasy that he has not entertained for years, and it seems to him that his wheezy breathing will awaken his grandson asleep across the room. When it first came to him he cannot remember, but it had been after the death of their second daughter, in the dark center of the sexual death that their lives had entered. The baby's death was *his* responsibility. Bridget's pregnancy had been *his* responsibility. *His* dirty needs, as she had phrased it, had sent the infant to her grave. May God forgive him.

Perhaps it had been after that night on which Bridget had allowed him, after so long, his desires. There had been an outing on the Fourth of July to the Rockaways and she had drunk two highballs and then, in the evening, three or four glasses of beer. Her mouth had opened. Her lips were wet and juicy and they had sweated together in the hot dark bedroom of the rented bungalow in Sheepshead Bay. She had licked and sucked his tongue to muffle her moans. He thought that their lives were changing, but that holiday expression of love had been an aberration, and they fell back immediately into their bitter celibacy. That may have been the time that his obsessive and recurring daydream began. It was so clear in his mind that he thought that had she looked into his eyes she would have there discovered it in impeccable clarity, a very picture of his shameful thoughts.

He is sitting in the leather Morris chair reading the paper after supper. Bridget has finished the dishes, and although Skip is asleep, she has not come to join him in their customary silence before he says, as he says each night, "About time to go for a pint." He suddenly looks up, and sees her at the door of their bedroom, smiling at him in unutterable lasciviousness. Her hair is loose, falling over her shoulders and back, her dark coppery hair, and her face is almost grotesquely bright with rouge and powder. Her lips are fuller, her mouth wider. She is wearing a white linen chemise, the low front bordered with pale-pink embroidered roses. Below this garment, she is naked, her belly slightly rounded with the weight she has put on since their marriage, her sex hidden in luxuriant hair slightly darker than the masses on her head. Her strong straight legs are set slightly apart and her white silk stockings catch the soft glow of the bedroom lamp. They are rolled to just above her knees and there caught tightly by pink satin garters. On her feet are the white patent-leather shoes bought for their dead daughter's christening and not worn since. She walks toward him, still smiling, her hips swaying, her face flushed with lust and her eyes softly virginal. Taking the newspaper out of his hands and dropping it on the floor, she bends over him, her knees drawing modestly together, her teeth wetly brilliant, and kisses him, their mouths awkwardly open. Her breasts fall out of her chemise and she laughs, her mouth still on his, and begins to stroke his hidden sex, laughing lower, and then she says filthy, forbidden things into his mouth, filthy, incredible things, which he begs her to repeat as he caresses her heavy breasts. She frees his aching phallus from his trousers and straddles him, one hand guiding him into her, the other cupping one of her breasts and pushing its stiff nipple into his slavering mouth. As he begins to suck at her furiously, she starts to pump up and down on him, sinking deeper and deeper onto his throbbing erection.

Skip was so goddamn het up about going into Hackettstown with that excuse for a man, Dave Warren, that John knew—wasn't she his flesh and blood?—that she was going to make a horse's ass of herself buying something or other to show off to Thebus. It better not be anything that makes her look like a cheap piece of trash, or by God he'd *really* put his foot down! He put on a long, sad face as he saw Billy come out on the porch and look across at him on the church steps, and then felt ashamed of himself, Christ, mixing the boy up in it, he must be getting dizzy. But the boy pretended not to notice him and went back inside, huh, she's got him dead set against me, the mean old grandfather, sure. When the boy is a little older he'll look back and be able to see himself what a shabby piece of goods this Thebus is. God forbid that he even remembers him!

When he'd told Marie that he was very upset about her going to that den of iniquity, the WigWam, she'd looked at him but said nothing, but he knew, oh how he knew that goddamn stubborn look that she'd got from her mother. The WigWam! He could have made his fortune a hundred times over, for the love of God, had he bet that if the son of a bitch asked her out anywhere, *that's* where he'd ask her. And she not even really divorced, not in the eyes of God. The last time John had gone to the WigWam was when? Ten years ago? And even then it was a nest of drunken floozies and five-hundred-dollar millionaires sniffing around their skirts like a pack of mongrels. My God, it was enough to turn your stomach. You can bet your bottom dollar that's where that little bastard would take her. And she, like the simp she was when that slimy article turned on his five-and-ten charm, by Jesus Christ, she thought he was doing her a favor, she

thought it was a compliment. No fool like an old fool. Oh, the dump
was the perfect place for him to give her the old soft soap, to the tune
of cheap rotgut booze and that nigger music that the young chippies
jumped around to, dancing they called it! With their behinds wiggling
around for anybody to see! When he'd gone a little further and said
that he really didn't want her to go, what do you even know about
this man except that he's divorced, and very pretty that is, isn't it? the
blind leading the blind, she set her face against him and said that she'd
accepted the invitation and that as far as she was concerned what
really got his back up was that he was scared to death of what the
other boarders would think about it and she was sick and tired and
fed up worrying about what a few relics that she didn't give two cents
for—and neither did he if he'd admit it—would say about *anything*.
And then she said she wanted to wash her hair and that was that. It
was easy to see that her head had been turned when she talked to her
own father that way. A spectacle, no two ways about it, that's what
she was making of herself.

She was a good-looking woman, anybody with half an eye could see
that, and he knew what a little bugger of a man like Thebus wanted
with her—not that Marie would ever disgrace herself by letting him
do—letting him get away with any smutty filth he'd cooked up.
Married and a mother or not, she was as innocent as a girl, it troubled
him even now to think of her and that greaseball she married doing
God knows what . . . Well, that's all over and done with and he'd seen
many a man stop and turn around to look at her on the street and
she'd walk along with her head up high as if they didn't exist. But
this one! He got around her with his Billy this and Billy that and his
sad tales of his own boy—all peaches and cream and snots and tears,
sure, now that he'd deserted him to chase sluts. Well, when she came
back from town he'd tell her a thing or two about her precious
gentleman admirer, and God bless Helga Schmidt for letting him
know about it. Now there was a woman, straight as a die. Oh yes
indeed, Helga Schmidt had the goods on the son of a bitch, and any
man who runs after the janes the way he did was not about to change
his spots just because he'd met a clean pure woman like Marie. By
God, he wouldn't put it past him to talk about marrying her, as if
Marie would ever fly in the face of God, but he wouldn't put it past

him to say *anything* if he thought it might allow him to take liberties.

The sun had finally flooded the whole expanse of the church steps and he'd gone across the road to the porch where he bumped into Ralph Sapurty, just what the doctor didn't order, and had to grin and bear it listening to his horse's-ass chatter about God-knows-what. Just yes the poor unfortunate gawm to death and give him a nice big castor-oil smile every now and again. Then he saw Dave Warren's car turn at the bend down the road and in a minute pull up and he watched Marie get out, loaded down with bundles to beat the band, like it was Christmas. She went past him like a ton of bricks, barely giving him the time of day, oh and how cute she was about it, saying that she didn't want to interrupt him and Sapurty, as if she had no idea in God's green world that the man gave him conniptions! Well, he talked with Ralph, if that's the word for it, for a few more minutes for the sake of appearances, and then excused himself and said that he had to go upstairs and do something that nobody else could do for him, that's the sort of remark that Ralph thought was more fun than Weber and Fields, the poor stupid man. When he reached Marie's room he heard voices and for a minute thought that Thebus was in there with her, by God, he'd—but then he realized that it was just Billy, and you can rest assured that she'd brought him something from Hackettstown, oh the boy was spoiled rotten without a father to put his foot down, did she expect *him* to be father and grandfather and breadwinner all rolled in one? It had been enough of a burden even when Bridget had been alive. *She* wasn't one to let things slide, when the boy needed to be taught a lesson she wasn't the kind to shirk from it. Well, he wasn't that kind and now, well, the handwriting was on the wall as far as all the good it had done him. He *should* have cracked him across the face once in while. Now they thought, the both of them, that they could walk all over him. Oh, it was grand for them. He pushed the door open hard and walked into Marie's room.

They both looked at him as if he was something the cat dragged in and Marie was right on the verge of harping about knocking on a person's door but he must have had a look on his face, there's life in the old dog yet, and she shut her trap, thank God for small favors. The first thing was to get the boy to hell out of there, he was entirely too acclimated to hearing every word that passed between them, turning into a little old man he was with a wise little face on him. Aha, and there it was, by God, wouldn't you have known it, a pair of shoes, nothing to them but a few scraps of leather, if you can call it that, and a high heel to show off her legs, the man has got her crazy as a bedbug, daffy! He held the door open and told Billy to go out and play, he had something to speak to his mother about, and she was about to open her mouth again but let it pass and the boy went out with some kind of a goddamn toy, another dollar thrown out the window, they thought he was made of money. Then he closed the door and started in on the shoes, what a pretty penny they must have cost, and for what? Could she even answer the question with a closetful of shoes not six feet away from her gathering dust? And a good time it was too to bring out what Helga had told him about young Lochinvar, that Romeo running after any skirt who looked in his direction, he never liked the cut of his jib from the first day he saw him running down off the porch all dressed in white like some horse's ass of a sissy with a pipe stuck in his mouth like a collar ad, all for show it was, couldn't she, for Christ sake, see what a fool he was making of her? Helga's cousin saw him with some painted slut on his arm lovey-dovey as you please, coming out of a rattrap of a hotel, a fleabag that you'd get the itch just to pass by. *This* was the knight in shining armor with his hair all slicked down with brilliantine like a regular gigolo? *This* was the man that was taking his daughter dancing, or God knows what he had in mind? John put nothing past such an article!

He wasn't prepared for her anger and spunk in talking back to him, and what did Bridget being sick all that time have to do with her letting this man be her escort, he'd like to know that, and could she tell him that? With a pair of high-heeled shoes meant for a girl of eighteen, not a mother who'd been married in the church at a high nuptial mass and in the eyes of God was *still* married. She sailed right by that and tore into Helga, that backbiting dutchie she called her, can't you see what's as plain as the nose on your face? That sauer-kraut-eater has, oh don't deny it, she has grand plans for you, oh my, *grand.* Why, you talk about what people, pardon me, the antiques here, think about Tom and me, Jesus, Mary and Joseph! Don't you think they can all see that woman setting her cap for you? And she'd say anything to play up to you, anything she thinks you want to hear, by God, she'll say it, in spades. He didn't mean to—maybe he didn't actually *say* it—but he forbade her to go out with that sly article and her face got as white as her shoes. She said she'd do as she damn well pleased! With a bleached blonde of a tramp he was seen, a whore! he said, and blushed. That's the kind of a man who's taking you *dancing*! Worse than that greaseball of a husband of yours, and bejesus he doesn't even have a bit of an ass on him! By God, it's one of the wonders of the world that the man can manage to sit down. She was holding the door open for him and wiping tears from her eyes. Oh Poppa, she said, what a spiteful thing to say, what a spiteful, mean thing to say to your own daughter.

He lay on his bed, smoking one Camel after another, thank God in heaven he wasn't the sort of a man with a filthy pipe stuck in his gob all day and his teeth black as the ace of spades. Ah Christ, she wouldn't have dared do this if Bridget were alive, that one would have marched right up to the little cock of the walk and told him where to get off and make no mistake about it. But with him . . . it was his softness that let her wipe her feet all over him, telling him that she'd been the maid of all work long enough and now she wanted to have some life, and what about him, didn't *he* have a right to some life? Hadn't it been John do this and John do that and John do the other thing and what do you need with an extra quarter for years and years and years? Was he denying her her goddamn life? It was that oily little mongrel he wanted her to hold at arm's length, didn't she know what he wanted from her? And there she was buying a pair of chippy shoes with a heel on them that was an invitation to any man with a pair of eyes in his head, and you can bet your last red cent that they wouldn't be lost on the likes of Mr. Thebus, oh no. And she's even beginning to lose all respect for anything decent, the nerve of her talking that way about Helga Schmidt! She was a good respectable woman, lonely like he was lonely, it wasn't as if *they* were gallivanting around in cars going to roadhouses and God knows where else.

When he woke from a short doze he heard voices from the lawn and got up to stand behind the curtain and look down. As he thought, it was Thebus and Billy, thick as thieves. You had to give the man credit for his gall. It was as clear as day that the boy—look at him now running around with that cheap tin toy in his hand—bored him

to death. Ah, but what a perfect foot in the door he was, you could
see that the man had the brain of your true salesman, he'd probably
sell goldbricks to some starving widow if the truth were known. John
had always hated salesmen, something good for the kikes to do but
no job for a man. But who said that this article was a man anyway?
Oho, and there he was, crossing the lawn to go and get himself all
dolled up like Astor's pet horse, ah, not yet. John craned his neck to
watch Tom and saw him walk across the road to his car and begin
to wipe it down with a rag. That's right, you little mutt, make everything all spic and span for the goddamn fool of a woman who's
probably admiring her feet and watching the clock. God help us all.
She's so ga-ga she may not even be seen at the supper table, I wouldn't
be a bit surprised if nobody saw hide nor hair of her until the great
moment. The old man pursed his lips in contempt.

But Marie did come down to supper, as cool as a cucumber if you
please, and bejesus, she didn't take her eyes off that little bastard's face
from the minute she sat down. She'd lost all sense of modesty and
shame, even that little chippy at the next table wasn't so bold with the
way she made eyes at that big gawm of a lifeguard she was making
a horse's ass out of. And his nibs looked back at her as bold as brass
himself, but what else could you expect of a man who had no breeding
whatsoever? John was so upset and annoyed that he didn't really
follow the conversation, but Thebus was doing his best, that was easy
to tell, to annoy everybody with ears to hear his ranting and raving
about what the Germans were doing to get us into another war, the
man was nothing more than a Mongolian idiot! Anybody with half an
eye could see that what Helga said, and the Stellkamps too, was as
plain as the nose on your face—it was the Jews who started everything, and by God, if there was another war who would profit from
it but the Jews? Maybe Thebus was really Thebowitz just like Roosevelt was Rosenfeld. He even looked a little like a goddamn mocky
with his little shyster lawyer moustache. Helga caught his eye and
smiled at him, oh, she knew what kind of shenanigans were going on,
this little mongrel was trying to get him into an argument so that he'd
wind up looking like he was defending Helga, the poor son of a bitch
thinks I was born yesterday! Ha! He'll have to get up pretty early in
the morning to fool me with his little tricks. But the gall of his

daughter! She was grinning away at her great hero so that you'd think her face would crack, and no attempt to hide it either. Oh, John was soft all right, too goddamn soft, and that was the trouble. If Bridget were alive, God rest her soul, she'd put a stop to this in a minute, even if she had to drag Marie away from the table by the ear like she'd done a thousand times when she was a little girl. Finally the patch on a man's ass stopped running off at the mouth and contented himself with mooning at Marie with his greaseball Valentino face on him, by God it was enough to turn your stomach to see it. As soon as John finished his tea he excused himself and went up to his room. He couldn't stand another minute of this vaudeville as God was his judge.

Oh, there they were on the porch, the great hero dressed to the nines, with that great ugly lump of a pipe in his face like some nance of a professor, well, maybe John would go down and maybe he wouldn't, but he'd be damned, whatever else he did, if he'd give them a goodbye, he wouldn't, for that matter, give them the sweat off an ice pitcher. Then he heard the screen door open and there she was, by God, dressed up like a little slip of a girl all in white with her new tart shoes and silk stockings on her. Ah, I've got to go down there and show my face, I'll not have it said that the damn fool's own father sneaked around like a rat in the dark while she paraded around like Cleopatra. When John got out on the porch they were about to start down the steps and Marie turned to look at him but he stood there without moving a muscle with his hands in his back pockets, she'll get no satisfaction from me! It looked to him like she was so embarrassed that she was blushing, well, she's got something to blush *about,* if truth be told, it was a wonder she hadn't gone around the past two weeks with her face as red as a beet. He watched them go down the path to the gate and then cross the road to the car, two damn fools all dolled up to go and spend their time in a dump that you wouldn't even let a dog die in. Thebus helped her into the car and closed the door, then got in the other side, Marie was looking out her window as the car started, and then she waved, and all the other goddamn fools on the porch waved too, well it would be a cold day in hell before John took his hands out of his pockets to wave to her after she had flown in his face and as much as told him straight up and down that he could take his opinion and put it in his pipe and smoke it. Well,

we'll see, we'll just see how far she can go with this damn fool idea
before I cut the legs out from under her. She was still waving as the
car moved out of sight. John went upstairs to clean his false teeth and
change into his spectators. He thought of that ten-cent Casanova
holding Marie in his arms and brushed at his plate furiously. She'll
soon find out the class of bozo he is!

When he finally came downstairs only Helga was on the porch,
sitting in a rocker and looking aimlessly across the road. Thank God
that dizzy Grace Sapurty wasn't monopolizing her—she was probably
locked in her room combing her wig, God bless the mark. He sat down
in the rocker next to hers and lit a cigarette. The woman was a
pleasure to talk to, a real lady and she had better manners, you can
mark my word, than half the so-called Americans he'd ever bumped
into in his travels. Hardly realizing it, they began to talk of Marie and
that oily gigolo and he told her that he'd warned Marie about him and
let her know about him chasing chippies, but she was blind and deaf
to anything he had to say to her, and suddenly he sobbed and tried
to cover it up with a cough, but Helga knew. What a wise and kind
woman. Without saying a word to him about it she suggested that
they take a little walk so he could, she said, get these things from off
the chest? He agreed and went in to get a sweater and a flashlight, and
also, it would be a good idea, his bottle of citronella. As he rose, Billy
came out, looking like a lost soul with his mother and his idol both
gone, and he told him that he and Mrs. Schmidt were going for a walk
and that he wanted no foolishness from him, he was to take a bath
and be in bed by nine-thirty at the latest. Helga was standing on the
path when he came out again, her sweater draped over her shoulders,
and as soon as she saw him she mentioned what beautiful stars were
out tonight, it looked just like the old country when she was a little
girl. He opened the gate and they started down the road.

She understood everything. How lonely he was, how he felt un-
wanted and unneeded, the fifth wheel, how he was the butt of everything now, he didn't mind telling her, Marie had fixed it so that his
own grandson sided with her on everything, Marie and that poolroom
Romeo who'd pulled the wool over her eyes. Anything, ja, but *anything* that Helga could do to help, she'd be only too glad, he understood of course? She had tried to talk to the young woman, she'd

known her so many years, but Marie had such a chip on her shoulder
this summer that it was like talking to the wall if you so much as
mentioned that Mr. Thebus was maybe not all he was cracked up to
be. They were passing under a clump of trees whose branches leaned
out over the road and Helga took his arm in her hand so that it was
pressed up against her side and bosom and he had a sudden image of
her straight, strong legs, her stockings in tight rolls that pinched into
the ample flesh just above her knees, and he felt himself turning red,
thank God for the dark. It wasn't his imagination, Helga was holding
his arm tight against her body and he let her. He felt oddly and
shamefully excited—how many years had it been since he had, with
Bridget, Christ Almighty, how many years? Yet here was the proof,
next to him, that he wasn't cold in his grave yet, this wonderful,
decent lady, this lady he had admired for years, a widow now, alone
as he was alone. Why not? Let Marie go and shift for herself if she
was so goddamn independent. Maybe. Maybe is all. Helga was saying
how much she understood his pain, oh ja, how children can hurt and
hurt even when they are grown big, they haven't got a thought in their
heads. And as far as she was concerned, this good, good woman, she
was praying on her hands and knees for the last week for Marie, ja,
for God to give her the strength she would need against this, how is
the word they say? this bum? He is just the sort of a man that in
Germany now Hitler is punishing, the trash running after good
women.

They had turned around and started back, no need for the citronella
this evening, and he and Helga as natural as you please and without
any self-consciousness, put their arms around each other as they
walked, nice and slow through the cool darkness and the sound of
crickets—there must have been thousands of them! Her heavy solid
hip and thigh brushed his leg as they walked, poor man, the worried
look on his face made *her* worry, and she would get down on her
hands and knees again this night and pray for him too and for that
poor fatherless boy. They discreetly removed their arms from each
other's waists as they neared the house, Christ, no sense in giving that
old woman Ralph Sapurty and his old woman of a wife anything to
gossip about, and as they got closer Helga said that it was none of her
business and as he knew after all these years she was not a busybody

with a long nose prying into private things, but she thought he should really put his foot down, a man like him, with an important job and in the prime of life, he shouldn't be aggravated by a grown-up daughter, but it was only a suggestion. But it was time to let Marie know who was the boss and tell her to stop giving him a headache. Ja? Excuse my butting in. And John agreed and agreed again, what a wonderful lady! And as they turned in at the gate he took her hand for just a second and squeezed it and Helga turned to him and smiled, her gold tooth shining.

Billy was asleep when he entered their room and he undressed and put on his pajamas in the dark, then reached under the bed and got his bottle of Wilson's, took a long drink and then another, might as well be a little pie-eyed as the way I am. He lay down and thought of Helga. It was terribly disturbing to feel this excited, Jesus Christ, he was an old man, probably, if truth were known, in his dotage! But he couldn't deny that he'd wanted to put his hands over her breasts out there in the dark, well, hell, he had a good job and enough money salted away for the two of them, why should he worry about this goddamn ungrateful snip of a daughter, mooning around all day long to make you sick. She'd see how it was without her fall guy of a father to support her and her spoiled-rotten son, see how fast Casanova would run when he saw the handwriting on the wall, ha. John dozed on and off, then took his watch to the window and saw that it was —what? ten after one in the morning! My God! The tramp! She knows goddamn good and well I expected her home by twelve, defying me! We'll see, we'll goddamn well see about it! He tried not to think of his feelings on the road with Helga because if that's how *he*—then what was going on with that little skirt-crazy bastard with Marie? Oh God in heaven, they were at it like two dogs in the alley in that car of his somewhere—he wouldn't put it past him to put something in her drink, oh hell, yes, he'd heard of it, hadn't his brother told him about girls, sweet and clean girls that had been given things in a cup of tea for Christ sake, and done things you couldn't even imagine? Was he to be made a complete horse's ass of?

He slipped out of the room and climbed the stairs to Marie's room, why? Hell, how in the name of God did he *know* why? He closed the door and shone his flashlight around, a slip on the bed, a pair of stockings in a tangle next to it, and there was, what the hell was it? Ah, yes. John put the flashlight down and opened the other bag that Marie had brought back from town—my God! A bathing suit, bejesus, that would show enough of her to get her arrested for indecent exposure. Oh my God, it had all gone far enough, too goddamn far. And this is what the little floozie thinks she's going to wear in public, with her behind sticking out of it like some slut in the *Police Gazette,* to go bathing with her little dirty-minded Romeo? By God, they'd have to carry him out in his coffin first! He put the bathing suit back in its bag, thinking of Marie in a car, her clothes all up and that mutt bastard—he heard a car then and quickly left the room, went down the stairs, and back into his room. There they were, and it one-thirty in the morning! The nerve, the *nerve* of them! He opened the window screen and leaned out, shining his flash across the road, oh, he was yelling, you're goddamn tootin he was yelling, and he didn't give a damn what they thought of it or what anybody the hell else thought of it either. He heard Billy call him and he turned toward him and told him to shut up, then shone the light down at the car again. A goddamn old fool, that's what they took him for? Well, we'll see who's the fool! He saw Marie get out and start quickly toward the porch, not looking up at the window. And there were some people up in the house, what in the hell did John care? They want an eyeful, they'll get one! Let's see how this little mongrel feels tomorrow showing his face to decent people. Marie thought she'd go out and do God knows what and then waltz in almost at dawn without so much as a by-your-leave? She had another think coming! He heard her pass the door and continue up to her room, crying she was, well let her. And tomorrow she could put that bimbo bathing suit in a drawer and forget about it. He was putting his foot down tomorrow, and if she didn't like it, well, she could lump it. If she didn't like what he had to say she could go back to the steam table, live on the street for all he cared. He'd get along, he was no cripple! He'd had enough of goddamn women to last him forever anyway. He saw a match flicker in the front seat of Tom's car, ha, there you are! The great lover and gent is so worried sick that he's having himself a lovely little smoke, just as if nothing had happened. Well, he'll have to see somebody else's behind in a slut bathing suit! Not an ounce of respect. And no respect from her and that boy either. After I've worked my fingers to the bone for both of them, and for her bitch of a mother too, God forgive me. He latched the screen and stood staring out at the soft white mass of the old church.

Everybody but Marie and John and Helga had gone to the first day of the Grange Hall Fair that afternoon and John was sitting on the porch alone while Helga talked German in the kitchen with Frieda. He felt good, satisfied. Helga and he had talked about how wise it had been of him to finally put his foot down on all the shenanigans with Thebus. Just before she'd left the porch she told him that he had done a great favor for his daughter, that she was sure to see someday how right he was, even though now she thought it was terrible of him. He was her father and everybody only has one father and she would forgive him and even thank him someday. This was the kind of thing she needed to give her some gumption and let her stand on her own two feet because it was a good experience and she'd learn from it what two-bit, is that how you say it? sports there are in this world. And it was time, well past time, that a woman her age stood on her own two feet and not expect her father to do everything for her.

Marie was remote and almost totally silent, still shocked and hurt and angry about him finding that trashy bathing suit, but she'd get over it, she'd better damn well get over it. John didn't really care a good goddamn now if she wore it or not with the assless wonder of the world gone. It wasn't very modest, but who was to see her? They only had a week or so left anyway here, then all the foolishness would be over and done with and Marie could come down from her high horse. She had never listened to him about anything, took after Bridget, stubborn as a mule! But by God she'd do what he told her about *this*. That goddamn little mutt with his business in the city! That was a good one, him running with his tail between his legs just like a cur. He hoped that Marie got a good eyeful of *that*. That cock-and-bull story wouldn't have fooled a six-year-old. Helga had put it right when she said that he'd run away when he knew he couldn't strut his stuff anymore. Now maybe Marie would realize that she was a *married woman* and act it.

Speak of the devil, Marie came out on the porch. She sat down in the rocker next to John's and said that Mr. Thebus—oh, he liked that! "Mr. Thebus"—had forgotten his tobacco pouch and that he wanted, well, and she handed him Thebus's note. The anger and contempt that John felt when he finished the note made his face almost blue. His lips were drawn back and his false teeth looked hideous. The son of a bitch is not welcome in my house and he won't put one foot inside it! But Poppa . . . he only wants to get the . . . and explain . . . I *want* to give him his personal . . . his belongings. She stood up, shaking, and took the pouch out of the pocket of her pinafore. His *pouch,* Poppa! My God, what do you take the man to be? My God! Poppa! He stood up too, and took the pouch out of her hand. Well, young woman! You want to fly in my face *again,* you go ahead and fly in my face! If you want to see that half-assed mongrel with his little smudge of a moustache you just make damn certain that you pack your valise first and take yourself and your boy with you. Poppa! Marie sat down again, her hands clasped in her lap. John shook the tobacco pouch in her face. And this sly little trick . . . This will be in the mail, *today.* The son of a bitch will not set foot inside my house and if you don't like it you can go and beg Katie to take you in off the street!

He banged the screen door entering the house and went up the stairs. In his room, he wrapped the pouch in paper cut from an old brown paper bag and then went up the stairs to Marie's room, pulled her address book out of her drawer and oh, sure, the silly jane had his name in her book as neat as you please, how sweet, how goddamn sweet! He addressed the package and went downstairs again, walked out on the porch and shook the pouch at Marie. I'm going down to the Post Office past the Bluebird and that will take care of Mr. Thebus! She sat and looked at him, her knees drawn together, her arms folded tight across her chest, her face blank and homely. By God, the girl was getting old! Running around like a little chippy and anybody with half an eye could see that she was no spring chicken. What the hell is the matter with her?

John walked steadily, keeping as much as he could in the shade of the trees, stopping every now and again to take a breather and mop his face. When he reached the Post Office, he mailed the package first class, and asked how long it would take to arrive. He was pleased when the clerk told him a day, at the most two. Then he started back, stopping off at the Bluebird for a glass of beer at the bar. Summer's almost over, the bartender said. Sure went fast. John agreed. Fella with the little moustache, always smoked a pipe, he gone back already? John nodded. Nice fella, said he was a salesman? John nodded again and said that it was time for all of them to put their noses to the grindstone again. That's for damn sure, the bartender said.

As he got near the house, he saw the Copans' car parked in front and the two daughters in their bathing suits putting blankets and towels in the trunk. They must have got bored with the Fair, John thought. No boys to shake their behinds at, and of course, those damn fool parents of theirs bowed and scraped and took the brats home and now, with it three o'clock already, *now* they were taking them bathing. Anything the princesses wanted—what they need is a good swift kick in the ass! Coming closer, he saw Helga on the porch, smiling at the girls and saying something to the older one, the little tramp. Next to Helga, and with a towel folded under her arm, stood Marie. She was holding a polo shirt out to Billy, who stood before her on the bottom step, tightening the belt of his trunks. Well, he was glad to see that she was going bathing too, instead of spending her time cooped up in her room with a face on her like death warmed over. Her robe was open and John could see that she was wearing her old flowered bathing suit. Good, he thought. Maybe she's got some sense after all. Helga Schmidt saw him and waved.

The mandolin learned as a boy. Deep pear of its body, rich and lustrous brown. Mother-of-pearl discs set between the frets. You've Been a Good Old Wagon, But You've Done Broke Down. On the stoop in the twilight after supper, picking out songs. Clear tenor voice. Hello! Ma Baby. Elegant white piping on his vests, boaters with black silk bands, spectators. In old Brooklyn, the farms and fields. Bridget dressed like a Gibson girl the first time he saw her. Heavy and solid bosom in a starched white blouse and perfect ankles in taut black silk. His twin brother Bill the ne'er-do-well in derbies pulled low over his right eye. Buttered his thick blond hair before he washed it. And the smell of whiskey on his breath. It's the hair that gets the janes, kid. And a little chee-arm.

She sat on the railing at Sheepshead Bay. There is a photograph to prove that her smile still had something of love in it. Celibate at that point for the past four years. The night of Francis Caffrey's wedding to that bucktoothed girl from Greenpoint, Agnes Kenny. He made her pregnant again and the child died. It was his fault, like an animal. Four years of smiling into cameras. Theresa dead of diphtheria, *something* the old bastard Drescher figured right. The judgment of God on his lust and Bridget carried out the sentence, oh Christ did she carry it out. Could she have known that Jimmy Mulvaney's seventeen-year-old sister made him crazy dancing with him? Softly straddling his right thigh each time they turned so that he could feel her young hot sex burning into him. Bill at the punch bowl smiling across the dancers at him. He mouthed Whoopee! Oh, Bill knew, the son of a bitch. Then pointedly danced with Bridget. The son of a bitch. Winked at him.

Had no heart for it so put the mandolin in the closet with the three
sticks his father had owned, beautiful shillelaghs, blackthorn and ash,
the handles rubbed smooth and almost ebony. Marie asked and asked
him to play some songs until one evening he took the mandolin out
and found that two of its strings had snapped.

His family Dublin Episcopalians originally from Londonderry.
They thought he had married beneath him for Bridget's people came
from County Clare. That's where the gawms live, his father had said.
Bog-trotters. But he was charmed nevertheless by Bridget. Tried to
stifle his sense of superiority after marriage but could not think of her
family, the Caffreys and Kennys, as anything *but* bog-trotters. Whiskey drinkers who fought and cursed and trembled before Catholicism.
And they thought of him as a Protestant unfortunate, mild, weak, a
man who worked, bejayzus, in a poor bloody office. And what was the
matter with the Police? She became enraged when he called them,
however lightly, shanty Irish. Oh but she cut him down to size all
right. That she did. He brought home the bacon and she gave him a
daily allowance. Subway fare, ten cents. Pack of Camels, fifteen cents.
Daily News, two cents. Lunch, thirty-five cents. The rest went into the
bank. How slowly and completely they both turned into misers. Finally, taking the neighbors' day-old newspapers off the dumbwaiter
no longer embarrassed him. The *Mirror,* the *Sun,* the *Journal-Ameri-
can.* One day he looked across the room at her and saw a sloven. She
was forty-eight. By God, she *was* shanty Irish. And was he any better?
No wonder Marie married a guinea. Something to break the spell. ·

You need any help, kid, send me a wire, Bill said. The wedding
breakfast was over and his bride had gone upstairs to change. He
blushed. Her shyness drove him crazy on their wedding night. Jesus
Christ. He didn't even know how to *do* it. Couldn't put it in her.
Bridget wouldn't touch him but lay stiff, her face burning. Dear little
girl, dear little girl. Repeated over and over as he strained and pushed.
Sweet Christ! Are they supposed to be so small? What would Bill do?
He almost did it but messed all over her thighs and the sheets. Fell
out, really, like some smutty joke. But Bridget was sobbing. You
shouldn't, you shouldn't, you shouldn't have married me. He kissed
her eyes. Her mouth. Do you want to get up and wash? No. Again?
John, again? She touched him with her thumb and forefinger. I'm

your wife. Her voice was so soft, girlish. Angelic, was the word he
thought of. And girlish, indeed. Jesus, she was more ignorant than he
was. I have to wait, wait a while first, he said. You do? Girlish, my
God, yes.

She used, oh God, how she used that girlish voice falsely, later when
there was nothing at all but those goddamn newspapers smelling of
garbage. To charm anyone, Tony especially. And of course, on the
phone, not that *they* had a phone. Won every battle and one day he
looked in the mirror and saw himself old. That night went through
his dresser drawer to find himself, ha! In bits and pieces. Fragments.
Of crap. Silver penknife, clay pipes from old-fashioned Irish wakes,
one from that idiot, Mark Caffrey's, shanty son of a bitch, even dead
he looked drunk. And the other clays with the green satin bows on
them, Erin Go Bragh, yes, and kiss my arse! The rusted knife with the
point broken off that she used for paring her corns till he couldn't
stand the sight of it and hid it here. Bejesus Christ, you'd think a
million dollars was lost the way she carried on. Tangles of string and
cord, clam shells. Matchbooks and stirring rods from dozens of roadhouses and taverns, coasters and napkins. Where in the hell did the
one with the pink elephant come from? Dizzy-looking article floating
amid glassy bubbles. COCKTAILS is all it said. And on the closet
shelf hats and horns from New Year's eves, a flowered pitcher and six
matching glasses from the Electra and its rotten movies, tarnished
watch chain and a broken old turnip in an envelope—that had been
Bill's. Inside the case was engraved *Excelsior.* Whatever the hell that
was all about. His mandolin, the shillelaghs, a green paper derby. That
had been Bill's too, wore it the last St. Paddy's Day he'd been alive.
The luck of the Irish, kid! Come on, have a ball with me! One goddamn ball won't hurt you! Right, Bridget? But there was no smile or
girlish voice for Bill.

In the Methodist Hospital he looked up at him, eyes dull in that
curiously flushed skeletal face. Bill, he said, and took his hand. I'm
on my way, kiddo. I'll give everybody your regards, especially good
old Mark. He died right in the middle of his soundless laugh. Then
he had to listen to Bridget tell everyone about how the whiskey will
do it to you until he came as close to killing her . . . well, not killing
her, but my God! Gave it the old girly-girly voice then, too. How he

had grown to despise it. It was soon after that he began to hide a pint of Wilson's under his shirts. Just a whisper, a hint of that phony voice and he could feel his throat begging for a swallow of that rotgut. It was intolerable precisely because it was such a perfectly monstrous imitation of the voice she'd really had. I'm your wife. Her small fingers wrapped around his penis, pulling it and squeezing it until he was ready. Again? Now, John? Sometimes, years later, he could feel her hand, feel just how it had been. Yeah? Have a cigar! What bullshit.

When did he stop singing? He hadn't been bad at all, at all. Sweet Adeline, Genevieve, Home Sweet Home. When You Were Sweet Sixteen. Old man Kahn used to come out of the butcher shop with that one, his walrus moustache and his few little hairs swirled around on his head and plastered down with hair tonic. The old Dutchman loved that song. Mister Johnson, Turn Me Loose, Bill Bailey, Some of These Days—he did a nice thing on the break, could *still* do it if he wanted to, hell. What else, oh Jesus H. Christ, he knew a lot of songs. Play That Barber Shop Chord, right! Waiting for the Robert E. Lee, Alexander's Ragtime Band, My Melancholy Baby, Ballin' the Jack, I Ain't Got Nobody, Pretty Baby—dozens more, dozens. All those old vaudeville songs that he got by ear. Sitting on a kitchen chair, his boater over one eye like Bill, picking away in his shirt-sleeves.

You put it in nice and slow, kiddo, take it from the man who knows. Bill leaned close to him and winked, then threw his whiskey down and sighed, took a sip of beer. Nice and slow and easy on the girl, don't be in a big hurry, me bucko. Then when you hear a loud pop you know you're on your way. He looked at Bill, his eyes wide and his mouth half open. Ah, nah, nah! Bill said, don't pay me any heed! There's no pop, bejesus Christ—can't your own brother have a little fun with you? But I'm on the level with that slow and easy stuff, take it from the man who was there, from the man who knows. Christ knows, *she* didn't know. While she was taking a bath their first night in a hotel he opened her drawer and kissed her chemises and drawers and silk stockings. When she came out of the bathroom her dark coppery hair was loose, falling over her shoulders and back. Under her white wedding peignoir the collar of her nightgown showed, white too, and embroidered with pale-pink roses. She blushed and looked away. He could see her heavy breasts shift as she smoothed the night clothes over her hips. Are you warm enough, John? I think it's a little chilly in here?

I've never been good enough for you, have I, Mr. High Mucky-Muck? Mr. Church of Ireland? Too much of a gentleman to be a man, a patch on a man's ass is all you are. Why God in His goodness knows you weren't but half a man on our wedding night! And you needn't gape at me. Go out and get another pint of beer, for God's sake! Ah, that got her back up—that she couldn't drive him to the whiskey but for a ball or two now and again. How she wanted to turn him into another Mick drunkard, but it wouldn't work. Walked around the house all day in her torn housecoats and broken shoes, the soles flapping, her stockings full of runs and twisted into knots below her knees. And he'd come into that, still impeccable in his starched white shirts and creased trousers, his heart dull and empty as he heard her: Wipe your feet! You're late! Talking to one of those cheap painted chippies in the office again? I wouldn't put anything past you! Later she'd sit across from him, cracking pretzels on her bottom front teeth and swilling her beer, lost in radio dramas, her feet planted on the floor, legs spread, so that he could look up to her naked crotch. God forbid she should put on drawers in the house and wear them out! It was disgusting. During the commercials she'd talk about how some old biddy neighbor of Aunt Lizzie or somebody had seen that bum of a brother of his fall in the gutter outside of Fritz's Tavern, the puke, by God, all crusted on his shirt front. Something, something about Bill. Or maybe about that "tramp" Whiting in the office. Oh, you had your eye on her, didn't you, you goddamn old fool? Jesus Christ almighty, Bridget! Don't be using God's name in vain with me, Mr. Big-Shot. And don't deny for a minute that for six months here there wasn't a conversation that the name of that tramp didn't come out of your mouth a dozen times. *Miss* Whiting this, *Miss* Whiting that, *Miss* Whiting the other thing. And no wonder, the tramp probably wears her skirts up to here and takes good care that you see plenty of her when she crosses her legs.

Odd and sketchy fantasies about Jean Whiting. But he was no fool. Not yet. The girl could have been his daughter, she was younger than

Marie. The night that Bridget had humiliated him in front of that goddamn flatfoot Jimmy Kenny and his common-law moron of a wife, Helen what's her name. Mentioned once, *once,* by Christ, to Bridget that she was a great help in the office to all the credit men in his section, a nice bright girl. Oh Jimmy, did John mention to you that he's gone ga-ga over some little chippy in the office? Why, you should see him, am I right, John? He goes to work every morning dressed up like Astor's pet horse, oh, fit to kill! And then that fat cop's laugh, the phlegm catching and tearing in his throat until he spit his filthy oyster into a grey handkerchief. And what did *he* say? The great strong hero, the lord of the manor, Caspar Milquetoast? Ha ha ha— she's a dizzy jane, cheap and pimples all over her face, God bless the mark. And you should smell the Woolworth's poi-fee-yume off her, my God, she's like a nigger on Christmas. We all feel sorry for her. He felt sick and drank off two more ginger-ale highballs as fast as Jimmy made them. But that licking of the floor, the dirt, kissing her ass, wasn't enough. Bridget squeezed the blood out and when it was gone she kept on squeezing. Insisted that he better his insults until Jean became their jointly invented monstrosity, their freak. And Jean moved then, even more strongly, in his fantasies.

But what would he ever have had to say to her? Her sweet face and mouth, her red hair? God, I hate a redheaded woman, Bridget said. And so proved that he had once, in innocence, told her the color of her hair. Everything was a weapon to maim and hurt. When would he learn anything in this terrible life? Could be her father, my God, younger than Marie. Well, Miss Whiting, Jean, I'm so glad that you could have lunch with me—I hope you don't mind eating at the good old Exchange Buffet, the Eat It and Beat It? Ha ha. Oh, she'd be a good sport. Her bright head across the table and other men looking at him enviously. I'm going to leave my wife because she forced me to insult you in front of a stupid ox of a gawm named Jimmy Kenny, a stupid gawm of a policeman. Then what? Now, Jean, take me somewhere, take me away, show me what to do, show me how to sin, do you want me to "keep" you? I've never ever seen a woman naked, do you know that? Oh my God! Not even when I was young, not even my wife, ever ever ever. It's true! Oh God! Now, my brother Bill, *there*

was a ladies' man. A little bay rum, kid, a few Sen-Sen, get the old
nails buffed and, oho! you win the cigar! The janes fall down and
woiship.

And when Marie and the boy came, beaten and broke, she became
more of a sloven than ever. Stopped cooking, tied her hair up in old
rags, ordered the girl around like she was a servant. Another Katie,
another poor Katie in the house. Took it all and worked like a slave
and he never once opened his mouth. And where would you be
without your mother and father to take you in and put a roof over
your head? Stink of garbage from the rattled *Mirror.* You see how
much that dago greaseball of a husband thinks of you, him and his
redheaded slut! Bud Halloran was *doing* it to her, the son of a bitch.
He wasn't much younger than he was! When she'd stoop to open a
bottom file drawer he watched how her skirt molded to the shape of
her sweet thighs. My sweet Jesus Christ. No, he couldn't be doing it
to her, she was too sweet, too fine, too clean. A virgin for sure. Too
fine. Oh Christ, I hope he isn't doing it to her!

Then started buying two quarts of Wilson's a week. He'd drink in
the closet, the bathroom, guzzle some when she went out of the room.
A kind of peace dropped on him into which came her first complaints,
then her illness proper. The old slob Drescher with his "anemia." He
drank his Wilson's and still went out for his pint in the evening, but
now he and Marie drank it, while she whined and complained from
the bedroom that they were glad to be rid of her now that she was
too sick to get out of bed. And he couldn't look across at his daughter
because he knew that they would find in each other's eyes the truth
of her complaint. How quickly she died after being admitted to the
hospital. A serious relapse, old Drescher, the horse doctor, said.
Right, sure, they call it leukemia. Goddamn horse's ass! Jean Whiting
came to the wake with Bud Halloran and some other people from the
office. And she sent a mass card. Back, he was back at work in a week
and felt nothing. He looked at Jean's thighs and bottom and felt
ashamed of himself. His lust for her had helped to kill Bridget.

He tried to talk to Marie one night, a couple of weeks after Bridget
was in her grave, about how much he had tried, you know, *tried,* with
Bridget, and then he began to cry and as she came over and sat by
him while Billy stood unhappily looking on, he murmured, over and

over again, oh Bridget, oh Bridget, God forgive me, oh Bridget. As Marie rubbed his back and sniffled and told him that she would take care of him now and that everything would be fine, he knew that he was crying for himself and for that lost alien girl who now, suddenly, appeared in perfect clarity to his memory in a starched white blouse. Her full bosom. Her thick coppery hair. Her slender ankles in taut black silk. We'll make a family, Poppa, you'll see, a real family. Oh Skip, Skip. He reached out for Billy and then hugged him tight around the waist, his other arm around Marie's shoulders. A real family, he said.

The meanest bloody thing in hell made this world.

—Brian O'Nolan

ABOUT THE AUTHOR

GILBERT SORRENTINO was born in Brooklyn, New York, in 1929, and studied English literature and classics at Brooklyn College. After serving two years as a medic in the United States Army, he devoted himself to writing. He edited *Neon* in the fifties, and was a member of the editorial staff of *Kulchur* in the sixties. Among his books of poetry are *The Perfect Fiction, White Sail,* and *The Orangery,* and his fiction includes *The Sky Changes, Steelwork, Imaginative Qualities of Actual Things,* and *Mulligan Stew.* He received a Guggenheim Fellowship for fiction in 1973.